Ever Lost A Dream?

A Novel By

Deborah Zvanut Drake

Copyright © 2022 Deborah Zvanut Drake
All rights reserved.

Barringer Publishing, Naples, Florida
www.barringerpublishing.com

Cover and Layout by Linda Duider

Paintings and Illustrations:
Darren Larkin Drake—*Peacock feather*
Nathan Joseph Drake—*Detective Bun-Cover*
Michael Thomas Fitzpatrick and Darren Drake—*Nevah-Tu-Latte*
Michael Thomas Fitzpatrick—*The Dream Spinner and Percy Press-on Verance*
Gail Marie Foster—*Renaissance Festival Shoe Slide and Destiny Depot Train Station*
Janice Schroeder—Book cover and *Seaphairies, Rough Terrain,*
and *Dream Garden Beach* watercolors

ISBN: 978-1-7352525-1-3

Library of Congress Cataloging-in-Publication Data
Ever Lost A Dream? Deborah Zvanut Drake

Printed in U.S.A.

To Ernie, my anchor,

And to Darren, Nathan and Catherine,

The navigators of this dream . . .

Foreword

By Linda Barrett

This is a magical story, just like its author. To sum up Deborah's effect on the world, I'd like to share my grand-children's response to hearing the early drafts of "Ever Lost A Dream?" She came to visit and my grandchildren were immediately drawn to her. Deborah relates to people of all ages at a very intimate level. She has an innocence of truth and caring that is so often lost when we reach adulthood. She values people and their feelings above all else. My grandchildren felt this. I knew she was writing a book about a young girl with an important message for people of all ages and asked her to share a little of the story. The children sat on the floor mesmerized as she read aloud to them. No one spoke but Deborah. When she finished reading the excerpt, my grandchildren had this response: "Grandma, she's magical! When will it be finished? I want to know what happens!"

That's the power of Deborah and her work. She sees the world from a captivating prospective. From newly created words like "direct-tionary" rather than dictionary, to deep insights into our most basic human needs, fears and wants, Deborah's writing draws you into her world.

I've known Deborah throughout her journey in bringing "Ever Lost A Dream?" to the world. Many naysayers have tried to be stumbling blocks, but she refused to give up. Her passion for nourishing human dignity drove her forward. The teacher of her first writing seminar told her, "I know one thing, young lady. You are never going to write a novel." Being Deborah, his comments fueled her determination. So, baby step by baby step, just like Anna Gwendolyn in this story, she navigated her way, overcoming all obstacles, to bring this enchanting, motivating story to you.

Yes! Deborah Is Magical! Enjoy her world!

Contents

Chapter One

Dreams for Sale

Anna Gwendolyn was suddenly wide-eyed, awake from her dream, and bursting with excitement!

"Oh, Pappy, remember when I thought I could get my dreams back—buy my dreams—from that dream machine? That Dream-O-Tron??

"Well, I just had the weirdest dream . . . There was this thief from that Dream-O-Tron info-mercial I saw on TV, who promised to make my dreams come true but really *stole* dreams instead—and I found this place called Rhibbonosphere full of crazy characters who kept telling me to never give up. My peacock wreath turned into a Peacock Plane and I climbed a ladder up to the sky and I had to make a parachute so I could get out of the plane! I parachuted out!!!!! Me!!! By myself!!! With a parachute I made myself!

"There was this guy, Pappy, Detective Bun-Cover who catches people lying to cover their buns and I fell into an Obstacle Multiplier—full of mean-talking bullies!—but I got out . . . I figured it out and I got out! And this woman, Nevah-Tu-Latte, with a red pillow on her head, was constantly saying 'It's never too late'—And, Oh Pappy, Oh! Oh!!

"There was a giant paper jigsaw puzzle of all my memories. My memories!! Plus, seahorses with wings carrying poor lost dreams and a funny flat guy named Percy Press-on Verance who got ironed in a mangle and preached persevering . . . Boy, did I have to persevere! I had so many obstacles! But I learned how to handle them. There were Clipper Ships with piles of lost dreams in crates and . . . and . . . an unending forest of tree trunks full of LOST DREAMS!! LOST DREAMS!! I'm not the only one who lost her dreams.

"And oh! Oh!! I saw Mama in the Dream Garden and Mama and me found my Dream Trunk and all my lost dreams were in there!!! Waiting for me!!!! Not a Dream-O-Tron in sight!!!"

Then Anna Gwendolyn finally took a breath . . . a long, big, deep one.

"Pappy, I've changed a lot since I've seen you."

The day before . . .

Anna Gwendolyn Shaw's grandfather, Pappy, was immersed in his usual pre-dawn fishing and frogging adventure at Alligator Bayou, about 20 miles from their home in Parkersville, Texas. Briggs, the dog, was sprawled sloppily on Pappy's chair, sound asleep. Anna Gwendolyn was alone. She could hunt for that info-mercial everyone was talking about. The info-mercial that sells dreams! Now was her chance. She could once and for all stop feeling like a failure, forget about her lost, unfinished dreams and buy herself a real, foolproof, guaranteed dream.

"Ha!" she scoffed to herself. Was there really such a thing? Whatever the case, this was her chance to find out with Pappy gone. At least it was worth checking out; she knew where the credit cards were kept for emergencies and drug store runs. Pappy did say she could use the card for an emergency, and this was certainly an emergency. She was desperate to find her dreams.

Anna Gwendolyn grabbed the remote and switched on the 1980 console TV Pappy had transformed into a digital model to get the best of both worlds. Anna Gwendolyn was ready. After a few hectic moments scrambling for the right channel. . . . Success! The announcer began:

"FAME, FORTUNE, BEAUTY, WEALTH, POWER, BEYOND YOUR WILDEST DREAMS! INSTRUCTIONS NOT NEEDED! NO LABOR INVOLVED; ARRIVES FULLY ASSEMBLED. GET YOUR DREAMS NOW!!" His voice boomed.

Then the info-mercial star whispered ever so faintly, "Please read the fine print." The camera moved in for a close-up of his face. Anna Gwendolyn felt the tension escape from her body, and her spirit came alive. She was convinced the announcer was talking directly and intimately to her. And with the house to herself, she privately took in every word.

The pitchman pitched, "Yes, Anna Gwendolyn, don't miss out on making your dreams come true. Order our virtual reality dream-maker from the convenience of your couch." A toll-free phone number flashed on the bottom of the old television.

"Hurry! Call within the next ten minutes and receive a free carrying case! Have your credit card number ready; it's only $49.99 per month for six months plus shipping and handling. Guaranteed or your money back," he bragged.

The totals *"12,347 sold, Only 523 left"* flashed across the screen. Then Anna Gwendolyn said aloud, "Wait a minute . . . receive what for only $49.99 a month? I sure wish I could record this! If Pappy wasn't so tight and old fashioned, we'd have a DVR. Hmmm, $49.99. That's not so much." Even though she was doubtful, she became intrigued as the announcer continued his high-energy hype.

"Order your very own Dream-O-Tron and take the drudgery out of working for your dreams. Yes, all of us here at Dream-O-Tron want to make YOUR dreams come true!"

Glued to the TV, Anna Gwendolyn was succumbing to the promise of a brand new, technological device that promised an answer to all her problems; she wouldn't feel sad and lost and a failure anymore; it was only a toll-free phone call away!

"That's it!" she declared out loud. "That Dream-O-Tron will do more for me than those useless inspirational songs and posters, begging me to reach for the stars and do the impossible! Ha! This could be just what I've been looking for. Just think! With the touch of a button, my dreams could come true—whatever I want. I could just type my perfect dream into the device. No blood, sweat, and tears. No waiting. No hard work. No endless wondering and imagining. I could be making my dreams come true, right here, right now."

For sure, the info-mercial star had done his job.

Anna Gwendolyn was ready to buy her dreams.

Chapter Two

You Can't Buy Dreams

Like fingernails across a classroom chalkboard, Anna heard the familiar screech as the front door swung open. Its scream for attention had been ignored for years. The info-mercial's spell was broken. Pappy was back.

Pappy sloshed in, tall and wiry with a contradictory round face. His dark auburn bush of hair and beard framed his sea green eyes. Deep lines of a long life creased his brow. His unexpected early return was not in the plan.

"Good morning, Anna Gwendolyn! Crappy fishing. Just what are you doing up at this hour? I've been outside putting away my gear.

"Ya' know, Anna, the truck windows were wide open and eavesdroppin' is automatic, so I couldn't help but hear that conversation you were having with the TV. What in the world are you up to? Couldn't help but hear . . ."

"Oh! Eh, ah, hi, Pappy." Anna Gwendolyn was both startled and shocked as she realized she'd been discovered. *Once again, my plans are all messed up.* She bolted across the room, almost crashing into the TV as she smashed the "OFF" button, which ended the virtual conversation with the announcer and forced her to focus on Pappy.

Anna grumbled to herself. *Darn! I was so close! Why is he home already? He ruins my plans every time. I was so close!*

But she answered in ho-hum style, "Oh, it's nothing. Just watching some old movies and stuff. There's nothing much on. I woke up early and couldn't go back to sleep. That's all."

"What do you mean, that's all? Never saw a movie asking for credit card numbers!" Anna Gwendolyn could hear the doubt in his voice. She had been found out. "I could hear that TV guy clear in the truck! Something about dreams?"

Pappy knew he was on to something because Anna Gwendolyn was now blushing. He'd clearly overheard "Buy your dreams here!" And he also knew that she had seemed very troubled about something for quite a while. Treading carefully, he didn't want to seem to be prying into her personal business, but he wanted to help.

Though incredibly creative, Anna's talents were often camouflaged due to her diagnosis of Attention Deficit Disorder (ADD for short), which challenged her ability to concentrate or follow through—even understanding instructions was difficult. *But she was always so creative!* Pappy smiled, reminiscing . . . *She used to always be creating 'somethings' from 'nothings.' A white stack of coffee filters . . . wa-la . . . a beautiful white chrysanthemum! A stack of dinner plates strategically placed under a sink became a miniature Niagara. There were paper towel roll log cabins and spice can skyscrapers. She even began building her own clubhouse out of scavenged river stones.*

Pappy thought on . . . *One day, Percy, their lifetime neighbor, who went from a talented handyman who could fix anything to an accomplished chef by way of his dogged perseverance—and then went on to take college classes—appeared at Anna's front door with a Santa-size bag of plastic building blocks, intertwined with odds and ends and thrown out what-nots. With those gifts, Anna transformed the unused dining room table into a fantasy land of castles, skyscrapers and planetary galaxies, all from those little, bitty colorful blocks that would end up under bare feet on the cold, tile floor . . . Ouch! That's where she had her first lessons in architecture, mathematics and perseverance, compliments of dear old Mr. Percy.*

Her ever-spinning mind was constantly creative. But now, buying a dream?

Pappy remarked, "Talk about dreams. How about a dream to remember things? I forgot my bait bucket this morning. Going fishing and I forget my bait bucket! Can you imagine that?"

Anna Gwendolyn pretended to sneeze and sneakily rolled her eyes. *I'm not going to say a word. I just hope my eye lids don't get stuck up there some day! What do you mean, imagine that? I don't have to imagine Pappy forgetting. He forgets all the time, there's nothing to imagine! All old people forget. And most of them are just sitting around with nothing else to do. We have the easiest, basic cable TV service and I have to help him use the clicker almost every time! Or, I have to find it!*

"I know you have dreams, darling," Pappy brought her back to the present, "everybody does. And everybody wants to sell you one, too. You know what my dream is?" Pappy asked.

What is he talking about? Anna Gwendolyn thought, with a fake sneeze and another eye-roll. *Old people already lived their lives. They're too old to dream.*

"My dream is to go fishin' from right here on this sofa. Then I wouldn't have to worry about forgetting anything. It'd all be right here at my fingertips: the pond, the water, the fish, the bait, and my tackle box. Plus that blasted clicker!" he said, now pointing to the TV. He leaned back. "Now, that'd be the life. Watchin' the World Series while catchin' a wide-mouth bass, right from my living room sofa.

'Ya' know, believe it or not, there really are moveable fishing ponds at some senior centers, Anna, giving people a way to be active and hold on to their passions. I can't buy that dream though!" he grinned at his granddaughter.

As he sat down, "You've had dreams, Anna. You were on your way to being a triple threat," Pappy reassured her. "You used to play Bach on the piano, belt out rock anthems, you were learning to climb the rocks at Big Bend! You spin like a top and can calculate and measure anything! I remember that really elaborate clubhouse you designed; boy, I'd sure like to see that finished."

Well, maybe one day, Pappy, Anna Gwendolyn imagined with a sigh. She always felt so bad about never finishing that clubhouse. But she'd lost her enthusiasm, not just for it, for everything.

"Well, speaking of finishing things, let me finish telling you my couch fishing dream. Maybe *you* could buy me *that* dream," he teased, as he walked into the kitchen for some coffee.

"Fishing's your dream, Pappy, not mine. I've got bigger dreams!" Anna Gwendolyn said, wishing inside she actually did—or at least knew what they were!

Anna suddenly flashed back to some of her young dreams, and how they were crushed right out of her by people with demeaning criticisms . . . She remembered their hurtful words:

- "Toe shoes? You dance as if they're more like hiking boots! I don't think so, Anna!"
- "And what piano piece have you prepared for me today? Oh no, Anna, you can't play that! Oh! You CAN'T play that at the GUILD! What would all of the other music teachers think of me?"
- "Can you not hear a word I'm saying? Is your head in the clouds? Do you ever listen to instructions, Anna? Do you ever, ever listen?"
- "You have to lie for us, Anna Gwendolyn, or we will shame you." (Anna remembered, *That horrible sleep over with the bullies. I never told anyone about the awful shame I felt, or how shocked and broken-hearted I was. I'll never go to another sleep over, that's for sure. No matter what!*)

To survive the sting of others' terminally embarrassing and hurtful comments, Anna Gwendolyn always pretended that the "head in the clouds" label they pinned on her was an endearing compliment, a great quality. Lacking the skills to speak up for herself, her "head in the clouds" living quarters were often her chosen refuge.

Staring at the now blank TV, Anna Gwendolyn wondered if things would ever change. Would she ever get it right? Would these scars ever heal? All of her friends seemed to have dreams about their future but her. Where were her dreams?

Pappy's long-distance prattling interrupted her thoughts, "Yeah, I know about dreams, darlin'. But you have to work for dreams to come true, real blood, sweat and tears."

Ignoring his comment, she shouted back to him, "Pappy, I think I've found the answer to my problem," with the sparkle returning to her eyes, "I can buy my dreams right here, right now, from our living room couch." Anna could feel his skepticism already oozing from the kitchen. She held her breath, then let it out, "You see, Pappy, I saw this info-mercial that sells dreams—it's called the DREAM-O-TRON!"

"A Dream-O-Tron! Jumpin,' stinkin' catfish! What will they come up with next?" Pappy almost jogged back into the living room and sat down next to her. *Better not let her catch me rollin' my eyes. She has to know, in spite of everything, that I do believe in her*, Pappy thought.

"Anna Gwendolyn, tell me all about this dream machine."

Ok, I've at least got his attention. He's actually asking me about the machine.

"It's not exactly a machine," she began. "There's an entire set of blue tooth programs, a question/answer blog, and the original *Virtual Reality Dream-O-Tron* manual, the patented state-of-the-art dream/destiny designer extraordinaire!" Anna said. "No more wondering; no more confusion! All the instructions are downloaded instantly to my cell phone. Just think of it, Pappy—a machine that directs me to select my dreams and gives me what I need to make them come true. And with personal 24/7 access to a Dream-O-Tron consultant, my ADD can't get in the way! Thousands of dreams to choose, right from the comfort of our couch!"

Oooh! He's not getting this at all!

Seeing the befuddled look on Pappy's face, Anna Gwendolyn switched gears. "Really, Pappy, I really need help and the info-mercial says the Dream-O-Tron will give me everything I need!"

She hoped he didn't ask questions.

"Is that what you want?" question number one, "to purchase your dreams? I'm getting dizzy from shaking my head in disbelief! Sweetheart, dream machines and dream potions have been around for ages—from Hollywood to Harvard—from fairy tales to Fantasy Island. But if somebody could concoct a potion or build a device that makes your dreams come true, they'd be a billionaire! The truth is, your own desire, commitment, and hard work with passion is the only road to your dreams. It's that simple!

"Dream-O-Trons don't sell passion. They can't guarantee your dreams will come true. Nobody can. Some people have been known to lose their entire life savings to false hope peddlers like this. I just want you to think before you're robbed. Use that creative mind of yours! Think about your passions. Before you decide to take a wild ride with this Dream-O-Tron, think how else you might find your dreams."

Pappy's gentle but logical words began involuntarily softening her teenage interior. Out of sheer exhaustion from bantering back and forth, plus her love for Pappy, she actually started to listen, not only with her ears, but also a little with her heart.

As poor a listener as she was, Anna Gwendolyn did remember her grandfather's stories about working hard toward his own dream of being a train conductor. And how, overcoming many obstacles, he made that dream come true. He even drove an historic steam engine now on display in Steam Engine Park in Parkersville.

She admitted life with Pappy, although sometimes challenging and often irritating, had been good. He'd stepped in when her mother succumbed to cancer long ago. Lost and traumatized in those early days, the love, comfort and support of Pappy, family, friends and the community strengthened her daily. But something was chipping away at her.

She wanted her dreams back.

Chapter Three

Making Something from Nothing

Anna Gwendolyn glanced at the clock. Would her friends be mad if she canceled going to to the Parkersville Renaissance Festival? Would it be worth it to stay behind and listen to Pappy talk about dreams? But if she were going, she needed to get dressed, and for her that was a backstage theatre operation. She could spend hours, glue gun in hand (forget needle and thread!), creating "costumes" that often ended up in a pile on the floor. The remnants of make-up, curlers, hair appliances and scrunchies would be scattered about in the aftermath of "getting ready" preparations. (Anna Gwendolyn had much in common with Texas hurricanes.)

From exhaustion, or maybe her sales pitch, Pappy was nodding off. She touched his arm, "Pappy, you've been up since dawn; you go nap out back near the Bling Swing while I get ready for the Renaissance Festival. We'll still have time, so you and I could do lunch. How about it? And Pappy . . . you can tell me more about dreams."

Secretly thrilled at the prospect of spending this time with his granddaughter, Pappy set off for the swing and a nap.

The Bling Swing was just that. A swing made of "Bling!" Anna Gwendolyn had entwined strands of discarded, sparkling necklaces to counteract the aged, rusty patches on the chains after Pappy had reinforced them for strength and safety. Ashford Park Elementary and Yellow School could be seen over the lush, green valley that came into the view of anyone who pumped their swing high enough into the air. Anna Gwendolyn and her friends had attended both schools. Pappy always loved afternoons in the backyard with the neighborhood kids taking turns on Bling Swing.

Now in her bedroom tossing everything backwards into a growing pile, Anna Gwendolyn dug through her closet. *That recycled dress from my cousin Penelope's wedding . . . that won't work! This old Halloween costume . . . no! Ah, how about if I wear this? No, not this old thing. I just simply have nothing to wear*, she said to herself, looking at the growing mountain of discards. She blared out in exasperation, "Oh, broken zipper! I can't wear that! And that dress needs the buttons sewn on. This skirt is too long; this petticoat needs fixing. I really have nothing to wear!"

Then, with a sudden surge of unexpected confidence, she perked up, "Wait a minute, aren't I the known *improv fashionista* of Parkersville Junior High? I'll just do some of my famous recycling."

Feeling better, she continued the hunt with enthusiasm, knowing what she had always known—that she would figure it out. In spite of terminal chaos, she'd always been able to pull it together.

She looked around at the mess. *I'll just braid my hair to get started,* she thought to herself, as if in control. (Anna Gwendolyn always put up a great *facade* to hide her inner feelings of being scattered and frazzled. She could have won an Oscar, she was such a great pretender.)

Time for the old train trunk, a gift from Pappy for dress-up. As a child, each visit to the faded, leather trunk had offered a new surprise. Reaching beneath a spider-webbed, encased package of crinkled fabric, she found the half-sewn taffeta dress she'd never finished in home making class, and remembered her teacher rolling her eyes in disgust. *My next project was a blouse . . . I remember that teacher making me feel stupid, "If you can't make a skirt, how in the world are you going to make a shirt?"* Cautiously, Anna Gwendolyn pulled the skirt out, being careful not to trespass on the pins, which were waiting to stick her. There it was—an unfinished dress of Caribbean turquoise adorned with lime green chiffon and satin brocade.

"This is good! This will work!" she yelled out loud. Anyone watching her would almost see math equations calculating in her head as she analyzed the material. She wrapped it around her frame and reached for her glue gun, her secret friend when it came to sewing. *Sewing takes concentration . . . glue guns do not! Of course, there was that time I burned my fingers . . .* In what seemed like minutes stolen, Anna Gwendolyn had constructed a mid-calf length, turquoise gown, with a lime-green underskirt. To embellish the bodice, she grabbed some beaded ribbon with loop-de-loops.

As a final touch, she glued a remnant scrap of blue and green satin, with velvet and lime-green ribbon, and wrapped it around her several times over to assure everything stayed in place. She was pleased, knowing she'd designed an original Anna Gwendolyn creation.

Anna Gwendolyn tempted her patience waiting for the glue to dry.

And then . . . lunch with Pappy. She couldn't wait to start talking about finding her dream.

Chapter Four

A Dream Direct-tionary?

"Oh, Briggs, Briggs, slow down, you silly dog!" Anna said to the midnight-black Labrador Retriever as he ran toward the Bling Swing. Pappy was awakened with a soggy, slurpy kiss. No, not from Anna Gwendolyn, but from Briggs, who eagerly washed Pappy's face.

Opening his eyes, gently pushing Briggs aside, he saw Anna Gwendolyn. "Ah, oh Anna Gwendolyn, you're a vision! The Renaissance revelers will fall in love with you! The knights will extend welcoming gloved hands to you, M'lady."

"Thank you, Pappy. I *am* going to the Festival, but first we can have lunch and a little talk." Anna Gwendolyn now felt the pangs of guilt from her ADD habit of not listening. She would do a better job starting right now.

Anna Gwendolyn had prepared lunch while Pappy had dozed in the backyard. "Here's your favorite picnic treat," she said as she handed him the avocado, peanut butter and jalapeno sandwich. "Oh! Pappy! Just look at my latest creation. Watch my dress twirl in a circle around me," pivoting into the chair next to Pappy. They ate in silence for a few moments. Anna Gwendolyn had a little scheme going. She wanted to talk more about Dream-O-Tron but she knew she couldn't just blurt it out.

"Pappy, are you ready to tell me where dreams come from?"

"Passion," he answered bluntly. "But ok, to begin with, what do you want to be when you grow up?" Pappy asked.

"I don't know; adults are always asking that. I used to want to be an architect, or world traveler. I loved building things, geography and working with numbers and rulers. But how am I going to be good enough do any of those? I don't even have an idea where to start."

He knew she wanted a "take a pill" kind of answer.

"Anna Gwendolyn, you're already ahead of the game. You know that you're missing something—a dream to pursue. So many people are not even aware of that. Grab my scratch pad and write down your interests. That's a good place to start."

Anna Gwendolyn began writing:

    Building things

    Rock climbing

    Traveling . . .

"Pappy, what do you mean, 'passion?' You said passion is the only thing missing from the Dream-O-Tron."

"It's not the only thing. But it's a very important thing! Passion is a feeling. It fires you up, like fuel in a rocket ship, to do things you never thought possible. It was that fuel— passion—that propelled you up those rocks at Big Ben."

"But the Dream-O-Tron promises me a dream now! And it didn't say anything about work, or needing stuff like passion."

Pappy couldn't believe what he was hearing. His grand-daughter was believing in hocus-pocus shams.

"*You* have passion! I've seen you bursting with it. I couldn't even watch when you graduated from the rock wall to the real thing on Big Ben. That alone, Anna Gwendolyn, is proof of your incredible passion. But now, something has stopped you."

I can't even look in his eyes, Anna Gwendolyn thought, hanging her head. Pappy knew that some trauma had re-surfaced. Some secret about bullying had drained her passions and self-esteem. Anna Gwendolyn had never told Pappy or anyone what had happened. He just knew that it had been a horrible defining moment in her young life and had derailed her dreams. Any reminder about the "secret incident" was met with Anna's tear-filled eyes and an immediate about-face of the subject.

"It's passion that propelled your Giselle leaps and spun you round and round doing your turns across the dance floor.

"And you believed you could climb up those rocks. It toughened your grip on those rocks, too! Belief that never gives up drives your passions. One secret though, Anna: You might have to *pretend* to believe at first," Pappy said with a twinkle in his eyes.

"So, besides passion, I have to . . . believe? What is this, a mystery? If I have . . . ah . . . or had this passion like you say I do, why can't I feel it? Where is it?"

Pappy knew he was going to need more than words to get his point across; his competition was a machine!

"Anna Gwendolyn, could you please run back to the house and get the Dream Direct-tionary on the podium?"

"Sure Pappy." She retrieved the book, all the while thinking *I need action like the Dream-O-Tron can give me! Not an old book. Old people always want to do things the hard way. They didn't grow up with technology! Oh well, here goes.* Anna Gwendolyn returned with the weathered, raggedy Dream Direct-tionary.

"Here Pappy, it's much bigger than I thought. I surely don't understand how this scrappy, old book is going to help me, Pappy, but if you insist, I'll take a look."

"Let's read here . . ." Pappy said. "The opening chapter: Definitions & Explanations."

Passion: a strong, barely controllable emotion and boundless enthusiasm that drives an individual towards a goal. Actions, fueled by passion, can unleash the power to do the unbelievable.

"See Anna Gwendolyn, it's not just me saying this, the Dream Direct-tionary says it. Let's read some more."

Commitment: The quality of being dedicated to a cause, activity, or goal.

"Without your commitment, Anna Gwendolyn, your dreams remain in limbo, floating aimlessly around, pleading for somebody to find them."

Perseverance: The ability to press on, without stopping, to pursue a goal in the face of any and all obstacles.

"Like me not finishing that clubhouse . . ."

Obstacle: Something, mental or physical, that blocks progress. Obstacles never disappear. Once overcome or banished, they simply refuel, multiply, and return to the scene of the dream to work their wickedness.

"Believe me, Pappy, I know obstacles!"

Visualization: Picturing a mental image, a vision of something in your mind that you want.

Mind Picture: The vision in your mind when you visualize a goal.

"Yeah, you know, Pappy, in the classroom, I remember I'd make my own personal movie screen out of the finger-smudged fourth grade classroom window. Then I'd imagine a metropolis of cities and suburbia on that cracked, asphalt playground, of course complete with castles and waterfalls. I had skylines to design, landscapes to create, journeys to navigate, and equations to solve the mysteries of the Universe. All this on my very own personal movie screen, outside that window."

Pappy knew she was listening! "Oh!! Oh! There you have it, Anna Gwendolyn! You probably have no idea that you were using the skill of mind pictures and visualization! Great work! Keep reading."

> **Dream Journeys**: The ongoing process (it can be treacherous!) of reaching your dreams, which fuels dignity, self-confidence and leadership.

"You can feel, Anna, like you are being led through dark, tangled passages, over countless challenges and obstacles, just like in rock climbing. But how do you feel when you get to the top of the boulder? What do you say? 'I did it! All by myself!' Eyes that rolled up at you now open wide with astonishment. All of a sudden people are listening to you! They look up to you. You might even inspire them to go after their own dreams!"

"I'm trying to listen, Pappy, really. Maybe I can find my passions . . ."

"Well, you don't find them in a Dream-O-Tron!" Pappy stated emphatically. *If the wrinkle in her brow gets any tighter, her eyes are going to be glued shut! It's painful to watch!* "Maybe you'll have to collide with your passions—before you recognize them!"

Anna was re-assessing this whole dream talk with Pappy. *This is a waste of my time. Commitment, perseverance, visualization . . . What good would they do?* she thought. *I remember working hard, being honest and following the rules. But that "incident" of unjust accusations and bullying destroyed my spirit. Why believe? It will only be destroyed by deceit, by kids lying or making up stuff to fill the space on social media.*

Back to reality, it had been Anna's plan to sell the Dream-O-Tron idea to Pappy during their lunch. All this talk wasn't working.

Chapter Five

Road Map or Dream Ladder?

Pappy suggested, "I hear the Festival calling your name."

"No, Pappy, I have time. Tell me more," Anna Gwendolyn still had hopes for her purchase.

"The Dream-O- . . ." she started to say.

"I know, I know . . . Anna Gwendolyn, that machine . . . But the work you do to get your dream develops commitment, self-belief, empowerment and courage, the tools to carry on, no matter what. They'll appear, sort of like magic! Then tackling life's challenges are possible."

"Magic! Now you're talking, Pappy! You about lost me there, but I could sure use some of that! Some of that magic you're talking about, Pappy, would come in real handy right about now. But, still, it sure would be easier to dream with that Dream-O-Tron," she added.

"Are you looking for your dream or for an escape?"

"How about some of that 'Magic,' Pappy, like I said. You've mentioned that a couple times."

"Yes, there's magic, but not the kind I'm lucky enough to pull out of a hat. Anna Gwendolyn, it's not time for the magic, yet. It's time for dream work."

That comment called for her well-honed, coping skill of ditzyness that always saved her.

"Pappy, one of these days, maybe one of those dream-keeper fairies who lives on a star is going to see my passion and my struggles from afar. She'll pass down a dream ladder—one I can climb up and it will lead me to my dreams."

"Do you need a dream ladder, or do you need a roadmap to discover your dreams?"

"I'll take the dream ladder," Anna Gwendolyn answered sarcastically.

And with a smile Pappy remarked, "Finding your dreams, Anna Gwendolyn, can be the greatest adventure of your life!"

Chapter Six

Dream Prints Hint the Future

"Before you go . . ." Pappy continued reading in the Dream Direct-tionary.

Write down your goals: Chisel the words of your dreams into stone, scribble them on a napkin, paint them on a canvas or picture them written in the clouds. Shout your intentions to the world.

Smile at your nay-sayers: Press on full-steam-ahead. (Half the world will look at you and wonder what the heck you're doing.) Commit to the work, fuel your dreams with passion, and then sit back and watch all that you have imagined come to life.

Oh magic! That sounds like magic!
In spite of time being short, Pappy had one more important thing to tell her.

"Have you ever heard of Dream Prints? They're like fingerprints but for dreams. No two are identical. Everyone is born with them. They give hints to your intended destiny. Listening to your Dream Prints will guide you to your destiny."

"What in the world? Did you say Dream Prints?"

Hmmmm, Dream Prints and Dream-O-Tron both sound kind of magical. Maybe I could connect the two subjects and bring them up to Pappy. She had not given up on the dream machine, and that's why she was sticking around.

Pappy continued, "Every human being has a Dream Print as a child. Johnnie obsesses with building blocks. Future musicians play anything that makes noise as toddlers. Baby engineers take apart anything that's not tied down.

"Anna Gwendolyn, your Dream Prints were evident when you were three years old. Even as a toddler, you were building skyscrapers and castles with boxes and scraps and anything you could find."

"So, I had these Dream-Prints? Do I still have them?" Anna Gwendolyn responded with surprise.

"Sure, why wouldn't you?" asked Pappy. "Everyone has them. They just have to be identified, acknowledged, and nurtured."

Looks like Pappy is the Master Advisor of Dreams. He's talking about dreaming like some kind of guru!

"You know, I didn't just wake up one day working for the railroad," he said. "As a three-year old, I wore overalls and my conductor's cap everywhere I went. I turned boxes into train cars, and charged five cents for rides around the house. Eventually, nurturing my Dream Print with hard work and attention, I became Conductor General of the Missouri Pacific

Railway. There were plenty of obstacles along the way, but my passion got me through.

"Anna Gwendolyn, your bridges and skyscraper castles created little cities in our living room. Your Dream Prints were alive and well . . . and still are waiting to lead you to your destiny."

Dream Prints. Wow. They really could help me find my dreams. This might be making some sense after all. It sure is a lot more work than the Dream-O-Tron, but . . .

"Wow, Pappy, time really flew by! Jake and my friends will be here soon."

"Maybe surrounded by all that Renaissance magic, you'll catch sight of your dream!"

Ever Lost A Dream?

Chapter Seven

If Cheshire Could Talk

Anna Gwendolyn heard the sound of Jake's car coming up the driveway. She was waiting near the remnants of her half-baked clubhouse.

Anna was excited about spending the day at the Renaissance Festival with her friends: Veronica, Gloria, Nevah and Jake, her cousin. The girls were like sisters to her. Jake lived down the street and had always been there when she needed something. They'd all grown up together. The girls were alumni of the first preschool class of the Little Yellow School, a magical place to learn.

Nevah, Gloria and Veronica piled out of the car; Jake waited patiently in the driver's seat.

The three festively adorned girls walked briskly toward Anna. They were brimming with anticipation.

"Are you ready to go? The Renaissance Festival awaits. We won't want to miss anything! Come on . . . Jake is waiting and he is impatient."

"I'll be there. I'll be there. Just remembering my dream of that clubhouse I started." Anna Gwendolyn knew Gloria just said that to hurry things up. She was the one known for being impatient.

"Think about all the Renaissance guys we'll see," said Veronica, a sparkle in her eyes.

That's what I need, thought Anna Gwendolyn—*a little fun at the Festival! This is the Renaissance Festival where everything is magical. I'm going to follow the magic!*

The wheels in Anna Gwendolyn's mind were turning. Gloria could berate her; her friends might fail to jump to her defense, but she wouldn't let that bring her down. She could make plans of her own. An idea popped into her head. *I bet this will stop Gloria. Maybe I'll just make some of my own magic; Pappy seems to think I have some. Then I won't have to put up with Gloria's bossiness.*

Pretending to be serious, she announced in her most lofty voice, "Hey all! Listen up! You've given me an awesome idea. You know how I love measuring sticks and rulers. Well, I'll just trade my love of "rulers" in for the RULER OF THE LAND, a prince who will become king!" Her teasing eyes gave away her motive. She could see Gloria fuming.

"And . . . I just love trains, too, so I'll trade Pappy's train in for a wedding train!" *Ha!*

Anna Gwendolyn's flighty and feisty way of thinking often stopped people in their tracks. And that's just what she was intending to do with Gloria.

The girls responded with the silent, expected group eye roll.

"C'mon, c'mon, she's a'rarin' to go, ladies!" Jake called, now standing by his car door. "Could you guys please step on it? We've been waiting here for . . ."

Jake, Anna's cousin, standing there in all his huskiness, was kind, handsome, rugged, and skilled at about everything there is to do in life. Sadly, Jakes parents, founders and CEOs of their "Heal & Soul" shoe business and dad and mom to six children, were killed in a horrific, head-on, auto accident. Life as they had known it had been destroyed simply because someone could not wait to text. The two had formed the shoe company and chosen the name "Heal & Soul" because they were firm believers that they could make a difference in underprivileged children's lives by providing them shoes, and consequently boosting their self-esteem and dignity. They wanted to heal souls . . . The children would know that someone believed in them.

Smirking, Veronica asked, "By the way, Jake, what's with the '*we?*' Who's with you? Oh, of course, your *car.* You consider your precious Cheshire another person. Sorry . . . I know, I always forget."

The aqua and white 57 Chevy, named the Cheshire, was Jake's best friend. Girls were barely on his radar. He had used his life savings from swim coaching, major creative home renovation projects, and teaching music lessons to purchase the old, classic car and refurbish it. Jake was used to waiting for girls. He had five older sisters and it seemed he'd been waiting on one or more of them for his entire life. The Heal & Soul family business made him a "chick magnet" even more than the iconic Cheshire Chevy. Heal & Soul Company made shoes of all kinds, from backpacking boots to Cinderella platforms. An unorthodox, unselfish ownership model allowed each family member to share all aspects of the business, but pursue his or her own dreams, too.

As always, this year's Heal & Soul exhibition at the Festival was donating shoes to children's charities. The founders believed everyone enjoys a new pair of shoes. But to some, more than the shoes' protective covering, new shoes can inspire feelings of belonging and being "cool," emotions that can act as a launching pad for a child's dreams.

Gloria and Veronica grabbed Cheshire's front door and climbed into and over the turquoise leather front seat and into the backseat, leaving the front seat for Anna Gwendolyn. She always wanted the rearview mirror in case she had to redo what she had already redone. They all settled in for the ride.

Jake was an Eagle Scout, avid back packer, triathlete and musician, and appeared to be on track so that whatever he became, he would make good use of his talents. Mostly, he was proud of his car.

It was a Jake original.

He'd turned the passenger seats and upholstery into a museum of previous excursions. He preserved leftover remnants of his passengers' memories—butter-stained popcorn bags, crumpled pizza menus and maybe a *boutonniere* from a prom.

The date and event of each remnant was noted. Passenger photos along with logos of favorite restaurants and pompom ribbons from football games were included. If the Cheshire could talk . . . His parents' tragic deaths magnified Jake's respect for even the smallest memory. A ride in the Cheshire was a ride down Teenage Memory Lane.

"Wake up! We're here!" Jake jostled. All four girls, Veronica, Nevah, Gloria, and Anna Gwendolyn, were suddenly bright-eyed. The long ride and the afternoon sun had lulled them into a short nap . . . well, almost a nap; at least the teen girl chatter had stopped.

The girls piled out of the Chevy, leaving one behind—of course, Anna Gwendolyn. She always needed one more look in the mirror. No matter how hard she had worked or fussed with her hair and make-up, she was always subject to a last-minute change. She said, "Guys, wait up, I'll be finished in a minute, I promise." The rolling of eyes could almost be heard.

Ever Lost A Dream?

Chapter Eight

The Secret

Lately, Anna always felt behind, not fast enough, not good enough, not pretty enough, simply, not enough. Always hurried. Always rushed. "Oops, oh . . . ! I wish they would stop hurrying me." The contents of her overloaded cosmetic bag had spilled. Through her tears she thought, *Oh, I can't let Jake see this*! Grabbing the strewn make-up and repacking it, "Okay, it's all picked up now and I've wiped up any powder," she calmed herself out loud. "Whew! That was a close one. There's not a drop on the floor." She headed toward her friends, putting a big smile on her face.

She wished her smile felt real.

Gloria's radar could pick up the tiniest detail and as she came closer, she noticed Anna Gwendolyn's typical far-off stare. Sure, she had a smile on her face, but her eyes gave her away. Gloria wondered to herself, *There she goes. What in the world is she thinking? We're here at this wonderful place and she's, once again, stuck in a maze in her head. She can't seem to get out.*

The four girls had known each other all their lives. Everyone thought Anna Gwendolyn was going to be an architect, world traveler, and mathematician. She was known for dreaming up solutions and it was assumed she'd find a way to blend together her many interests. But then, that incident happened. She referred to it as "The Incident," but never said much more. That's when everything about her changed; no more excellent grades, no more exemplary conduct and no more enthusiastic, bubbly personality. Anna never told anyone the details, including Pappy. What was known was that Anna Gwendolyn had experienced an injustice—a betrayal from bullying—and the incident could have gone viral. Her refusal to tell anyone prevented any possible resolution, but her friends respected her right to keep her secret.

Chapter Nine

Game Plan

Excited to finally enter through the massive Renaissance Festival gates, the girls all started talking at once. They each had a special place they wanted to see, but of course, it went without saying that the Shoe Garden was on everyone's list.

Nevah's first stop would be for coffee, her favorite beverage. She needed it, often appearing dysfunctional without her time-scheduled latte. She regularly pulled all-nighters to keep up with school and the lattes had become a staple of her diet. Nevah had dreams of becoming a best-selling author, lawyer, or congresswoman . . . maybe all three. Her head was a perpetual landing site of her contested brainstorms. Nevah was known to rise at 3:30 a.m. to siphon ideas from that brain on to paper. To her friends, she was lovable, but a little loco. Underneath it all, she knew exactly what she was doing, bent on surprising everyone. But right now, she knew she needed a latte and made sure the girls knew that, too. "Once that is accomplished, I'll be more accommodating," she proclaimed, as she headed off, following the aroma of fresh-brewed coffee.

The other girls couldn't stop squirming and chatting as they tried to work out a plan. Gloria, of course, took swift action to get them on track. Ever fastidious with a mind like a Swiss time piece, Gloria could drive a sloth to agitation. Taking leadership of the group, she said, "Okay, ladies, we're going to plan and not miss anything." The eye rolling started on cue.

"Grab that map over there to read off the program, and I'll put the schedule on my phone, so we won't miss anything."

"Let's go to the Peacock Tea Garden, the Marketplace, and of course, the Heal & Soul Shoe Garden," suggested Veronica.

"I know y'all can't wait for the Heal & Soul Shoe Garden, but let's stop at the Peacock Tea Garden first," said Anna Gwendolyn.

Jake interrupted, "Okay, ladies, I need to get to my shift at the Heal & Soul. Please, y'all stay together, and meet me at 5:30," he warned.

"We know, Jake, we're all supposed to stay together," Nevah sort of yelled out, walking toward them, with an extra-large coffee in her hand.

"Come on, Nevah. We're headed to the Peacock Tea Garden," Anna Gwendolyn called out. Nevah went to scout out more coffee instead, saying she'd catch up.

"There it is. See that giant peacock on the sign? And oh, look up ahead; it's the entrance." A sparkling, multi-colored, 3D peacock graced the gate, mesmerizing the girls as they strolled through.

The magic was beginning. . . .

Chapter Ten

Peacock Picnics & Shoe Slides

Once inside the Peacock Tea Garden, make-believe became believable. Peacocks strutted around the grounds, declaring ownership. They could have been carrying signs that read, "We are beautiful, and we know it!" The girls spun in circles, trying to take it all in.

"Look at those waterfalls!" Anna Gwendolyn exclaimed. She was remembering the ones she built in her backyard. *I could build them everywhere.* "And those peacocks—I've never seen so many!"

"May I offer you a seat at one of our waterfall tables?" asked the waitress.

"Can we have that one over there?" Anna Gwendolyn pointed with both hands. Her enthusiasm spilled over, just like the waterfalls. She was re-energized by them. The muffled but exhilarating sound waterfalls are known for was exactly why Anna Gwendolyn had fallen in love with them. The table was perfect.

"Fair maidens, I have the pleasure of taking your orders. Here's our menu. Just check off what you'd like," she said, handing out four whimsical looking scrolls.

"Okay, y'all, let's order." said Gloria. "Wow, check out this food!"

- Damsel Takes a Rest plate with double cream cheese swirls
- Raspberry Rapunzel smothered in cinnamon-sugar crunchies
- Lady-Fingers in Waiting with blackberry vanilla whipped cream
- Peacock Passion Picnic Platter a combination of everything!

As usual, Gloria made the decision for all of them. "We'll have one Damsel, one Lady-Fingers and two Peacock Picnics, thank you."

Anna Gwendolyn turned around to watch the peacocks as they strutted by. She could have cared less about food; how could anyone think about food with these amazing creatures so close . . . She felt drawn to them, but why? It was almost as if they were trying to showcase their magnificence just for her.

Nevah appeared. "Hey, wow, you guys are missing all of the cool, latte places at the fair. This place has international coffee flavors on every corner and it's hard to decide which one to try!" She'd found her own personal treasure chest at the Festival.

"And I'm sure you tried all of them, Nevah," Gloria smiled, already knowing the answer from watching her friend fidget.

The food arrived to an applause of approval. It was pure Renaissance gourmet. Muzzling their mouths, lively chatter was traded for relaxing conversation between bites.

Anna Gwendolyn, distracted, concentrated on the peacocks parading about the Garden. *I know what everyone is going to say . . . , but I'm going to say it anyway,* Anna Gwendolyn bravely exclaimed to herself.

Then, out loud, "Look! Just look at those peacocks; I know it's crazy, but they look like they're trying to fly! Watch how they run up and down that flagstone path. Like a runway—it's as if they think it's a runway! Do you think . . . ?" asked Anna Gwendolyn.

Almost in unison, the girls cut her off, "No! No way, Anna Gwendolyn."

Gloria spoke for the group, "We don't think, and you don't either. Those peacocks are NOT going to fly."

"Yeah, peacocks fly a little. But they don't really fly like robins and blue jays," said Veronica, backing up Gloria's absolute statement.

"And they are NEVER going to," Gloria said. "Besides, I think all those yard-stick long feathers would get in the way. Don't ya' think, Anna Gwendolyn?"

"Oh, I don't know. Pappy says you can do anything if you put your mind to it. Maybe they just haven't tried hard enough. I'm sure he also meant peacocks," her eyes twinkling.

They rebuked her with a collective "Hah!"

Starting out from the Peacock Garden with Gloria's cell phone map in hand, the girls dodged revelers, musicians and more than a few knights.

Their bellies now happy, they turned to Gloria for direction. It was time to check out the Shoe Garden everyone was talking about. "Okay, the map on my GPS says Heal & Soul and 'a little shoe magic' is up ahead. Look, it's that way and three venues to the right," she continued, pointing to the screen. "Okay, gang, let's go."

Approaching the Shoe Garden, something ahead was large and unrecognizable.

"There's a big sliding board up there! What is that thing? A giant . . . shoe! No, a giant high heel! And it looks like it's even on a platform." Veronica pointed.

"Jake didn't tell us anything about this," Anna Gwendolyn said.

"That shoe has a platformed, high heel! You're right! And look! Look at that platform. It's a garden. It's like a terrarium inside the clear platform, under the shoe. How weird!"

"And take a look at the heel. It's a staircase to the top of the shoe!" Nevah was intrigued.

The clear platform terrarium was something they'd never seen. Finally moving toward the entrance, they saw the shoe up close. It was a giant depiction of a Renaissance shoe, with all its straps, beads and, yes, its platform. And, as if the giant shoe was not enough, a colorful signboard welcomed visitors into the Garden.

Welcome To Heal & Soul Shoe Garden
We donate a wardrobe of new shoes for deserving children, providing a launch pad for their dreams!

Jake's booming voice in the distance gave revelers all around a reason to visit the Heal & Soul Shoe Garden. "Every year, Heal & Soul presents children with a wardrobe of shoes. This year, the focus will be athletic and performing arts shoes, to inspire the children to explore new adventures and arm them with the confidence to do it."

"Okay y'all. Let's go! The staircase leads to the top of the shoe, and then—look at all the kids!—they're s-s-s-sliiiiide down the shoe into the Garden!" exclaimed Gloria.

"Swoosh!" smiled Nevah.

"What a hoot! This is going to be a blast. Time to climb up this thing." Gloria's quick assessment had a plan in place for the girls. "Okay, everyone, time to pay our donation. Over there, that knight is taking money."

Caught up in her own thoughts, Anna was imagining how this giant high heel had been built and was visualizing her own embellishments. Jarred back to reality by their laughter, she followed the group.

The girls, still in awe of the colossal high heel, handed the knight their donations and fell in line at the bottom of the staircase. They could see the terrarium-like interior within the confines of the giant, high heel platform. Tickets secured, they climbed the staircase and with a "swoosh"—they were inside the Heal & Soul Garden.

Jake's voice, booming over the loudspeakers again, welcomed one and all into the Garden. "Time to give away some shoes. Heal & Soul is now famous for their belief in, and support of, deserving kids by providing new shoes, to help make them feel 'cool.' We all understand that believing in kids directly affects their self-esteem, their dignity, and their ability to dream. Hey, kids!! We believe in you!

"Now, Lords and Ladies, the history of platform shoes . . ." He saw the girls from the corner of his eye. *Good,* he thought. *They are all together just like I told them.*

"Jake knows all this stuff." Gloria commented as the group walked toward him.

"He really had no choice," Nevah laughed. "He grew up in a 'shoe box.' Then, put five sisters in the mix and of course he's an expert!"

Anna Gwendolyn and Nevah were checking out the knight who had suddenly appeared. He was not a Knight of the Round Table, but just a high school student getting extra credit for a history project. The ambience of this magical garden, and his kind voice and grand gestures, convinced them that he was straight out of King Arthur's Court. Jake and his brilliance were quickly forgotten as they watched the knight move through the crowd. They could have followed him forever but . . .

Gloria called, "C'mon girls, it's time for shopping."

Now headed up to the Mall of Merchants, it was time to check out the booths. Not fully listening, combined with trying to follow directions, Anna was overwhelmed. Then there was the distraction of the knights all around her, collecting donations and getting her further off-track. "Good luck on your amazing journey, my lovely lady," one knight had said with a wink.

For a second, Anna Gwendolyn had been captured by the knight's attention. She was intrigued and thought to herself, *Hmmm . . . amazing journey . . . ? a sign . . . ?*

Ever Lost A Dream?

Chapter Eleven

Treasure in the Bargain Box

The girls headed to the center of the fairgrounds. Gloria was drawn to a booth covered in scarves and shawls from around the world. A handsome, young knight approached them, "Hello, and welcome to Royal Rags. How may I help you? What color scarf are you looking for today?"

"Psst! Hey, this guy looks like a Roman prince. None of us really want a scarf, but he is definitely worth sticking around for," Veronica whispered.

Oh no, here we go again, Gloria said to herself.

"You surely do have a lot of scarves and so many colors—so many choices," Veronica said, flashing her best imitation of a teen magazine smile. Picking up one of the scarves, she asked, "Where does this one come from, kind sir?"

Watching Veronica openly flirt with the knight, Nevah asked herself, *The knight or the scarves? She needs to learn a little subtlety.* Looking around, *Yes, this place has knights from every corner of the globe! Anna Gwendolyn got the attention of the Shoe Garden Knight. So maybe it's my turn to choose a scarf . . . and a knight.*

Anna Gwendolyn walked around the small space picking up scarves of her favorite colors. She swung them in the air and playfully wrapped herself in them. Several matched glittery, teal-turquoise throws back home in her dress-up trunk. And the sequins . . . *How those would have made Mama smile!*

"Pappy would like these, too," Anna Gwendolyn told the girls, oblivious to the fact that the girls had no idea she'd been thinking of her mother. Then another turquoise scarf caught her eye. Ever drawn to weathered and worn objects needing attention, Anna Gwendolyn spotted the sparkly scarf beneath a heap of discounted scarves, in a dilapidated wooden crate. Even though almost out of sight, its sparkles peeked through the mish-mash of bargains.

"Oh, it's beautiful and look at it glisten, as it falls through the air. I've just got to have this! Y'all just be quiet for a moment," pleaded Anna Gwendolyn. No need to hush Nevah; she was staring at the knight . . . and a scarf, of course. (At least, that's what she wanted the knight to think.)

With the shimmer of wannabe gems, the scarf's untangling created a commotion throughout the shop. It was that beautiful. "Ah, I can't seem to a find a tag. How much . . . how much?" Anna asked.

"How much would I be willing to take for it?" asked the Roman-looking knight.

Anna Gwendolyn replied, "How much would you be willing to sell it to me for?"

"For sale at $24.99, reduced from $40.00. Shall I wrap it in tissue or would you like it on a hanger?"

Anna Gwendolyn said impulsively, "I'll take it. Look! It matches this dress that I glued together. Teal green turquoise . . . my favorite color."

Sharply aware of Anna Gwendolyn's spending habits, Gloria gasped and the girls chimed in "Awfully expensive," but to no avail. While Anna Gwendolyn was making her purchase, the others continued shopping. To the dismay of the charming knight, each bought one of the smaller scarves. They were saving their money for the jewelry merchants.

Anna Gwendolyn was aware they were skeptical about her purchase, but she knew exactly what she would do with it. Her beautiful scarf was just what she needed to carry out her earlier threat. She was now determined to pretend to turn her love of "trains" into her future wedding train. "Couldn't this scarf be a wedding train??" Of course, she knew that statement was outrageous, but it was fun teasing Gloria about it. Besides, who knew? Someday, maybe it *could* be a wedding train.

Gloria just rolled her eyes. Gloria lived her life wound tighter than the second hand of a clock. Everything had to be in order and on time, precise too. Gloria rarely imagined her dreams; not having dreams was all Anna Gwendolyn thought about.

They left the scarf booth and headed for the artisans down the Merchants Mall. The girls' intentions not to spend all their money in one place was about to be tested by yet another handsome knight.

Ever Lost A Dream?

Chapter Twelve

Throw-away Jewels & Grapevines

"My Lords and Ladies alike . . . come and feast your eyes on our beautiful Renaissance crowns. Custom made by hand while you watch, and accented with jewels," tempted one knight.

"Oh, yes, look. I love those headpieces," Veronica said, the knight's words catching her attention. "I've just got to have one! Let's head over there. See, over there next to that huge tree, with all the hanging wreaths?"

This time the temptations were beautifully woven grapevine wreaths to be worn as crowns. The tangled, almost braided, grapevines were interwoven with wildflowers and jewels. They all seemed similar but looking closely, you could see each adornment held its own mystique, Renaissance-flavored. Each crown oozed magic. The girls wanted to feel that magic.

"Step up, if just for a moment. Select a crown, or for a few dollars extra, we'll custom design it to your specification," the knight said.

The girls were taken by all the choices. Jewels, ribbons, fabulous bits and pieces of glamour were everywhere. Veronica,

Nevah and Gloria each bought a headpiece, carefully selecting colors and trimmings that best complimented their personalities. Putting the crowns on, they took turns posing in front of the mirror, loving their Renaissance looks.

Anna Gwendolyn fumbled through the hanging wreaths and dug through the boxes of used ones under the table. She was always rummaging for a bargain. (Considering her spending habits, that was a good idea.) She delighted in knowing she could custom-design her own wreath, but at the same time dreaded not being able to afford one. Her money was about gone, and she still needed to pay Jake for gas.

Anna Gwendolyn reluctantly said to herself, *Nothing under twenty dollars here. Well, I don't even have five dollars, so I guess I'll just have to . . .* Turning, she saw the girls with their new treasures. *Gosh they look so Renaissance,* as she watched the girls preening. *I love my scarf though. Besides, I'll probably get more wear out of a scarf than a grapevine wreath anyway,* Anna rationalized half-heartedly, with more than a little pout.

"I can do this," she countered under her breath, gritting her teeth and determined to find a solution. Out loud but to only herself she added, "I can figure this out and no one will have any idea how I managed to get a wreath. Let's see, I'll pretend to do without . . . but then . . . but then what?" *It will come to me,* she thought. *I just know it . . . just like Pappy's Direct-tionary said, "Persevere." Well, I will persevere and keep my eyes open.*

Chapter Thirteen

From Down to Crown

Anna Gwendolyn pretended to hide her disappointment from the others. Pretending was one of her gifts and she'd nurtured it a great deal lately. She'd become accustomed to people nagging at her to "listen," "pay attention," or "get it together," but she was expert at acting as if their words didn't bother her, expert at pretending. She knew exactly how to pull this off.

"I really wanted one of those wreaths, but I have my scarf and that will be enough for me," she proclaimed. "Y'all look so pretty, like Renaissance fair maidens." Secretly, Anna Gwendolyn was counting on one of her legendary schemes to get what she wanted.

"Thanks, Anna Gwendolyn," Veronica smiled, thinking to herself that surely, she would catch the eye of a knight with her beautiful wreath. "Let's see what other goodies we can find today." Off they sashayed down the fairway as crowned Renaissance princesses.

Suddenly remembering something she saw while at the Peacock Tea Garden, Anna Gwendolyn excused herself to go the restroom. "Girls, I'll be back in a flash. You go on." She knew that with the lines at the Festival, she could buy herself at least thirty minutes away from the group. She intended to use this break to revisit the peacocks and scoop up their strung-about feathers.

Gloria, Nevah, and Veronica hesitated to leave her behind, but their shopping spree beckoned.

The owner of Peacock Tea Garden was more than pleased to have Anna Gwendolyn tidy up a bit. She gathered as many feathers as she could hide inside her scarf's bag. She knew her friends would have a thousand questions. More simply put, they might laugh at her for picking up "trash" off the ground. But that didn't matter; she wanted a beautiful wreath and she was going to get one. Like most teens, she yearned to be like everyone else. She knew exactly how she was going to turn this "trash" into treasure; recycling was her lifetime obsession.

Gathering what she hoped would be enough feathers, Anna Gwendolyn spotted the jewelry merchant. A bin behind the booth contained scraps of copper and gold-looking wire, broken glass beads, and fasteners. Bits and pieces of jewels and beads had also fallen into the grass. Anna Gwendolyn asked, "Would you mind if I picked up a few of these scraps? I'll pay you for them." She hoped two dollars would be enough.

The jewelry merchant answered, "All those little pieces are such a pain to pick up. If you have a use for them, help yourself." He handed her a paper bag. "I'd love to see what you're going to do with our trash."

All Anna Gwendolyn needed was a table and some wire cutters, which the merchant immediately offered her. In a few minutes, she fashioned a wreath of exquisite peacock feathers, weaving in the colorful jewels and beads so they peeked through the feathers every couple of inches. "A custom-made masterpiece, just for me," Anna Gwendolyn whispered to no one in particular.

The merchant, impressed with her creation, praised her ability to throw together a beautiful original wreath. "That's ingenious!" he said. "Wow, you could really make yourself some money. Are you going to study design?"

"No. Actually, I'd love to be an architect—like the builders in the Renaissance."

"You have a natural eye; I'm sure you'll be amazing at whatever you do. With an imagination like yours, you'll be building castles, just like the ones in the Renaissance, right along with your headpieces."

His praise is just what I need to hear! Anna Gwendolyn thought. *I can't wait to show my friends. They'll probably want me to make one for them!*

"You could open your own booth next year!" the merchant called out, as she turned to walk away.

Anna Gwendolyn proudly declared, "I could call it 'Crowning Glories' by Anna Gwendolyn."

Anna Gwendolyn remembered Pappy had always marveled at her resourcefulness. Now, maybe, she was beginning to *believe* what he'd been saying.

Bringing her thoughts back to the moment, Anna Gwendolyn realized, once again, time had gotten away. She'd better hurry back to the group.

"Thank you," she called to the merchant, as she took off down the path in search of her friends. Yes, they were used to her getting sidetracked, but she'd promised not to be gone long. Seeing them up ahead on the main promenade, "Here I am," Anna Gwendolyn yelled.

All eyes were on her wreath as she ran toward them. It was beautiful and quite different from any they had seen in the merchants' booths.

"Where did you get that? Did you charge it on your Pappy's credit card? Where did you . . . just where did you find that beautiful thing?" asked Gloria.

"You only had a few dollars left. Look at that gorgeous wreath. It must have cost a lot more than ours," remarked Veronica.

"I thought you were all out of cash," quipped Gloria.

With her head held high and her shoulders back, Anna answered, "You're right, I was almost out of cash. So how in the world did I find such an extraordinary wreath? Do I look like one of those models in the Renaissance Fair flyer? Do you like it? Didn't cost me a dime."

Anna Gwendolyn pranced—throwing her long, flowing scarf around as if it were a train for her dress, the wreath's feathers enveloping her head like a halo. Though annoyed by their expected interrogations, she was feeling victorious. *They all love this thing on my head, and they have no idea where it came from!*

She was pleased for not giving up after spending most her money on her scarf. She could have pouted all day, but instead put her thinking cap on, kept her eyes open, and, yes, she had even done a little work. Now she had a beautiful one-of-a-kind wreath, maybe even extraordinary . . . a wreath that the others envied.

"How did you do that? Where did you get it? How could you afford it?" Gloria kept firing questions faster than a ricocheting pinball.

"Do you like my peacock feathers as much as your grapevine crown? I had little cash, so I 'made do' like you guys are always telling me to do. It's a bit ingenious, isn't it? That's what the guy . . . I mean the knight, told me," she mused, pleading somewhat for approval but with a renewed dignity.

Gloria cut her off, "Yes, it's really nice. I know you picked up peacock feathers from the ground, but where did you get the jewels and wire?" She challenged. "Did you ask for them? And, did you ask the peacocks for their feathers?" Anna's illogical ways always confused her; here Anna had managed to outdo everyone without spending a dime.

"Yes, of course I asked the peacocks. But they were too busy practicing flying to answer! And as far as the other stuff, I asked the jewelers. They were just bits and pieces I found on the ground." Just once she wished they didn't look surprised at her accomplishments. *No wonder I doubt myself,* she thought. *Where is their belief in me?*

Anna Gwendolyn continued, "I just stopped and asked the owner about picking up the feathers. He was happy to have them removed. And, I asked the jeweler about using his scraps. After he saw my finished creation, he told me I could open my own store. I could call it 'Anna Gwendolyn's Crowning Glories.' Do you want more details?" she continued, feeling a little indignant again, as she countered Gloria's barrage of questions. "I don't take things without asking. The merchant was thankful that I cleared his grounds of wires and stones that are harmful to humans and animals."

"But, those feathers—the jewels are one thing, but those feathers belong to the peacocks. You said you thought they were trying to fly. How are they going to fly without those ridiculous feathers?" teased Veronica with a gentle smile. Everyone laughed. Once again and, as always, Veronica had lightened the mood.

Anna Gwendolyn summarized, "We've dined with peacocks, slid down a colossal, high heel into a garden of shoes and helped some children feel better about themselves. Then we shopped til we . . . what's next?"

It's almost time to meet Jake and go home," Veronica announced. "Let's head that way. Jake will be there already."

Anna Gwendolyn turned suddenly, feeling a pull on her train and thought to herself, *That must be some mischievous child.* Then she exclaimed, "Oh my goodness!" To her surprise, it was one of the knights from Heal & Soul. Anna Gwendolyn stopped in her tracks.

"M'lady, your creation is a work of art. It's the buzz of the Festival. I'm impressed by you. Your talent and belief in yourself could turn those wreaths into your own Renaissance business."

Anna Gwendolyn, almost speechless, stammered, "Ah . . . ah . . . really. Are you talking to me? You mean me? Oh, no one's ever noticed that in me, except my Pappy." Her face turning red, she thought, *Great, now I'm rambling on about Pappy. He doesn't want to hear about Pappy.*

"You've created a buzz throughout the Festival, M'lady, and I wanted to make sure you knew it!"

Dumbfounded, Anna Gwendolyn said to herself, *This is what Pappy was talking about—my creativity, my ability to make something out of nothing.*

"Thank you, sir. But I need to get back with my friends."

"You are welcome. Good day, M'lady," he said, bowing his head to her and leaving her standing there, staring.

Anna caught up with the girls, thinking *Wow, maybe this is another sign. Maybe I could go after my dreams without the help of a Dream-O-Tron or whatever that thing was. Just like Pappy said, maybe I have all it takes. It wasn't only Pappy talking; now this guy at the Festival is telling me!*

Gloria interrupted her thoughts, "Let's go, girls, the shopping spree is officially over."

Ever Lost A Dream?

Chapter Fourteen

When I Build My Castle

"So, what was so interesting that we lost you back there, Anna Gwendolyn?" Gloria asked, as everyone caught up with Jake.

Anna Gwendolyn thought she had escaped Gloria's relentless probing. Sighing, she replied, "I told you all already what happened. The knight just happened to think my wreath creation was so good that he thought I could make money selling them. Actually, another knight told me my peacock wreath creation was the talk of the Festival."

"You can't just flirt with strangers," Gloria scolded.

Anna Gwendolyn couldn't tell if her friend was really concerned or just jealous. "I wasn't flirting. The knight was telling me what a great job I did on my wreath. That's all. Yeah, you guessed it, he was really cute, but for one thing, he had a princess with him who was probably his girlfriend, his Cinderella."

Anna Gwendolyn smiled to herself. *My friends do not understand the future blissful life of luxury and privilege for which I am destined—if I can ever figure out how.*

Why shouldn't the knight have sought me out? When I'm sitting in a turret atop my castle, where will my friends be? Anna reverted to her most favored defense mode: a little evasion, denial and fantasy.

Then she boldly announced, "I want to build castles, waterfalls in suburbia, and travel the world. Think of it. I could build a castle with an indoor waterfall, a heated swimming pool and a closet the size of the entire teen department at Macy's!" The compliments Anna Gwendolyn had received had gone to her head. She knew she was off on a tangent, but she was caught up in the feeling of confidence and dignity the knight had inspired—feelings she hadn't felt since the secret bullying incident.

"So, what will you have to do to accomplish that?" Gloria asked.

"I'll have to go to school, of course." Anna Gwendolyn answered emphatically, forgetting that usually she couldn't even think about making that decision.

Though slightly bored with the girl talk, Jake decided to join in, joking. "Will your castle have a moat? One full of trout?"

"Of course, just like the real castles," Anna Gwendolyn countered, noticing his smile.

"I can't wait for an invitation to go fishing. Bet you'll even have a few sharks in there," Jake quipped.

"Yep, sharks for sure."

The group's fading energy definitely signaled the end of the day.

Happily exhausted, the girls exited the stadium and headed towards the Cheshire. Anna Gwendolyn led the way, with her new-found dignity. Today had been a good day for her.

"Come on, gang, the quicker we load into the Cheshire we'll get on the road before the rush. Maybe we can stop by Memories Park and take a ride on the Dream Spinner," piped Veronica. Everyone's eyes lit up.

"Okay if we stop by the Dream Spinner?" they asked in unison.

"Ok, sure," Jake agreed. "Maybe we'll find our dreams there!!"

Ever Lost A Dream?

Chapter Fifteen

The Legend of the Dream Spinner

Jake called, "Wake up, ladies! We will soon be touching down in Memories Park, home of the Dream Spinner. The temperature is a cool, Texas 82 degrees. Please return to the vehicle in sixty minutes, at which time we will prepare to travel home."

Waking up with eye rolls at Jake's banter, the girls collectively yawned, stretched and refreshed themselves for a ride on the Spinner. They tumbled out of the Cheshire, one by one; no need for last minute hair and makeup checks.

They'd been playing on the Dream Spinner since they were small children; it was like a best friend. They walked down the river-rock strewn path toward the Spinner in silence, as if to honor the ancient piece of machinery. "We've been coming here since our pre-school days, and look, it gets better every time," Jake said, his rare sensitivity allowing him to display his respect for its beauty and history. As always, as if to honor the Spinner, he read the writings on the historical marker out loud.

The Dream Spinner Legend
If you fall asleep while swinging,
the dream you dream will come true.

The girls listened with teen-age impatience, as he read. They'd heard these words before, but Jake was right, they could never be said too many times. It was magic. The presence of the Dream Spinner brought back a collage of memories, from childhood playgroups to pre-teen mischief.

The group moved closer to the Spinner. The swings were supported by steel, octopus-like arms extending from the engine's machinery in the middle. Each arm held one swing, hung by massive, braided, steel cords. The swings were actually seating boxes, painted gold, and each box was fashioned in early 1900s facades. Bars slid up and down the supporting chains for entry, exit and safety, as they had done for more than one hundred years. Seat belts had been added thirty years ago, with the tightening of amusement ride regulation.

What better way to continue the magic of their Renaissance day, then to take a twilight ride on the Spinner? Now it was time to see who would fall asleep, dream, and test the Legend of the Dream Spinner.

Lining up at the Spinner's gate, the five tired revealers were seated in the Spinner's swings. Once the safety checks were complete, the countdown began, and the attendant pulled the "ON" lever. Each swing began its ascent.

Within seconds of the pull of the latch, legs became horizontal and feet became rudders, scooping upwards through the air. The race was on as the friends pretended to challenge each other to see who could "fly" the highest. Actually, once propelled, all the Spinner swings soared close to the same level, but no one cared. As Anna Gwendolyn pumped her legs, the swings gliding through the air brought a breeze to her face and glee to her psyche. This was a welcomed relief after the day in the sun.

The moving steel hinges went from squeak to song, while familiar muffled, clanking sounds created the backdrop for the melody of the Dream Spinner's official chant. This masterpiece of workmanship and labor of community love was now in full flight . . . as it spun around to the legendary song, "Ever Lost a Dream?"

"Ever Lost a Dream?"

Dream tonight by starlight,
Or while the sun is shining bright,
Catch a ride upon Dream Spinner,
Time to catch your dream in flight.

One hundred years of witness,
The life-long legend can't be wrong,
Listen to the melody,
The lost dreamer's anthem song.

Fall asleep upon the Spinner,
Your dream, the grandest show!
That dream your heart's been guarding?
The Dream Spinner might just know!

The Spinner's on a mission,
Slumber's magic, dreams come true.
Pick a swing to take you dreaming,
Swirling light whispering the clue.

The legend's age-old question—
Ever lost a dream or two?
Where did they disappear to?
Would you like to take a view?

A brave view of possibility,
Visions growing 'til they gleam,
Whirling winds of passion calling,
Your dreams now waiting to redeem.

Find your dreams! Find your dreams! Find your dreams!

The rhythmic melody inspired a tempo, directing everyone's legs to push faster and faster.

Ever Lost A Dream?

Chapter Sixteen

Dreams Aflutter

Jake and the gang were whirling with eyes wide open with each round of their Spinner seats. But Anna Gwendolyn's obsession with the Legend directed her differently. She might as well see what might happen if she fell asleep. Climbing higher, and higher, spinning faster and faster went on for a while. She was waiting for sleep. Although her friends teased frequently about her scattered brain, today they had been impressed by her ingenuity. Her confidence was soaring.

This is my chance. I'm on this magical Dream Spinner. I'll fall asleep, I will dream, and when I awake my dream will come true, Anna Gwendolyn thought as she impatiently awaited sleep.

Hundreds of dreams coming true for Parkersville residents can't be wrong. And to think this morning I was all ready to buy that Dream-O-Tron, that dream-making machine. I was actually going to buy one of those! Maybe Pappy was right about that outfit. Now it's Dream Spinner's chance to prove its legend, she thought to herself.

Pumping harder and harder, blasts of air lifted her, all the while twirling her round and round in the Spinner. *Wow . . . the Spinner still has it!*

The victory of her peacock feather creation crowned her with a boost of needed self-worth. Her renewed spirit lifted as the power of her own legs and imagination directed the swing higher and higher, faster and faster, unleashing a freedom in her flight. She felt the wind on her face and heard the flutter of her makeshift, sparkling scarf, her prized Renaissance purchase, as it unfurled powerfully behind her. It was designing itself into a superhero cape—*or maybe even a wedding train,* she thought sarcastically.

"Look at me, world! I'm flying now!' Anna Gwendolyn continued sky bound. One, two, three spins melted into six . . . seven . . . eight.

Each spin began teasing her to sleep, then jostling her, as compacted air made speed bumps against the circling swings. "This thing is too bumpy; *I . . . will . . . never . . . fall asleep . . . sleepy—so very sleepy.* The now muffled Spinner machinery finally lulled her to sleep. Her eyelids gave way. All was dark.

Leaning back, goose bumps in slow cadence began marching up her spine. A silky sensation brushed her neck. "Oh, that . . . my scarf must be . . . oh, that's my scarf!" Too drowsy to capture the wayward scarf, sleep came. The early evening stars clocked in, keeping perfect time with the Spinner's lullaby.

"Oh, ah . . . Soon she was fully asleep. Would she dream? And what would the dream be?

Chapter Seventeen

From Feathers to Flight

Slowly, methodically, the individual swings beside her seemed to begin twirling round and round, showcasing a glowing colorful swirl like multi-hued taffy being stirred in cylindrical glass mixers. Each swing of her friends was mysteriously transforming itself. The individual seats, one by one, had materialized into spot-on replicas of her friends' actual, treasured dreams! All those dreams, the talks at midnight tell-alls during sleep overs, were now in front of her. Smitten, and within the glorious confines of her sleep . . . Anna Gwendolyn waited to see hers. She was patient.

Look, there's Jakes dream—he's a fighter pilot! Before her very eyes, she was seeing a state of the art fighter jet, cockpit, pilot's seat and steering wheel. *Oh! Jake is sitting in the seat!*

Oh, and what's all that clutter? It just had to be Nevah's writing desk complete with a stack of coffee stained pages! *Just look at that stack of her latest bestselling novels! WOW!!!*

So, is my dream next?

No, it wasn't . . . *Gloria,* Anna thought, *our very own "Controller in Chief" event planner, wedding planner, organizer of the lives of her near and dear* . . . Gloria's dream was represented by a huge, majestic clock on a "Glorious" chaise lounge, from which she could do her beloved controlling. Gloria even had one of those gold scepter things that a king uses to rule his countrymen.

"OK, there's Nevah's and Jake's and Gloria's dreams; where's Ver . . . Oh, there it is, I guess that's it."

Veronica's seat was empty with a sign that read "Undecided." There was a list, penned in red, that listed all her various dreams. It totally fit. Veronica had so many dreams, she wasn't even close to declaring.

With her excitement for her friends fading, Anna Gwendolyn really just wanted to see her dream. *Pappy told me I have to be patient.*

But where was it? The dreams of her friends had so magically appeared in front of her eyes. Could this be a sign? Were her fears to be confirmed?

Maybe I really don't have a dream. Or maybe my dream is just lost forever.

Frantically looking about, turning her head back and forth, she began searching all the swings on the Dream Spinner for even a sign of her dream. Watching her friends' dreams "coming to life" had turned from frivolity to torture.

Was the Dream Spinner confirming her belief that she really did not have a dream, that her dreams were lost forever?

As Anna Gwendolyn's train unfurled recklessly behind her, tears clouded her vision. Now fearful and exhausted in her pursuit, her failure to find her dream was devastating. It was not what she'd been taught all her life about the Spinner. It was supposed to be a chance to find her own dream, not to watch others live out theirs. Confused or disappointed? Anna Gwendolyn wasn't quite sure.

Still in flight, Anna tried to calm herself, fearful of the judgments of her friends regarding her tear stained face.

A peculiar sight flashed into the tiny opening of her eyelids. Just like when a bird flies by your open window and you see it and even "feel" it in the corner of you eye. "What, ah, ah, what was that? What's going on?" Then it was gone.

"It's not fair! Where is my dream?" Anna Gwendolyn whined aloud. This was not what she had signed up for. Again, the tears began to flow. And the Spinner, with its carousel of personal dreams, continued to revolve.

Faster and faster, every "dream swing" continued in flight, not unlike a sortie of planes in position. Through it all, the Dream Spinner melody continually replayed "Ever Lost a Dream?" *Okay, so maybe I'm not supposed to marry a prince, but where is my dream of architecture or world travel? Why is there not a drafting table . . . or my geography maps, or massive rocks to climb?* As if to answer her plea, a faint figure seemed to materialize from the glint of light she'd seen earlier. Curiosity silenced her complaints. *Oh, what now? The sky! What is that in the sky?* It seemed to be coming closer. Feeling a little frightened, she demanded, *Well, if you are my dream, present yourself now!*

Certainly, she was hallucinating. She tried to refocus her eyes, realizing that something wasn't right. Something was in her eye; something was falling apart. Was her "train" falling off in the wind? Was it secured? Was her head full of braids—

adorned by her masterpiece wreath—now taking on the antics of a bobblehead doll? Those wayward strands of hair were surely the culprit. That was it. The train had unfurled and some hair was blowing into her eyes. She reached up to move it and was startled. A tickling over her brow made her squint. She panicked, *I can't see! I can't see!*

The force of the wind seemed to be rustling her peacock-feathered wreath. Or was it some other unknown force? Brushing the obstruction off her face, something still fluttered around her. *Oh, what is going on? Will someone please help me?*

Okay, the swings have transformed themselves into dreams; my friends are experiencing them and mine must be lost. This doesn't feel like fairy dust, but my, oh my . . . something is happening above my head. It's going to hit me. "Help!" she cried out into the chaotic space, now cluttered with maddening visions of others' dreams. Though frightened, she was fueled by the intrigue of what was happening above, below and beside her. She was surrounded by chaos that somehow felt eerily magical.

And what . . . what in the world! Oh . . . oh . . . a blur of teal and purple . . .. wait. Those are peacock feathers! My handmade wreath, the masterpiece that I created . . . it's falling apart! Or, is it coming apart? Could it be? . . . All I want is for my swing to show me my dream . . . just like the others. Whatever is going on, please, I don't need anything but to see my dream!

Oh, my goodness!!! It's . . . what in this world? What! It's a peacock! Her handmade peacock feather creation was falling apart. No, it was de-constructing, turning into . . . was growing . . . was fluttering, growing bigger and bigger and was transforming into a . . . PEACOCK! But not an ordinary peacock. It was growing these massive wings. Not ordinary wings. It was growing peacock wings. As if . . . as if it was turning into some kind of . . . *What is it doing? Is it . . . is that way above me . . . a plane?*

What is happening to me—to my head? It's so loud! My ears! It's too loud! Startled and confused, she worked to decipher what was really looming above her head, making all the commotion. It was indeed some kind of plane, but it still looked more like a peacock. With the roaring sound of a 747 and the legendary hues of teal and purple, the majesty of this peacock plane left her with a feeling of awe she did not understand.

Could it be? Is this somehow part of my dream? Someone must think I want to be a flight attendant. Or work in a bird sanctuary. What is this? Why can't I just have a dream like everybody else?

Anna Gwendolyn's hunch was right. The peacock feathers of her original Renaissance wreath had been somehow transformed before her into a magnificent airplane, a Peacock Plane.

The Peacock Plane climbed higher and higher and began drawing circles and loop-de-loops in the air. Anna Gwendolyn covered her eyes, convinced this bird-plane was going to crash right into the Spinner. *Some dream this is! This is crazy!*

Then, due to her curiosity and without warning, searching for her missing dream was slowly abandoned.

Was there something about this in Pappy's Dream-Directtionary? Had she missed something due to her poor listening skills?

As the strange peacock-like plane spread its wings, wind gusts from the flapping wings of the magnificent bird-plane increased the speed of the Dream Spinner. Anna Gwendolyn watched wide-eyed as everything swirled into a blur. Thankfully, the dizzying spin slowed down a bit, allowing her to gain her composure. She thought she saw words in the distance. In the air space beyond the circle of the dream swing, alongside the peacock-like plane, was a glowing neon sign:

Daily Departures, Non-Stop Flights
Just remember, in the matter of Dreams,
as Nevah-Tu-Latte says . . .
It's Never To Late!

Huh? Never too late for what? Anxious and frustrated, Anna Gwendolyn made sure she was reading correctly, reading it over and over again. "Daily what? . . . daily departures, but to where?" Anna Gwendolyn asked aloud, "Non-stop flights, but to where . . . and who in the world is Nevah-Tu-Latte, anyway? What have I gotten myself into? Another sign—this must be another sign. Just like . . . maybe like what Pappy was talking about." *Surely these visions are not random,* she thought. *Could Nevah be behind this, with the help of Gloria?*

A voice spoke suddenly, "Anna Gwendolyn . . . Anna Gwendolyn, wake up. We're all ready to leave. It's time to go. Wake up, we need to get back before it's too late and Pappy is looking for you. Jake's ready to go."

Who is calling me? Anna Gwendolyn was wedged in the in-between state of dreaming and waking. Hopelessly lost in the unexpected drama and magic of the evening, she wasn't quite ready to leave this chaotic, confusing, magical place.

Reaching tentatively up to her head, *There, I'd better make sure my feathers are still on my wreath.* She assured herself that her peacock feather creation was still intact. Indeed, it was . . . not a feather out of place.

Chapter Eighteen

Dream Spinner Re-Do

Anna Gwendolyn awoke the next morning in her bed, still wrapped in her Renaissance dress. Her friends had taken her from her swing, placed her in the front seat of the Cheshire and drove her home. She could not remember getting home or climbing the stairs to her room, but she remembered her dream.

She also remembered all the fuss that her peacock wreath creation caused all over the Festival and how good it made her feel about herself.

Her mind drifted to the Peacock Plane. Wow! She had one heck of a dream. Could she remember any more of it? She closed her eyes and hoped for a replay.

How did the Dream Spinner's strange production relate to her dreams of being an architect or world traveler? That big sign about non-stop flights . . . that crazy, peacock plane . . .

Any hope for an instant replay was interrupted by a burst of morning sunlight.

Not bothering to change her clothes, Anna Gwendolyn rushed downstairs. Pappy was sitting on the couch, utterly engrossed in the annual Texas Regional Fishing competition. Briggs, half-asleep at his feet, lifted his head and yawned when Anna Gwendolyn entered the room.

"Hi! Briggs, come give me big slugs!" A slug was simply a nickname for Brigg's sloppy, wet kisses.

"Finally, maybe, I have found that passion you're talking about, Pappy. I think a magical peacock plane inspired me to travel. That's it! I do have a dream about traveling. After all, I've spent much of my life on your trains. That Legend of the Dream Spinner . . . it really does work!"

Putting his doubts aside, Pappy was smiling inside. It was the first time in a long time that Anna Gwendolyn had shown any interest in her future. Maybe yesterday's dream teachings had helped jostle Anna Gwendolyn out of her rut—and made her ditch the idea of that crazy Dream-O-Tron. The Renaissance Fair probably helped, too.

"Oh, Pappy!" she said, as she sat down next to him. "I want to visit exotic places. I want to fly all over the world. I want to see how everyone else lives!" (The words "Never Too Late" flashed in her mind. She remembered the "Never Too Late" sign she had seen in her dream.) "Right now, Pappy, I've got to go find out more!"

She jumped up from the couch and hopped double steps up the stairway. She changed from her festival clothes into skinny jeans, polo shirt, and sparkly flip flops, adding a touch of "Fired-up Orange" lip dew and line-defined eyes. Her peacock feather wreath was the final touch. She was ready to choreograph her future—or so she thought.

Chapter Nineteen

When Peacocks Fly

A couple of minutes on the swing will get me started again, Anna Gwendolyn thought, and hoped. Her impulses taking over, she searched for "her" swing. There were only a few other morning riders, so she was able to sit in the very same swing, the one she thought she'd been in the evening before. The attendant checked each rider for safety and pulled the huge engine lever.

Instinctively, Anna Gwendolyn began pumping her feet, arching her back in celebration of the moment. After all, she seemed to be headed in a new, more positive direction. As the swings lifted up into a circular motion, one could almost envision Mother Nature's remote control conducting chirping birds and singing crickets. The song, "Ever Lost A Dream?" played, all was good, and Anna Gwendolyn waited.

Lulled by the melody, she searched for answers to the questions of the evening before. She would watch for even the smallest sign that what she had witnessed was returning.

For now, she would pretend to be asleep. She was way too nervous for the real stuff. Real sleep or not, those colors in the sky seemed to be reappearing.

Teal and cerulean blue streaks blurred between the swings, surrounding the middle engine of the Spinner. Mother Nature's remote control gently hushed her symphony. In Anna's excitement, as always, she began pumping her legs, trying to propel her swing faster.

But pumping her legs exhausted her. Anna Gwendolyn was falling asleep.

As eyelids draped themselves reluctantly, there was a shaft of light slivering through from above. Then, the sign she was waiting for:

Daily Departures, Non-Stop Flights
In the matter of dreams,
as Nevah-Tu-Latte always says,
It's Never Too Late!

Something happened. What was that? Then something else happened. "Oh. OH! There it is, it's come back! Oh, come down! Can you see me?" In awe, as she wiped away happy tears to clear her focus, Anna peered upward. Her disbelief threatened to blur the developing vision. A starburst of teal, blue and purple, squeezing through a gust of lavender wind, grew steadily in size until the burst of teal took full reign.

An eerie quiet whispered the question, "Is this really happening?" Anna Gwendolyn was not going anywhere until she could find out. Amidst the scene, came repetitive bursts of purple and green and blue that seemed to go on and on, making loop-de-loops designs in the air.

This better be good! She could hear Pappy's teachings about patience in the back of her mind.

First, it was that banner! And, then, it was the plane. *It's all happening again! The Plane!* It was still made out of peacock feathers, just like the evening before. *Spectacular! It really is a plane made of peacock feathers. As crazy as it seems, the plane's feathers peculiarly look just like the feathers from my Renaissance wreath.*

And there it was again! "OH! OH MY . . . it's, it's come back! There it is!" Anna shouted.

The plane began circling overhead, round and round until coming to a complete stop, in midair, as if it was on some kind of runway. This plane really looked just like a peacock—graceful, commanding and over the top haughty. But its size was massive! *The head of the plane, or I guess peacock, is a bit higher in the air than that of a normal plane. I know these peacocks could strut their stuff up and down the flagstone path at the Festival, but I did not think they really could fly!*

"Yikes! My gosh. It's . . . Uhm, something is happening!" On the left side of this strange aircraft, a large, wide door opened. A rope ladder, secured to the floor of the plane, was thrown out the hatch. The ladder twisted and turned as it tumbled sporadically down to the Spinner.

What is that thing? Why in the world! "Who's up there? Who threw out that ladder? Please, please someone answer me!" *I joked with Pappy about choosing a dream ladder from dream-keeper fairies rather than a roadmap to work on my dream. Is this that ladder? No.*

I wonder what's in that plane anyway. Is it a real peacock? It looks just like the plane my wreath turned into last night.

Wow, good thing Gloria's not here. Please don't let this be my worst nightmare! All I'm doing is looking for my dream!

Anna reached up to straighten her wreath. It was all but gone! Only a few remnants of feathers and wires remained. And, at that moment, her skinny jeans and shirt were transformed into her Renaissance gown, with all the layers and layers of taffeta and chiffon. *How did that happen?*

Anna Gwendolyn sat frozen in the swing. *I bet I could climb up that ladder, if I still had my jeans on!* she thought to herself. *But what's up there?* She said out loud to no one, "What should I do? If this is . . . of course, it's a dream. So, if it's a dream, it won't matter what I do, will it?" Frowning, she thought, *I guess I should have been more specific about what I wished for.*

Pappy's teachings had emphasized that Anna had to be bold and do brave things to find her dreams. She thought to herself, *I can do this . . . I'm petrified but I've got to know what's in that plane. I'll hold my breath and circle around in the Spinner three times. Then I'll . . .*

Chapter Twenty

Luv-Ern Talks Rib-bon-os . . . huh???

Circling round on the Dream Spinner, nervous but determined, Anna Gwendolyn began calculating her move. First, she would pump her legs much harder to gain momentum and increase the height of the swing. Once in flight, she figured she'd be close enough to grab the rope ladder. *Well, here goes . . . One . . . two . . . three.* And with that, on her third revolution, Anna Gwendolyn reached her arms upward and outward, grabbed the last rung of the ladder and held on for dear life. She was terrified, wide-eyed, but brave beyond belief!

With all of her might, which seemed to be decreasing with every move, she hoisted herself up the sagging rungs of the ladder—one by one. Step by unsteady step, holding onto both sides of this surging ladder, the Dream Spinner below became smaller and smaller and the plane became bigger and bigger. Had Anna Gwendolyn's extreme curiosity replaced her common sense? "What in the world will I see? Am I safe?" Safety had not even crossed her mind until now.

Pappy's lesson about pretend confidence had gotten her up the ladder, but now what?

"Welcome aboard! Ms. Anna Gwendolyn! Welcome aboard Peacock Airways. I'm Captain Luv-Ern. And this is Penelope, our flight attendant. We've been anxiously awaiting your arrival!"

"Wait!!! Wha . . . what . . . what in the world??? What do you mean . . . you've been waiting for what?"

"Oh. We'll get to all that later. First, let's get you acclimated to your new surroundings. Just relax a bit and we'll take you on a tour of our Peacock Plane. To your left is the cockpit, and to the right our passenger cabin complete with recently enlarged, reclining, passenger seats! You must be exhausted! Go ahead and try one!"

"To heck with your seats, ma'am, I've got to get back home!!!"

"Anna Gwendolyn, it's time to prepare for the ride of your life—to retrieve your lost dreams and secure your destiny. Again, I am Captain Luv-Ern, and we at Peacock Airways are at your service. Any questions?"

"Oh right. Yea, I might just have a few. Like . . . why am I here, and how do I get out of here and back to Parkersville and my Pappy? Ah, excuse me, but did you say something about lost dreams? Look, all I know is, I got on the Dream Spinner to find my dream. And this is definitely not it!"

"Oh, come on now, we deserve a chance, don't we? You might want to re-consider such a premature exit. We have lots to share with you. Seems you know exactly what you're doing, even though you're not taking responsibility for it."

"Excuse me. Who are you, again? I'm sorry. I'm not a good listener," Anna Gwendolyn said. "Can you just slowly tell me again, who you are and what you are doing flying around and above Memories Park?"

"Let's start over . . . Good morning, Ms. Anna Gwendolyn, our lovely, lost dreamer. This is Captain Luv-Ern speaking. I am the one and only Captain Luv-Ern, CEO and owner of Peacock Airways. We extend our warm and sincere welcome to you, Miss Anna Gwendolyn."

"What do you mean a 'lost dreamer?' How do you know my name? How did you know I was coming?" Completely confused, Anna Gwendolyn looked around for something that seemed normal; something to help her figure out if this was a dream or had she been delivered into some strange entity. *Or is this Luv-Ern lady my worst nightmare?*

Stepping into the cockpit from the cabin, the captain continued, "Our sole mission is to identify lost dreamers and put them on a path to retrieve their long-lost dreams. Please listen carefully. It's all very simple. We had a bird's-eye view of the Renaissance Festival, saw you making that exquisite wreath and witnessed your belief that peacocks could fly. Your unwavering faith in us has literally outfitted Peacock Nation with our long-awaited wings. Your brave gesture in the Peacock Tea Garden gave me the power to unleash an entire fleet of flying Peacock Nation 747s that had been grounded for ages.

"And yes, we all have one unified mission, to help you find your lost dreams. We know this is hard for an earthling like you to understand, but it's the simple truth. We've lost more than a few dreamers because they just don't get it. Now, are you ready to give us a chance?"

"CEO, uh? You must make a whole lot of money! Is that it? Do you get some big fat bonus for every sad, lost dreamer you fly around picking up?"

"Not quite. The C stands for Confidence, the E—Excellence and the O stands for Ostentatious. Confidence is my fuel; I pursue excellence in all I do and yes, I am the pure definition of ostentatious. So, there you have it. Not quite like some earthling CEOs."

"So, you're saying that my belief got me here? Really, where's here? I think I need to go back home."

"Well, your belief got you started on your journey, at least. Your destination is top secret, Anna Gwendolyn. Buckle up and prepare yourself for the greatest adventure of your life!"

Anna Gwendolyn thought to herself, *Greatest adventure of my life?? Where have I heard that before . . . Oh, wherever am I? Why did I just have to climb that ladder? Did Pappy ever mention this Luv-Ern lady? She says she's some sort of pilot. I've never seen a pilot like her. And how do they lose some dreamers, anyway? They must just throw them out!*

Anna Gwendolyn gulped. "I've never told you my name or where I came from. Are you some kind of lunatic that flies around picking up every lost kid on the planet that might have had a bad day? Do you think I'm just going to jump into this plane and follow your orders? That's crazy. My Pappy is probably frantic by now, looking for me."

"May I remind you, dear, you climbed up that ladder of your own free will," Luv-Ern pointed out. "No one coerced you.

No one bribed or chided you. It just may be your destiny. You cannot blame us for your predicament."

"Well, uh, I was just on my way . . ." started Anna Gwendolyn.

"On your way to where?"

"I am looking for my dream. Th . . . that's it. I am here to find my dream," Anna admitted.

"Yep, we know all about your dream search and that Dream-O-Tron. We've helped more than a few of their unsuspecting victims."

The mention of the Dream-O-Tron shocked and intrigued Anna. She decided she might just stick around for a bit, to see if this character was for real.

"I must have fallen asleep on the Spinner. This must be my dream," Anna Gwendolyn said, realizing that this could even be part of the discovery work Pappy had told her about. Then she looked up.

On your way to find your lost dreams?
How did you lose them?

Those words, in sparkling, golden letters, were plastered across the wall above the entrance to the cockpit. "But really I need to go home. Enough of this dream stuff," she said half-heartedly.

Luv-Ern continued, "Well, you must have gotten really lucky, with the stars being aligned just right, because you are now . . . uh . . . finally on your way to your dreams—the ones you lost or somehow gave up. Now it's time to try something different. Nothing else has seemed to work, has it?"

"Well, uh, how do you know all this stuff? And how did you see me making my Renaissance wreath and how in the world did I get into this plane?"

"First of all, your belief power transformed your wreath into this 747 Peacock Plane, and secondly, to be exact, you chose to climb up here to us. That's how you got here. By the way, you are precisely where you need to be to begin the journey to retrieve your dreams."

"Okay, then, please tell me . . . where can I pick up my dreams and how do I turn them into reality?" Anna Gwendolyn asked, dead serious.

Luv-Ern paused, took a good look at Anna Gwendolyn, then said, "Sounds like you've been watching some 'instant dreams for sale' info-mercials. To make your dream a reality, you have to believe you have the power to do it. That's one of the first tasks. Of course, there are many others."

"What other tasks?"

"It's what I'll be explaining to you. Once you learn from various tasks, challenges and problems you solve, you'll have proven your worthiness for dream fulfillment."

Anna Gwendolyn questioned, "Planes from peacocks . . . dream rescue . . . Where is it going to end?" Then, silently, *Thistle Ern lady has a comeback for everything. This plane has huge picture windows and a sunroof. None of this can be real. I still just need to go back home.*

As Luv-Ern continued to talk about all the difficult tasks and strange travels ahead, tears welled up in Anna Gwendolyn's eyes, her new bravado quickly disappearing. She was trying to be brave, but she was in way over her thirteen-year-old head. The new air of sophistication she and her friends had adopted—and were good at faking—was not enough to carry her through this weird experience. This was way more than she bargained for.

Luv-Ern said sympathetically, "There, there, Miss. We have known since your birth that you would be arriving here someday. It was just up to you to decide when. Now, let me help you get acclimated to the flight. High tea will be served at top altitude. That should calm your jitters."

High tea, uh? On a plane that looks just like a peacock!

"Jitters! You call what I'm having the jitters? I've had all that I can take! Excuse me, Ms. Luv-Ern or Verne or whatever your name is, but I am terrified!"

The captain offered Anna some tissues. "Looks like you're going to need these.

"It's not surprising that you've never heard of Peacock Airways. Just settle down and relax. Let your wish be our command for a while. There'll be in-flight dining after lift-off."

Anna Gwendolyn spoke up, "Wait a minute. What do you mean 'after liftoff'? We're already floating in the air. We are so already lifted off!"

"There, there, Anna Gwendolyn, it's OK. You see, we lift-off from the earth's airspace for a trajectory into the Rhibbonosphere. That's where you're headed."

"WHAT? Where in the world is the Ribbon? How did you say it? Ribbon . . ."

"Rhibbonosphere, dear. It's so far away from our galaxy that few people know of it or have even heard about it. It's a sacred secret of the universe. And, it's your destination."

Anna Gwendolyn said more calmly, "Oh, is that so? And you've not told me anything about this riboprobe!" *Okay.*

There's a runway in the air. They're taking me to some place made of ribbons. And . . . how did they know that I love in-flight dining? Sure, I dressed up my Barbie Doll like a flight attendant. Well, yes, the flight attendant uniform was my favorite outfit for her. But that didn't mean I wanted to be one. Yes, I want to travel but . . . this must be one of the dreams coming true. Yes, looks like I'm in training for just that. I am going to be a . . . flight attendant. But that's not really what I want . . .

Anna Gwendolyn was overwhelmed. *What have I gotten myself into?* she asked herself for the fourth or fifth time. She hit the call button above her head and held it until the flight attendant, Penelope, appeared. Her long, straight hair was parted in the middle, and she had a giant peace sign hanging on a gold, red, white and blue ribbon around her neck. She looked to be straight out of that ancient place called Woodstock, something old folks had talked about. Penelope reminded Anna Gwendolyn of the hippie she'd seen in old *Life* Magazines.

"Again, my name is Penelope. How may I help you?" she asked. "I am here to make this the flight of your life."

Some flight—"I don't mean to be rude, but the pilot's eyeglasses look like the bottom of soda bottles. How old is this Luv-Ern anyway? And can she even see to pilot the plane?" Anna Gwendolyn questioned.

Overhearing the conversation and annoyed at being referred to as old, Luv-Ern jerked the plane into a sudden nosedive. "I'll show her!"

"Oh my!!! Gulp!!!" Ah uh . . . Yikes!" Anna Gwendolyn turned white with fright.

After again climbing in altitude, Luv-Ern laughed, "Yes, I know your kind! You don't mean to be rude. Then why are you? Ha! About my glasses, yeah, I'm so blind I have to wear these extra thick lenses. I think they call 'em coke bottle glasses where you come from. But don't worry, I fly this plane with the avid assistance of my co-pilot, a seeing eye dog named Briggs."

Briggs! Anna Gwendolyn said to herself. "That's Pappy's dog . . . our family dog! What! Who? What's he doing up here?"

Ignoring Anna's queries, Penelope offered, "You may have free range of the entire aircraft as long as the green overhead light is on. I'll tell the captain that you might be visiting the cockpit."

"Visiting the cockpit would be cool!" exclaimed Anna Gwendolyn, with a sudden change of heart.

During the take-off in mid-air, her stubbornness was magically transformed by the vision ahead of her. She was certain that no one on Earth had witnessed it. Overcome by awe, her fear and aggravation melted.

The spectacular light extravaganza at the back-bay window must be the Rhibbonosphere that Pilot Luv-Ern kept talking about. Anna Gwendolyn stood dumbfounded as she watched a light show of rainbows, lightening, sunrises and sunsets and cerulean blue and emerald green working together as if an orchestra. It stretched out in huge, misshaped circles, outlined in dark lines of sparkling, black light.

Anna Gwendolyn's fear abated as her adventurous heart took over. For an apparent lack of other options, a slowly evolving belief in Luv-Ern's intentions crept into her still stubborn mind. Anna unknowingly was taking the reins in what would turn into a wild ride indeed.

She boldly walked towards the cockpit.

"I've never seen anyone quite like you," Anna Gwendolyn said to Pilot Luv-Ern. "How did you get to be a pilot? How did you end up on this planet? Did you invent peacock planes? Where do you live?" She popped one question after another.

"Oh, child of little faith, I am the one, the only, Pilot Luv-Ern who, because of your belief in us that we could fly, now guides deserving passengers to their lost dreams and destinies. That's all I can tell you."

"I didn't really know that peacocks could fly," Anna Gwendolyn confessed. "It's just that my friends were so, well . . ."

"So negative?" Luv-Ern filled in.

"Ah. Yes . . . negative."

"Well, you certainly must have done some believing, because that's how you got here; you believed that peacocks could fly! Believing is an important requirement for finding your dreams. In the face of the adversity and the eye rolling of your friends, you stood your ground at the Peacock Tea Garden. And we loved it when you picked up our feathers and re-used them in your head dressing; that made us feel important. You believed we could fly. You believed in us!"

"What else should I believe in?" Anna Gwendolyn started to really listen to this unusual character. Besides, obviously, this trip wasn't ending anytime soon. "Luv-Ern, how did you end up as the pilot of this airplane? Do you do this all day long? Do you just go around picking up . . . uh?"

"Picking up lost dreamers? I like your curiosity. You can't dream without it, or without a lot of other things which you'll learn," Luv-Ern encouraged.

"But still, I don't really believe that peacocks can fly! It's a scientific fact they can't! Well, they can a little, but they can't fly like a plane!"

"Look, Missy, you'd be wise to stop and listen. And some gratitude would be in order. I literally have offered you a chance of a lifetime. A chance to discover your lost dreams. And all you can do is insult me and doubt me to the point that Peacock Nation would be once again without wings to pick up lost dreamers," Luv-Ern said with hands on hips.

To make her point, Luv-Ern decided to teach her another lesson. She grabbed the controls and sent the aircraft into a dizzying spin.

Oh . . . Ohhhhh . . . now . . . again . . . Who is this mad woman?

"Here, dear, you are going to need some more tissues."

Anna Gwendolyn defiantly pulled out some tissues and noticed instantly that the peacock feather motif was on each tissue. She shouted, "Everything . . . is everything around here a peacock design? Could I please just have a normal white tissue?"

Taking notice of Anna Gwendolyn's cries, Pilot Luv-Ern had mercy on her.

"There, there now. I'll admit this is all new and scary and rough, but this is what you must go through to find your dreams. You have a lot of work to reclaim your destiny. That's why you're here.

"You need to straighten your back, hold your head high and remove the fog from your eyes. And, oh, here are some more tissues," Luv-Ern said, gently surrendering to Anna's Gwendolyn's request for plain tissues.

Following Pilot Luv-Ern's directions to take three deep breaths while stretching her arms and legs, Anna Gwendolyn's mood lightened. "Okay, you win, Miss Luv-Ern. Tell me what I need to do," she said with a whimper.

"You must prove you are committed to finding your dreams. You'll be tested and tried all along the way, but the rewards are many if you stay the course."

"Why is my final destination a secret?"

"Because if I told you about the road you must travel, you would refuse to go; it's a treacherous, laborious trip full of challenges. To get through it you'll need perseverance and commitment."

Oh, not that again. "It sounds so scary. Why does it have to be so scary?"

"Self-empowerment often times is. But it's your ticket for this flight. And your genius is the flight plan," Luv-Ern responded.

"Excuse me, did you say genius?"

"I certainly did. Why are you surprised? You can't tell me no one has ever noticed the genius in you."

Anna Gwendolyn admitted, "Well, uh no, no—not really."

"Perhaps you've not been listening. Probably busy rolling your eyes. Up here, one can always hear the sound of rolling eyes; it is often mistaken for thunder."

Anna had to think about that for a minute.

Luv-Ern interrupted her thoughts about thunder. "On this journey, if you pay attention . . . learn the lessons . . . do the work, you can find your wings!"

"Me? I never dreamed of flying. I love trains," Anna Gwendolyn said, mind wandering. "I plan to ride trains all over the world. My Pappy was a conductor of the Missouri Pacific

Railway for many, many years!" Anna bragged. She was proud of Pappy and wanted this Miss Luv-Ern to be impressed.

With no reaction Luv-Ern went on, "Flying is just a figure of speech, dear. Flying, well, it's like removing the shackles, the obstacles, that kill peoples' self-confidence and their dreams."

"I think I understand," hoping she really did.

"Gaining self-confidence is like changing a burning candle into a raging fire that refuses to be extinguished. You need to ignite your self-confidence."

That sounds just like Pappy.

"You can label life's obstacles 'terminal' or you can transform those very obstacles into fuel to meet problems head on, instead of crashing into them. The lessons of the Rhibbonosphere will help you do that."

"Obstacles? Terminal what? Lessons? How can I handle all this?"

Luv-Ern knew Anna needed a break. "It will soon be time for your initial challenge. But first, time to rest. Breath deep. Now, reach into the overhead bin above your seat and pull out the satin covered pillow that has your name on it. Enjoy your reclining seat. And go ahead and press the massage button! You'll feel great after some rest."

Anna Gwendolyn complied meekly. *Everything in this plane is a mystery.*

"Listen for the song of the Dream Spinner. You need to be rested for your treacherous journey. Sweet dreams."

Treacherous? She didn't like the sound of that . . . she was going to need that fake confidence. Staring out the airplane window, Anna Gwendolyn wondered again how Captain Luv-Ern knew about the Dream Spinner? *She seems to know everything*, she thought, as she drifted off, however reluctantly, into a peaceful slumber.

However, moments from sleep, she was jolted awake. Another Luv-Ern nosedive! *What is going on??*

Anna Gwendolyn's mind was racing. She murmured, "Is the plane on fire? Was it hijacked? Have we entered restricted airspace?" Anna cried out, "What's wrong??? What's happening???"

"No Problem, Miss Anna Gwendolyn. We were a bit overwhelmed awaiting your arrival, and forgot to check the fuel gauge. We are simply stopping to re-fuel . . . Ha! . . . make that *re-feather!*" Penelope said with a chuckle.

"Oh yeah, ha, that's really funny," deadpanned Anna.

No sooner had Anna Gwendolyn jumped up when she heard Captain Luv-Ern announcing her pit stop for refueling. "Make that re-feathering," the captain corrected herself. The daredevil in Luv-Ern could not resist making another dramatic "landing," once again in mid-air.

Anna's body drained from excitement, she was ready to return to her reclining seat by the window.

By now, Pilot Luv-Ern was confident she had done everything possible to convince this wayward dreamer of her pure intentions. Now, if she could just get Anna to build her own parachute . . .

Chapter Twenty-One

Just Figure It Out

Luv-Ern soared through the atmosphere, deeper into the outskirts around the Rhibbonosphere. Enjoying her new-found wings, Pilot Luv-Ern put the plane into a nosedive again, purposely to awaken Anna Gwendolyn, to show her the incredible views and prepare her for what would lie ahead.

Once awake, Anna Gwendolyn watched nature's fireworks out the cockpit window. She anxiously remarked, "You mean that's where I'm going to find my lost dream? I don't see any dreams out there."

"That labyrinth of ribbons is the path you'll take, but you'll need to conquer dark and foggy areas along the way. Each of those foggy ovals has lessons you must learn. The ribbon-like borders of the Rhibbonosphere are your paths, which total 2,650 miles. Construction crews recently re-paved the roads with sparkling granite, which will guide you through each of the ovals.

"You will cry, laugh, scream, with both glee and fear. You'll be frightened; you'll be frustrated; and you will sometimes be alone. But you'll be prepared to reclaim, nurture and protect your dreams, and introduce yourself to the person you are meant to be."

"You'll go with me, right, Captain Luv-Ern?" Anna Gwendolyn asked timidly, missing the mileage reference entirely.

"No, I'm sorry; this is something you must do on your own. Besides, I must log more flight miles. So, I'll just drop you from up here and move on in my search of other lost dreamers."

"What, wait a minute, wait a minute . . . what do you mean, 'drop'? YOU CAN'T just drop me out of this airplane! Have I been kidnapped by some deranged bird maniac? I have to get out of here! Even if some of this makes crazy sense, I just can't . . . I just want to be . . . well, normal."

Luv-Ern trumpeted assertively, "This is not about being normal, Anna Gwendolyn. It's about being extraordinary. And, besides, stop worrying. You'll have a parachute."

Anna Gwendolyn sneered, "Ah, 'besides!' Oh Wow! I get to use a parachute! You said, 'Besides!' Thank goodness for that. Hey! Parachutes can break!!! And I'm sure you do not have a real parachute company up here!"

"Calm down now. Navigating the ins and outs of the Rhibbonosphere will strengthen you spiritually, physically, mentally, and emotionally. This is a requirement for lasting dream rescue. You've already climbed up our lousy, unsteady, rope ladder and climbed into this plane. You can do anything!"

Grasping for any kind of reassurance, Anna Gwendolyn replied, "Do you really think so? How would you know how strong I am? This has nothing to do with my wreath making."

Anna Gwendolyn had to push aside the feeling of being scared out of her wits. Tears ran down her cheeks as she tried to pull herself together. She had few options up here, wherever she was, and no other place to go. The "parachute" exit seemed inevitable.

"Skydiving? Me? I can't breathe . . . the thought just takes . . ."

"Your breath away," Luv-Ern added.

"Yes . . . and makes me petrified!"

"Penelope and I are going to help you. You are not alone. We're rooting for you. Now, as we approach the Rhibbonosphere, you will exit the aircraft for your first challenge."

"Exit! Exit where? You mean after one of your mad-man pit stops? Why does it sound as if you're set on just throwing me out the plane? I'd have been better off with the Dream-O-Tron! I do not believe you!"

"Because you are not listening," Luv-Ern answered quietly.

"You're really just going to drop me off at that place you call the Rhiba . . . Rhibon . . . ?"

Luv-Ern continued, "Well, to be honest, and as your Pappy might have mentioned, you're going to have to be "catapulted" to embark on your dream. Now, grab onto your self-confidence, because you're going to need it."

Anna Gwendolyn again looked around for an escape. There was none. *I'm stuck here. No one is going to save me. I was kidnapped by an old, mad woman who can't see, in a plane that's a peacock.* She thought to herself how crazy all that sounded. *Oh please, dear God, can you help me?*

"You can do this," Luv-Ern assured her. "Look into my eyes, Anna Gwendolyn. You have proven yourself to me, and you can prove it to the world."

"Thank . . . you, I guess."

"Oh, and by the way, so does your Pappy. Now pull yourself together and reach into the overhead bin and open the door marked Exit Info. There is something waiting for you—a specialized kit to make a parachute," Luv-Ern instructed.

"Kit? Kit? Wait a minute!! What do you mean a parachute kit? Do you think I'm going to strap that thing on my back and jump out of this plane?"

"I don't think you will jump. I know you will jump," Luv-Ern said emphatically. "It's your destiny."

"Now I know you are bonkers! Yep, I've been kidnapped. Do I have any freedom of choice in this?"

"Well, I guess you could fly around with me in this 'pop stand' into infinity. I know I'm exceptionally entertaining, but you'd probably get bored soon enough," Luv-Ern smirked.

Anna Gwendolyn was not amused by Luv-Ern's teasing. She strained her muscles along with her eyes, stood on her tiptoes, and reluctantly reached into the overhead compartment. "I don't see a parachute," she complained, as she peered over the edge. All she saw was a bluish-green fabric. "This isn't a parachute, it's just a bunch of fabric."

"I know. That's what I meant when I told you about the kit. You are definitely talented enough to make your own parachute."

That stupid wreath! I'm sure they got this wacko idea from that wreath I made.

"Oh well, look at it as another chance to display all that creativity you have, Anna. Just think of it—you can make a pile of peacock fabric turn into a parachute or what we call a Dream-Chute, as they're known in the Rhibbonosphere!"

Anna Gwendolyn protested, "So, you think I'm going to make a parachute, or whatever you call it, to jump out of this plane! My life will depend on it."

"Exactly."

Anna Gwendolyn finally grasped that this was real. She was seriously expected to construct her own parachute. The construction of her Renaissance festival costume was proof she could create something beautiful out of fabric, but functional? Anna was overwhelmed at the thought.

"Just where are you preparing to drop me?" Anna Gwendolyn asked, showers of tears rolling down her cheeks.

"I am not in charge of that; Penelope is," Luv-Ern said.

Penelope emerged from the galley to join Anna Gwendolyn and the Captain. "How are you feeling?" she asked.

"Well, how would you feel if you were about to jump out of a plane, with your own handmade parachute? I'm going to throw up!"

"I could give you t-shirts or posters with sayings like 'Reach for the Stars' or 'Go for the Gold,' or 'Dream the Impossible Dream' to make you feel good, but they won't get you to your dreams," Penelope advised.

"You sound like Pappy when he was warning me about the Dream-O-Tron. How do you know so much?"

"We've seen all kinds of dreams advertised on the black market internet—for a price," Penelope said. "None of them work."

Anna Gwendolyn, still fearful, was forcing herself to understand what all this meant. *I wonder if that Ribboning place has something for me.* She pondered out loud, "Maybe I can really learn something from the lessons. Will I be completely alone? Will I be graded on these lessons like in school? How long will this trip take? Is there like a virtual tour of the place you keep talking about?"

"No, dear, we have no virtual tours. But there's a lot to do to prepare you for the journey. We're now in the process of simply waiting for the 'ALL CLEAR' from Della of Delphinium, so all is prepared for your arrival."

"Arrival where? When do I . . . jump? Just where is or what is this Delphinium? And, who is Della?"

"Anna Gwendolyn, I have received the latest data regarding your DROP. At our present speed of 21,000 measures a minute, I calculate your landing to be precisely at 01:09:01. Delphinium is the outer most oval of the Rhibbonosphere, at an altitude of 1,027 feet precisely twenty-four hours from our present trajectory—although all measurements are guesswork on Peacock Airways!"

Luv-Ern projected, "After Dream-Chute construction, a sound twelve-hour sleep will prepare you for the DROP to Delphinium.

"Della, the Docent of Delphinium, has received the appropriate text. She will receive lost dreamer Anna Gwendolyn at precisely, 01:09:02 following her DROP. Della is anxiously awaiting your arrival."

Luv-Ern headed to the cockpit. "It's now time to put that incredible creativity and mathematics skill to work."

Anna Gwendolyn said quietly to herself, *Now I know why everyone keeps calling it a drop! It's up to me now. It is all up to me. But if I was truly empowered, I would have found the strength to refuse to do this, no matter what the consequences would have been. But then there's this little voice telling me to trust Captain Luv-Ern. A gut feeling??*

"Anna Gwendolyn, you are experiencing a normal reaction. Fear is part of this process. Just pretend you know how to do this. Now, run on down to the back-galley quarters with your kit. You'll find everything you need there."

Secretly rolling her eyes was beginning to be an Anna habit. She heard thunder every time. *Remember, your life depends on it!* she moaned to herself.

Taking a deep breath, along with a change in attitude, she went down to the galley area of the plane to start work on the parachute. Although on the verge of tears, she immediately was stopped in her tracks by two, massive sewing tables. A big, beautiful box full of giant, golden, sewing needles sat atop one of them. She had found what Captain Luv-Ern was talking about: needles, a cord, giant spools of steel and gold thread, a stack of beautiful silk fabric. Under the material was a yellow envelope. *This pile of peacock fabric and tools are my vehicle out of this crazy plane. It sure better take me to my dreams.*

Anna Gwendolyn surrendered to the whole bizarre idea of what was happening.

She gathered all the items and placed them methodically on the smaller table. She held the needles up to the light of the sunroof and threaded them. By standing in front of the table and holding the fabric up with her arms like a spread eagle, she was able to ripple it through the air until it landed smoothly on the table. The peacock fabric was now ready, but Anna Gwendolyn . . . still not quite.

"Oh brother. This is difficult. Where is Gloria when I need her? She would have already finished this," Anna Gwendolyn said to no one in particular.

She opened the purple package and pulled out a giant, plain piece of thin paper. It was the kind of pattern paper she had used in sewing class. She remembered pinning the unruly tissue-thin paper to the fabric with her classmates. Pin pricks happened often. She unfolded the huge piece of paper and laid it out on the table, experiencing the same frustration she had in school. And there, in the center of the paper, were the directions:

Directions for Dream Searcher Miss Anna Gwendolyn Shaw:
1. Use your imagination
2. Incorporate your ingenuity
3. Envision your purpose
4. Then just figure it out

Perfect. Very specific directions! Anna Gwendolyn thought ironically to herself.

She drew out four, huge, identical pieces on the pattern paper. It so easily tore that she had to use tape to repair it. Then she placed the pattern pieces on the giant table over the peacock fabric. Inching her way, she side-stepped around the circle of fabric, pinning the pattern paper to the fabric and occasionally to her fingers. Ouch!

Anna Gwendolyn began sewing her Dream-Chute. She fumbled with the fabric, twisted it, tied strings, loosened the strings, and fixed the fraying with Fabric Fray Stop. She continued to fold, measure, cut, and shape it. Soon she was picking up the giant needles like a doctor about to do open-heart surgery. Then, as if her life depended on it, she began stitching this huge absurd parachute together. Actually, her life did depend on it.

Thankfully, the body safety harness and backpack were prefabricated. Was this a bonus? Maybe this was a reward for her hard work. What a relief! At least, she didn't have to worry about that anymore; there was an actual harness.

With the construction completed, Anna Gwendolyn added her own special trademark, by making use of a gorgeous little pile of peacock feathers. Had they fallen off the peacock plane? Who would know? But she decided they needed a purpose. Without waiting for permission, she stitched each one of them to her new creation—her Dream-Chute. She even used the steel thread to embroider her name on the project as "Anna Gwendolyn Shaw."

Then with extreme caution, Anna methodically maneuvered and folded the fabric and placed it into the backpack of the harness. She carried out three checks to ensure the safety of the Dream-Chute. *Well, it looks good,* she said to herself, but the big question, *Will it work?*

Anna Gwendolyn had used a big dose of pretending to complete this task. And, almost magically, as the parachute came together, she felt she knew what to do. No instructions, and yet there she stood with a totally finished, functional Dream-Chute.

Maybe there is something to this pretend confidence, she silently said.

And, then it was time. She could hear Captain Luv-Ern walking down to the galley area. The twelve-hour window was almost over. Now, she needed twelve hours to rest and prepare for the morning DROP.

"What a beautiful job," Captain Luv-Ern said, seeing her completed project. "Absolutely amazing. You truly are a genius," she added.

"Thank you," Anna Gwendolyn said, her eyes swelling with tears. "Happy tears, Miss Luv-Ern. I did this all by myself. I created this. Isn't it beautiful? I made the pattern and used my imagination for the design, and I used my math knowledge and wisdom for the technical necessities. You told me to figure it out. I just saw a vision of the finished product in my head . . . plunged in, and figured out what I needed to do," Anna Gwendolyn babbled, exhilarated, but again acknowledged the fear she felt deep inside—no matter how much she pretended. "But I'm still scared."

"Fake being fearless," Penelope encouraged, joining them. "It works." She, too, was impressed with the job Anna Gwendolyn had completed. "Now go get some rest. I'll wake you when it's time."

Not even worries of being dumped out of this weird peacock plane could keep Anna awake. The satisfaction of a job well done worked better than any sleeping pill.

Allowing the full twelve-hour sleep, Penelope gently awakened her. "Anna Gwendolyn, it's time for your leap of faith."

Seeing the fresh fear on her face, Penelope continued, "Respect your fear and fake your courage!"

"Are you ready, Anna Gwendolyn?" asked Captain Luv-Ern.

The three, walked back to the galley and positioned themselves in front of the left galley exit door.

The hatch opened with the press of a button. Against a christening gust of cool wind, Anna Gwendolyn once again tried faking her fearlessness. As she peered out the hatch, trembling, the faint multicolored ribbons of the ovals could be seen, beckoning her. *That must be the beginnings of the Rhibbonosphere!*

"Uh . . . nan . . .uh, I can't do this. I don't want to do this. I'm terrified. I want to go home . . . please. Oh please, where is my Pappy?" *Or Gloria or Jake?* she added, without moving her lips.

"Ok. Miss Anna Gwendolyn, believer in the flight of Peacocks! Creator of beauty from trash and reformed listener to her elders . . .You can do this. We believe in you!"

With a stubborn gulp, Anna Gwendolyn swallowed her fear. Her breath was now . . . well, gone. She looked back at Luv-Ern, her eyes wide with reluctance.

"Fake it till you make it! The distant Rhibbonosphere winds will encircle you protectively during your plunge. Close your eyes and visualize floating," Luv-Ern advised. "Della, the Docent of Delphinium, will help you with your initial challenges. Ask questions. Ask for help."

The three of them counted in unison, "10, 9, 8, 7 . . ." Then Penelope burst, "Oh wait! . . . her scarf . . . she still has her 'train' on. It will make a tangled mess! We have to cut . . .we are running out of time! We should have thought of this . . . her . . . her scarf!"

Anna Gwendolyn screamed, "No! No! You can't take my train. Oh! Oh! Don't cut off my train. It is my only worldly belonging. I have to have it! I have to have my train. Stop! Stop! Do not cut the train!"

Captain Luv-Ern continued "4, 3, 2, 1!" Then, with the help of a little shove from the captain, Anna Gwendolyn soared out of the Peacock Plane—well, not exactly.

Chapter Twenty-Two

Robot Della and My Jig-Saw Diary

The initial jump was terrifying. However, when the free-fall began, Anna experienced the "magic" paratroopers sometime feel. She was floating, weightlessly, through the air, until a burst of turbulence rudely re-awakened her. Now she was tumbling! *What is happening?* The Dream-Chute was performing beautifully, but her treasured train had tangled itself in the parachute strings. Anna Gwendolyn had to make a critical choice. As she tumbled erratically through the air, she remembered, *I don't have Pappy, my friends, or my home. All I have is my prized possession—my train! Time is running out. But how can I untangle the mess above me now?* "It's my only material possession from my world—Parkersville!" she screamed.

"You cannot let this material item control your destiny."

Is someone talking to me? "Who's there? Hello!" She had less than thirty seconds to remove the train so her Dream-Chute would open freely and save her life.

Remembering her wreath, Anna Gwendolyn reached up for the remaining wire remnants, thinking she could shape a large wire loop to lasso the menacing train away from the parachute strings. *Will I live through this?*

In what seemed a split second, she entwined the shorter pieces of wire to the longer ones, struggling nervously, and created one large lasso-like circle. Then, her breath held, she hurled the lasso, hitting her target victoriously on the first try.

While gravity pulled her downward, she held her breath again, reached up with the wire, but accidentally snapped the train off, freeing the parachute strings but sending the scarf hopelessly floating away! "Please, No! No!! Gone! Forever!"

No time to mourn, she was heading to fall point blank onto a slender protrusion rising up from what seemed the ground. It looked like a giant steeple of reflective papers, shooting off colorful prisms in every direction . . . and the reflections had words in them.

Peering down, the letters "COLLIDE-A-SCOPE" startled her.

Suddenly, with a jolt, she was dangling by her dress at the top of Delphinium's Collide-A-Scope! She discovered the fabric of her skirt had hooked itself to it. Fearing she could dangle there forever, she tightly wrapped her arms around the steeple.

Pappy had said something about me having to collide with my dreams . . .

Anna Gwendolyn looked around to assess her situation. She hung for what seemed an eternity. "Ugh! Oh, could someone please help me?" she yelled out into the quiet. No answer. Starting to shake, she shouted, "Luv-Ern! Now what am I suppose to do?" This was too much! *Calm yourself,* she thought. *I have to think.*

Then she heard that voice again. "Believe in yourself."

All I have is me! she thought. *I have to believe in myself . . . That's it! I know what to do. I know how to rappel!* This wasn't going to be rappelling exactly, but she had to try. Gingerly, she released her skirt from a jagged point. Slowly, inch by inch, she worked her way down the steeple, until she caught sight of the ground. With each downward step, the steeple appeared to be shedding its covering—the shining paper was turning into small pieces, almost shreds of shiny, mirror-like paper. They made it hard to grip the steeple. Finally, abruptly hitting the ground, she looked down at her billowing skirt. *Well, good thing I took my time making you; that could have been a very hard landing.*

She looked around and was quickly overtaken by the sights. Standing among growing piles of paper peeling off the Collide-A-Scope, she had a new place to figure out. Maybe her train would float down, too, with the pieces now falling like rain.

Instead of the view out of Luv-Ern's back window, Anna Gwendolyn now had a panoramic view of everything described by Luv-Ern and Penelope about Delphinium. Nothing had been exaggerated.

Small seeds of belief and self-confidence were sprouting, even if Anna couldn't see them.

I fell asleep on the Spinner. It did its job. I climbed into an outlandish Peacock Plane on a dream ladder. I was introduced to Luv-Ern's tailspins and nosedives and I made my own parachute, with which I was catapulted out of a plane—due to a shove actually.

But now . . . I'm lost all over again!

Exhausted, Anna Gwendolyn fell asleep, sitting against the base of the Collide-A-Scope, in the midst of piles of glossy paper.

Oh! Where am I? Now almost awake, *Boy, the sandman's really busy in these parts! I can't see til I get this stuff out of my eyes!* Slowly taking in the surroundings, she remembered a "plane ride" and the free fall, with a Dream-Chute strapped to her. In spite of the trauma, she felt a wondrous freedom. *Maybe I'm one step closer to my dream. How long did I sleep?* she wondered.

"Oh! The ride on the Spinner!" she almost shouted. Jolting herself back to reality, she panicked. "I can't just sit here, wiping my tears, daydreaming my life away. No one is coming to help me. I have to do something."

The mystery of this experience frightened her but fueled her mischievous curiosity. The growing ocean of paper pieces from the Collide-A-Scope blanketed the ground.

Noticing her soft bed of torn papers, "Well, at least it's sort of cushy and comfortable here."

Seeming to have a conversation with herself, Anna went on, "It feels good; it's kind of refreshing to run my hands through this all these paper scraps, sounds kind of like waterfalls. I wonder what they're for. There must be hundreds . . . and they keep coming! There's handwriting on them!" Picking up the paper pieces, one by one, *This is going be good! I guess Delphinium has its own version of Twitter!*

"Oh no! What the heck does this mean? These words are about my life! My private feelings! All falling around me! . . .Yes, I remember doing this, and oh, I remember doing that. Oh! What is going on here?"

The more she studied the pieces, the more she began to comprehend. *These memos are moments in my life! If this is what I think it is . . . oh, what in the world?*

"Where did these come from? How did they get here?" Some were tattered or close to shreds. One large one was in Pappy's handwriting.

"Piece it all together—piece it all together," that voice whispered.

Just what am I supposed to do now, Captain Luv-Ern?

"Piece it all together . . . piece it all together . . ."

"Is that coming from Pappy? Are you here, Pappy?"

Since brazenly ascending the rope ladder, Anna's world bordered between bizarre and magical happenings. Adjusting to abnormal being normal was becoming a honed skill.

Anna Gwendolyn swished around in the heaps of paper and selected one.

Sitting in the midst of the piles, she flattened the palms of her hands on the cool ground to reposition herself and get comfortable, as if that was possible. Then she squinted her eyes, trying to focus on the piece in her hand.

"Well, here goes . . ." Hey! This can't be! This looks . . . why . . . I remember when this happened to me! I remember that day!" *How did . . . How on earth did my life's memories find me here in the Rhibbonosphere? And why?* She continued reading. . . .

One May morning, after breakfast, five-year-old Anna Gwendolyn sat transfixed on the delicate, symmetrically patterned crocheted tablecloth. Armed with spontaneity and a pair of carelessly misplaced scissors, she cut out five identical doilies from the century old family heirloom. Placing them back to back and with a squeeze in the middle, she created a flower and handed it proudly to her Pappy.

The vision of the family heirloom that had served as a beautiful backdrop for generations of family celebrations, now with five gaping holes, shocked Pappy. He gasped at the surgery of symmetrical cuts, but instead of chastising his granddaughter, with a compassionate lesson in scissor safety and respect for other's personal belongings, Pappy praised Anna Gwendolyn for her precise cutting and creativity. (Pappy understood she was too young to know better, and that it was his fault the scissors had been left out.) She had learned an important life lesson, with her self-confidence and self-esteem intact.

Calmly, her Pappy had said, "It's time, Anna Gwendolyn, for you to have your own art supplies. About the tablecloth . . . We'll just piece it back together," patting her hand. Pappy knew the tablecloth could be, and eventually was, mended. But it is so much harder to mend the torn threads of self-worth.

Anna's first lesson in discipline was made survivable by a merciful dose of dignity. Through this incident, Anna Gwendolyn received the message that she was more important than an antique tablecloth. She was the treasure, not the heirloom. That thought brought her comfort now. She was reminded of the kindness and wisdom of Pappy, and how he had preserved her feelings of accomplishment.

Anna Gwendolyn entertained the idea that "picking up the pieces" might be a theme for her life, even at age thirteen. Maybe that feeling was literally born with the cutting of the tablecloth, making something useful without getting yelled at for doing it. *Ahh . . . maybe that could be like a dream-print . . . that must be what Pappy was talking about. My first dream-*

print—making something out of what might be called damaged goods.

With a new-found understanding of what the Collide-A-Scope paper pieces were trying to tell her, she picked up another. *Look at that,* she thought, as she held out one of the larger pieces. It was a miniature version of one of her childhood drawings; one of her favorites—an abstract drawing of swirling, intersecting lines of large and small, misshapen, black lines bordering the vibrant colors within the loops. To no one Anna said, "I know I've seen that somewhere recently . . . too recently . . .oh yes, (*now this place is really getting weird*). My favorite childhood drawing looks very much like the view out of Luv-Ern's plane . . . that place she called the Rhibbonosphere!"

Anna's imagination had come to life in her present reality. *What a magical thing!* she thought, smiling to herself and for a moment forgetting the treachery and challenges that Luv-Ern had warned her of. *How lucky am I?*

Anna Gwendolyn propped herself up once again against the base of the Collide-A-Scope, intrigued enough to explore this new environment.

Then, without warning, a shiny red, robotic creature appeared right in front of her.

"Hello! Welcome to Delphinium! I am Della, the Docent of Delphinium." The robot spoke in typical robotic voice tones, with colored lights flashing across her chest with every word.

What a strange creature; should I be frightened or . . . entertained?

"Miss Anna Gwendolyn . . . once again . . .We welcome you to Delphinium!

"I am Della, the Docent of Delphinium. Oh! I am beyond thrilled to meet you! And I'm grateful to Captain Luv-Ern for getting you here. I have been waiting for you!"

"Getting me here? Ha! I got myself here, by myself, thanks to the Dream-Chute I made by hand, thank you very much! How about some credit where credit is due?" Anna Gwendolyn protested. *Not sure I should trust this robot . . .*

Della had robotic arms and legs, a stylish '80s, quite lovely hair-do and a flashing data screen on her chest. *Well, what do ya know! Hey, maybe this robot is part of the Dream-O-Tron!* Excited by the prospect, Anna Gwendolyn jumped right in. *That's it. This is my dream. Finally, we are getting somewhere; the Dream Spinner did its job!* she thought to herself.

"Miss Anna Gwendolyn, we have a lot to introduce to you. Delphinium is the first stop in the Rhibbonosphere. Its sole purpose is to re-connect you with your Defining Moments and show how they affected your dreams."

Anna's hopes were smashed. "But what about my dream? And what may I ask is a designing moment? I can design a lot of stuff, is that what this is about?"

"Well, first of all, they are Defining Moments, not designing moments.

"And, feel free to ask any questions. I will do my best to explain their importance," answered Della. "It is complicated but vital to dream rescue. These Defining Moments can occur throughout your life; they either derail or boost your dreams."

Anna couldn't help but frown.

"Just how does anyone know if they have these so-called Defining Moments? How would anyone know any of mine, if I happen to have them? And if I do have them, what exactly am

I supposed to do with them?" Anna's eyes were beginning an upward roll.

"Miss Anna Gwendolyn, let me help you understand why you've landed here on Delphinium.

"First, using this keyboard, please input your name, phone number, birthplace, birth date, schools attended, likes, dislikes, and anything else that will assist us in helping you retrieve your dreams."

With her enthusiasm riding a roller coaster of ups and downs, Anna Gwendolyn completed the requested task and handed the keyboard back. Within minutes, Della the Robot lit up like a Christmas tree!

"What's happening?" Anna Gwendolyn asked, surprised at the light show.

Della's eyes sparkled and she smiled mischievously. Words literally marched across Della's data screen with the speed of a '60s secretarial pool's shorthand scribbles, letters and numbers jumping up and down as if they were excited to see Anna.

Thrown off track by the jumble of flashing messages, and wanting to slow things down a bit, "Again, what's a Defining Moment? I don't listen very well. I think maybe Pappy might have mentioned them once."

Della softened her voice as she explained, "As one progresses through life, there are moments that either crash or encourage a person's direction in life and how they feel about themselves. They are life-changing, life-rearranging moments.

"Understanding your negative Defining Moments and how they've affected you can repair your damaged self-confidence, self-esteem and self-worth—and help you find your dreams again."

"But, what about the things I've done so far? I parachuted out of a plane, using a Dream-Chute that I made by myself. I was fearless! I should be ready for my dream right now. I don't have the time." Anna Gwendolyn struggled to find some order in all this captivating fantasy. Someone was not listening.

"You do not have time? Is that what you are saying? That is at least seventy-five percent of the problem with lost dreamers. The other problem is failure of people to face their negative Defining Moments and persevere. That is why few actually get to the Dream Garden," Della responded robotically, no emotion evident. "Some try but give up. Which group are you going to be in, Anna Gwendolyn?"

Della must have been talking to Pappy!

"Did you say Dream Garden? Just tell me where I can find that."

"That is precisely the point. Your destiny is blocked, until you come face-to-face with the negative moments in your life that left harsh marks on your ability to dream."

"How long does that take?"

"Oh, just long enough to understand what stopped your dreams. How are your study habits? Do you mind a little homework?" Della persisted, her light board dancing.

"I was never crazy about homework, but ok," said Anna Gwendolyn.

"Well, up here we call it Dream-Work."

Oh! Dream-Work . . . was that in Pappy's Dream Direct-tionary? I can't remember.

"To start, tell me something bothering you about your past. Anything," Della coaxed.

"Well, I quit all the things I loved to do—building, dancing and rock climbing. Oh, piano, too.

"And all other dreams stopped also?"

"Well, yes—more than stopped. They disappeared." Anna almost whispered.

"Anna Gwendolyn. Everything, your mind, your imagination, your dignity, and your dreams, can be once again under your control. Now is your chance. Take it!" Della almost commanded, her neon data screen alive with erratic blinking.

"Okay, I guess you win," Anna Gwendolyn sighed, trying to decipher the neon, and continued. "Oh . . . I guess I should tell you I have a really hard time listening, due to my Attention Deficit Disorder. I've been told I wasn't listening to this or that, just about every day of my life. The fact is, they were right. I wasn't listening. I was pretty good at faking it—smiling, shaking my head, and looking straight at the speaker. All the while, my mind was on an adventure in some far-off galaxy, daydreaming, and having a blast. It was not on purpose. My mind just drifts away," Anna explained.

"Well, there you have it! Congratulations!" Della exclaimed, more enthusiastic than a robot should be.

"Congratulations for what?"

"It must be humiliating to be constantly told you are not listening. You've just named one of your negative Defining Moments. Maybe we can help you deal with the sadness that that has caused you.

"Not to change the subject," Della switched gears, "but how about hearing about your hotel suite, your Defining Moments Movie Suite?"

"What suite? You mean like a real hotel room with amenities? Did you say movie?"

"A needed comfort on your journey, but not quite like you might be imagining."

"Okay, Miss Della, I could really use some rest. Where exactly is this hotel suite."

Della reported, "A nice surprise awaits you. Come, walk over here and look down the winding trail. You can almost see the sun succumbing to the horizon. See that structure's faint shadow against the streaks of orange and yellow sky?"

"Yes!" Anna answered. "Is that a . . . that's a castle!" Just over the ridge, the outline of a castle shown rising through the early evening haze. The imposing structure boasted turrets, towers, a drawbridge and, of course, a moat.

Wow! Something I can really get excited about. Wait till I tell the girls. This place might not be so bad after all—A castle? Really?

"Before our walk to the castle, take this basket over to the Collide-A-Scope and scoop up a smattering of your life," Della interjected.

"How do I know which pieces to pick?"

"You will instinctively select the ones you need to address. It just works that way."

Shortly, Anna returned with her basket full of papers and she and Della strolled to Candlewood Castle.

"Oh! This is really . . . a castle! A castle with a moat! Well, my friend, Gloria, would never believe this! I can just hear her now. 'Oh! It's just a bit too opulent for Parkersville, isn't it?' Yes, Gloria, and that's why it's a castle, and someday I'll be living in one of these glorious places!" But, as always, Anna Gwendolyn was thinking secretly that she wanted to build them, not own or live in them, just build them. She remembered her own lost dreams.

Why are castles just for royalty? Why aren't they in suburbia? If I can find my dream, in this wild place, I will be building castles in suburbia so everyone can enjoy them. And . . . of course, just like in the homes I build, sparkling waterfalls will refresh the lives of the inhabitants! Ummm! . . . . And maybe a few peacocks!

"Anna Gwendolyn," Della demolishing her daydream, "I will show you to your room.

"This palatial suite will provide the comfort and emotional support you need, as you sort, study, face and learn from your Defining Moments. Some handmade tapestries of Parkersville, Pappy, Briggs and the Bling Swing grace the walls to help you feel at home."

Wow! Just like in the movies! Jeweled satin everywhere. Look at that! That's a real silver tea set, ready for afternoon tea. Or maybe breakfast in bed! I'm sure to feel like a princess, sleeping in that gorgeous bed! The four posters . . . they reach up to the ceiling!

"Anna . . . Anna Gwendolyn . . . Anna!" interrupted Della, getting Anna Gwendolyn's attention, shaking her out of her trance. "This is what you are here to do now, review your memories," emphasizing a massive oak table labeled Thinking Table. "Place them on the Table."

Re-adjusting to her opulent surroundings and, as if laying out precious fortune-telling cards, Anna began carefully spreading her scraps of paper—her memories—across the Thinking Table.

Proudly, she took a deep breath, then grimaced.

Chapter Twenty-Three

How I Lost My Dreams

"I'm not sure I know what to do, Della."

"Trust your mind, but listen to your heart."

"I wish my friends were here, especially Nevah! Our resident aspiring author would help me get through this pile of writings." *I wonder if I'll ever see her again.*

Della sat down next to Anna Gwendolyn, hugging her (as difficult as that was, considering she was a robot). Anna began the initial sorting task. Soon, she was pushing herself into an strange yet intriguing zone, almost forgetting Della's presence, as she dove into the project. One by one, after sorting a handful of paper scraps—remnants of her life—Anna was amazed by how they were fitting together chronologically. It was like working a jigsaw puzzle. Soon, the correct life memories, one after another, began jumping into her hand, guiding her along as she worked. *Is this table bewitched?*

After a few hours, Anna Gwendolyn's head reluctantly began to bob with emotional exhaustion. She protested to herself, *I'm re-experiencing the moments of my life. Some good . . . some . . . I just have to see how this ends.* Shaking her head awake, she begged Della, "It's not time to stop, is it? I can't stop now! There's so much to do!"

"This has been the perfect introduction to the monumental task ahead. Yes, miss. It is time to close down for the evening and get some sleep. Tomorrow is ahead; you will be refreshed and ready to decide on three of your most important Defining Moments."

"What happens after that?"

"You'll learn," is all Della would answer.

"Starting tomorrow morning, at 9:00 sharp, you will have twenty-four hours to acknowledge, study and learn from three of your Negative Defining Moments. By day's end, you will be one step closer to reclaiming your lost dreams." Those blinking lights again . . .

"Della, it sounds kind of scary. I'm not sure I want to see the bad stuff. The negative stuff."

"We are not just throwing you to the wolves, Anna. This memory work can be painful, but I am here to hover over you. You walked over that drawbridge and you saw that moat; it's simply full of harmless goldfish. You will have many other bridges to conquer, as you search for your lost dreams. And some of the moats or waterways will not be full of just goldfish. We will equip you with the tools you will need to succeed on that journey," Della said, without a tad of emotion.

"So, I really get to sleep in that gorgeous bed? Anna asked, only half listening.

"It is yours to rest . . . and recover from all you have been through."

Oh . . . so Della is finally understanding that I have been though a lot! It's about time!

The beautiful tapestries, indeed, reminded her of Parkersville; warm thoughts of Pappy comforted and strengthened her. They were doing their job. Without warning, as if sneaking up behind her, everything that had happened since boarding Luv-Ern's Peacock Plane was beginning to make sense. She was being given a chance to visit the good and bad, positive and negative, life-changing and life-rearranging moments of her young life, as Della calls them, Defining Moments (DMs for short).

The goal, I guess, is to understand the impact these moments have had on my life.

For the first time, Anna Gwendolyn, thought that now, just maybe, she was in the right place at the right time. Somewhat resigned to her present scenario, falling asleep on this princess bed in a real live castle enticed her. Snuggling deeply into the comforting embrace of white, down-filled covers, she was lulled to sleep.

The burst of dawn's colors painting the sunrise on Delphinium awakened Anna Gwendolyn, and, once again, returned her to the reality of her present, self-initiated predicament.

"Wow, they do believe in sunshine around here," she stated to her room. "Oops . . . oh my goodness. Things just show up around here, don't they? But who needs a warning for breakfast in bed? Well, would ya look at this! Oh, delicious! A tower of pancakes! Waterfalls of syrup and a perfect little garden of raspberries all sitting atop a silver platter perched on oak tree branches! I feel like a princess at the Renaissance Festival!"

She picked up the ringing phone and was relieved to hear the responding voice. "Della, after stuffing myself with pancakes, I'm sitting myself down at that gorgeous Thinking Table. Can you come over and just stay until I get started?"

Putting her empty breakfast tray aside, she stared at the now organized puzzle of her life memories on the table. *Ok. Let's see. I'm supposed to pick three Defining Moments . . . the negative ones. How will I ever do that? There are too many to pick from!*

"Oh, there you are! Great, Della, you've come to help me!"

"Good Morning, Anna Gwendolyn . . . How was your night? Were you warm enough? And have you selected your three negative DMs?"

"Oh yes, very cozy, thank you! I'm trying to do that right now, but it all seems pretty impossible!"

"No, no, not impossible. That's the reason for the movie screen in the adjoining room. Our state-of-the-art technology literally takes the words from your memory pages and transmits them as videos on the screen. Simply said, the 'movies' re-enact your most impactful negative Defining Moments."

"What . . . that's impossible! How in the world?"

"It is all possible here," Della said flatly, her voice never changing tone. "It is a step beyond virtual reality. All we ask is that you trust us."

"I'm learning to do that. Just not totally there yet. Ah . . . oh . . . yes . . . so that's what the movie screen is for. So, you're telling me the three DMs I select . . . will be like . . . made into a movie?"

"Yes, Anna Gwendolyn, it is the most successful method in existence to explore Defining Moments. Have you selected your first Defining Moment memory? Just place it in the carved-out circle at the top right of the Thinking Table."

"This is kind of creepy, Della . . ." The table almost selected the piece of paper for her.

"Oh! Look on the screen! It's me! That's my eighth-grade music room. Oh, I remember. I feel someone's frown on me. She's disgusted with me. And mortified at what I'm doing! All I'm doing is playing Norwegian Concerto for an audition for the County Guild Festival."

Anna remembered, "I had worked so very hard on it. That teacher made me feel so stupid. And embarrassed! The whole class was staring at me, some snickering while I was trying not to cry. I felt sick. I felt someone yelling at me. I didn't understand why. I heard the words, 'You can't play THAT at the Festival! It's not Guild-worthy! What would all the other teachers think?' I later figured out why; the piece was an arrangement, and the Guild does not allow *arrangements*, only original pieces. But no one had told me!"

Anna Gwendolyn was still visibly devastated by the humiliation so vividly experienced years ago. She knew in her heart most teachers were wonderful, but this one had had an awful wounding effect.

"How did that hurt you?" Della asked, startling Anna Gwendolyn as she re-experienced and reacted to her first, very painful Defining Moment movie.

"The moment permanently branded me with feelings of stupidity and embarrassment," Anna said thoughtfully.

"And it damaged your self-confidence, self-esteem and dignity," Della analyzed. "A compassionate change in the teacher's tone of voice, or further explanation about Guild

Rules, could have changed this. She could have listened respectfully, complimented you and then, in private, explained the Guild rules about arrangements. She was probably following rules, made a vicious and hurtful error in judgement, as we all occasionally do. But she should have apologized to you, not berated you."

"I'm going to have to think about that," Anna Gwendolyn said, not convinced that Della was getting this one right. *What would a robot know about apologies?* she thought.

"Ok, time for your next Moment." Tentatively, with the Thinking Table's guidance, Anna Gwendolyn placed the second memory page in the carved circle. Again, a movie . . .

"Oh. That's ballet class. It was 'Toe Shoe Measuring' day. We're practicing pirouette turns, and I really loved dancing," Anna Gwendolyn murmured, turning her attention to her picture on the movie screen, her eyes misting over.

"I can barely hear you, Anna Gwendolyn. You were a ballerina, too? You've done a lot in your short life."

"No, I wasn't a ballerina, just maybe trying to be one. This movie is about toe-shoe day—for everyone but me."

"Are you ready to tell me about it? How old were you?"

"Almost ten. I am standing at the ballet bar, facing the mirrored walls. I hear the commands as the positions and steps are called out."

Anna recalled, "I was trying hard to listen and focus and then I could feel a searing gaze from behind me. My ballet slipper-covered feet began twitching, making tapping noises on the wooden floor. The commands grew louder and louder. My hands began to shake. Without warning, my ankles were grabbed in tight fist holds; then, I heard those words shouted and repeated over and over and over—'Back, side, front . . . back, side, front, the other right foot! The other left foot! The other right foot, Anna Gwendolyn! Don't you ever listen?' The classroom of students stopped what they were doing and stared at me. That person is still in my nightmares. I can still hear his voice in my ears, every time I doubt myself."

"Oh. My goodness. Yes, that qualifies as a Negative Defining Moment, most definitely a life-changing and life-re-arranging Defining Moment. What did you do?"

"I froze. I turned red. My face was so hot it hurt. My tears were melted by my beet-red skin as they paraded down my cheeks. I knew that I was not getting my toe shoes that day. I had to listen to all of the ooh's and ah's as my classmates were measured for theirs."

How did that affect you afterwards?" Della asked.

"I was humiliated. I dropped out of ballet immediately. Pappy couldn't understand why. I think up in heaven my mother was devastated, too; she had had her own ballet school at sixteen! But she was gone and I couldn't tell her—or Pappy—what had happened; I never told anyone. I figured it was my fault, my stupidity. That experience colored everything I attempted, not just ballet. Every time I doubt myself I still hear his voice screaming at me . . .

"OK, Della," Anna Gwendolyn's tone changed and she straightened up, "I understand how seeing and talking about my negative moments maybe can help heal me, and I'm glad I did it. But, whew . . . glad that's over. What now?"

"Not so fast! How about your third negative moment . . . the one that's still in your clenched fist? You didn't even need the Thinking Table to choose that one. Take a deep breath and open that fist . . . your third Defining Moment will appear on the screen. If it helps, don't watch. Just explain to me what happened, as the movie is playing."

Della's not giving up! Well . . . here goes . . . But this memory has haunted me all my life, even more than the others.

"I'd met these older girls at Steam Engine Park and wowed them with a special tour of Pappy's train and some of my favorite treats. Days later, I was invited to their pajama party! I felt so important. (Pappy had said 'No!' but eventually gave in.) I arrived, overnight bag stuffed with new PJs and treats to share, and settled in with their social media surfing, the Mean Girls movie, pizza and more surfing. It was fun. But, before long, the surfing turned to whispering and gossip, sounding kind of cruel to me. I was thinking . . . 'Is this what big kids do in high school?' To change the mood, I handed out my treats. That worked for a while, but then . . .

"They motioned me to the back door, to follow behind them. They were sneaking out. I said I'd better not. Giggling, they teased, 'C'mon, go with us, be brave, and do bring your treats.' Out the door and down the quiet, dark street, I followed. As if on cue, the texting and ringing of cell phones began. Steam Engine Park was just a block away. I thought, yeah, that's it, they've made plans to see Pappy's Engine again! I handed out my treats, motioning towards the Park. But hearing their whispers, I nervously discovered they were making plans, not for the Park, but secretly to meet up with some boys. I had no interest or intention of doing that. But (lucky for me), their plan was foiled . . .

"Blaring lights!

"The boys split.

"I remember the Suburban's blinding headlights and these two ranting parents—the parents hosting the party. We were herded into the car; the ranting continuing until we were back at our PJ party.

"All the girls pulled into a huddle, desperately conniving a scheme. And it involved me being the cause of it all! Not true!! But what was I going to say? That had already been decided for me . . . without my consent!

"I remember the parents' footsteps, then squinted eyes, pointed fingers and stern questions. As I listened, I froze. One after the other, each girl answered, saying stuff like: 'It was Anna Gwendolyn's idea. She said we had to see Pappy's Engine. She made us go. It's all her fault.'

"In disbelief, I thought to myself, 'Huh?????!!!!!'

"Each girl testified that I insisted on showing off Pappy's Engine. No, there were no boys involved at all. By the time the parents got to me, it was written in stone that I was the guilty one.

"I remember every single word . . . 'So, young lady, you might be really proud of your Pappy's Engine. That's fine! But horrible things could have happened to all these sweet girls and you'd be to blame! It would be your fault! Shame on you!'

"Unable to speak, my humiliation silenced me. I was scared, of the parents in front of me, and of these lying so-called friends. I tried to stop sobbing. My head hurt from crying. Then the dad patted me on my back, and the Mother hugged me. They said some calming word about apologies due and left the room.

"Pretending like nothing had happened, the party resumed . . . I wanted to disappear. Mortified, I put on my pajama top, laid down and silently cried myself to sleep. (I'd forgotten the bottoms, but was too upset to notice.)

Morning came; the girls woke me up with donuts and milk, and were being very nice. They told me everything would be fine . . . all I had to was lie and apologize to the parents. I was told how 'very cool' these parents were, and that they would not call Pappy if I apologized. All I had to do was lie . . . go along with their story, take the blame . . . and apologize.

"Trying to speak up, I told everyone that sneaking out was not my idea and that I would not apologize. They warned that I might want to think about that. They surrounded me, all sneering, each holding items from my overnight bag: jeans, T-shirt, PJ bottoms, bra, toiletries and treats. I'd have to apologize to the parents to get my clothes back. I was helpless in my underwear, pajama top and a blanket. And they threatened it could have been worse . . . they had taken my picture! I knew what that meant: the internet. Shaking with fear, I promised to back up their lies and take the blame. I got dressed, walked upstairs, sat down, and waited.

"Both parents sat across from me, staring. I believed they had made up their minds about me. I was the instigator. I was no good. I should be ashamed. Again, I remember every word: 'Anna Gwendolyn, your Pappy's train is great. But there is no reason, ever, for young girls to go out by themselves at night. Our daughter would never do that on her own. That was a terrible idea! What do you have to say for yourself?'

"I apologized. I thought I had no choice and I lied. I didn't defend myself. I didn't speak up. I couldn't or wouldn't find my voice, Della. Why was I so desperate for big girl friendships that I let them use me like that? I've never completely trusted anyone ever since, even my friends. Being betrayed and forced to lie still haunts me . . ."

Della knew the damage bullying inflicts. "Anna, bullies like those girls use shame as a tool. They're victorious when they've shredded confidence and beheaded self-esteem, never realizing the long-lasting harm that can do to a person.

"I am sorry that you have lived with the effects of these painful experiences running through your head, daily chiseling holes into your self-confidence and self-esteem. People, teachers, bosses, friends and family make mistakes; they have bad days. Anna Gwendolyn, there is always history for the way a person behaves. But that does not give them an excuse to bully you into lying or make you apologize for something you didn't do. No one has a right to bully anyone."

As Della put her arm around Anna Gwendolyn's shoulder, Anna murmured, "I thought we were also going to look at my happy memories."

Della reminded her of the crocheted tablecloth art project. Oh yeah . . . Anna Gwendolyn smiled.

"The way we are treated, spoken to or believed, can forever scar our self-worth and dignity. In order to move forward, sharing a negative incident with a supportive listener, and acknowledging the hurt, can begin to heal the wound.

"The ultimate goal is to develop an armor of steely self-confidence and self-esteem to deflect bullying, find your voice and move forward," Della responded. "I can tell you have never spoken to anyone about this memory before. These moments are often so disturbing they have to be 'dug up' because we've buried them so deeply. All this is Dream-Work, my dear."

"Ah . . . just like Pappy told me."

Ever Lost A Dream?

Chapter Twenty-Four

Stepping Onto the Granite Path

Sapped of energy after her Dream-Work with Della, Anna Gwendolyn executed a weary swan-dive with a heavy plop into her queenly four poster bed. Sleep came in an instant.

Awakening, she was still wrapped in the luxurious, terrycloth robe she'd chosen as PJs. Beside her bed, she found a surprise. *Oh look! Skinny jeans! And T-shirts. And . . . of course, all in peacock colors! Oh, these sneakers look so comfortable!"*

With a knock on the Suite door, Della entered.

"Good afternoon, Anna Gwendolyn? Were you able to rest your eyes a bit?" Della said.

"Afternoon? It can't be afternoon," Anna replied wondering just exactly how this robot defined morning. Certainly, it could not be that late.

"Hurry now, time is wasting. I will be working on your Lost Dreamer Itinerary for the continuation of your journey!" Della declared.

"My own custom-made itinerary! That sounds . . . a . . . wonderful! But isn't there more Dream-Work to do?"

"Oh that." Della responded in true robotic flat tones. "My dear, that is over and done with. You met with your Defining Moments last night. Recognized them right off! And I must say, I have never seen anyone put those paper memory pieces together so quickly. You observed, listened and worked with your mind and heart, and began the sobering task of understanding the impact those situations had on you. Good job, dear, great job." Della applauded with a rainbow set of lights, lights looking much more excited than her voice proclaimed. "Time to move on, young lady. Come on now and have some lunch before you leave."

All the dread Anna Gwendolyn had felt the day before was slowly vanishing. She was filled with hope and anticipation.

"At your service, Madame Anna Gwendolyn. What would you like: juice, lattes, tea?" Della pretended formality as she led Anna to the Dining Garden. Anna Gwendolyn selected The Rapunzel, and the Lux-Latte, with its marshmallow mountains of whipped cream. "Ah . . .oh . . . and Raspberry Rapunzel . . ." *I had one of these at the Peacock Tea Garden.*

"For anything else, we are here to serve you. Your pleasure is our purpose."

After the Lux-Latte in tribute to Nevah, and gobbling down the Raspberries Rapunzel, plus Castle Cakes and Bow-Tied Bacon, Anna returned to the Defining Moments Suite. Magical Marzipan Mini's and Train-Stop-Truffles were waiting on the Thinking Table.

Grabbing a mouthful, Anna bathed in the Waterfall Basins, and dried in an exhilarating "Wind-Room" that could make towels obsolete.

Maybe I am destined to live my life, right here in this castle on Delphinium!

Anna changed into the pair of skinny jeans, with purple stitching and yellow *Fleurs-de-lys* on the pockets. A colorful, tie-dyed t-shirt and a pair of red, polka dot, high-top basketball shoes completed her "retro" look. She reminded herself of pictures of her mother long ago, and a poignant smile crossed her lips.

Another knock on the door was followed by an anxious "Come in" from Anna Gwendolyn.

Walking into the suite, "I have your Rhibbonosphere Itinerary."

"Oh?" Anna Gwendolyn said, coming back to the present. How had she let herself get so caught up in the daydream of a castle and all of its amenities! Brought suddenly back to reality, she knew it was time to continue her trek. The luxurious surroundings had made everything comfortable and easy, but she worried that was about to end. Pappy's words rung in her ears. "Dream journeys can be treacherous." And every character she'd met so far had said the same thing.

"Are you coming with me, Della?" Anna Gwendolyn asked, hoping for a little support.

"No, it is a solo trip," Della said, handing her the itinerary.

Looking down at the scroll-like document, Anna held sort of a map with some blurry routes and faded, vague wording. "Where am I supposed to start? How will I know the way?" she asked, thinking that this journey had been puzzle enough so far. "I feel lost already."

"We are without Wi-Fi up here, so you have to rely on your own brain, your instincts and this old-fashioned paper map, like the one your Pappy used when he conducted his trains."

"I guess I could pretend I was born during the Renaissance," Anna Gwendolyn replied, more a question than a statement, trying to rationalize the situation.

"Good idea." Della was glad to see Anna Gwendolyn was making an effort to find a solution to her perceived problem. At least, she hadn't brought up that ridiculous Dream-O-Tron in the last twenty-four hours. *Yes, progress is underway,* Della said to herself.

So, Anna Gwendolyn began her next journey, map in hand, not having a clue of where she was going.

Putting one foot in front of the other, Anna Gwendolyn began, very slowly, walking into this strange world she had become reluctant friends with. The sky above looked much like the sky out of the Peacock Plane.

While taking in the view, she noticed something in the sky, and it was moving. *Even in this crazy place birds don't fly like that. Oh, I hope it's not something or someone else coming to get me! Should I hide? Is there a place to hide?*

Could it be? It was!! Her treasured train that she lost in her jump from the plane was floating down from the sky! With a mind of its own, it wrapped around her shoulders and waist! Its tail was left to flow softly through the air with each of her steps forward. "OH, my Festival scarf, my train . . . my train!!! This is like a warm hug! Somebody around here knows what this means to me."

As Della watched her walking away with each step, she was touched by the joy spread over Anna Gwendolyn's face. "Godspeed, my dear, and may your wildest dreams come true."

As Anna Gwendolyn embarked on yet another mysterious passage, a gust of wind swirled the leftover Collide-A-Scope papers into a twirling funnel of her Defining Moments. And then they became mirrors again, reflecting her hopeful face and flowing scarf. The funnel followed her joyfully to the horizon.

Anna Gwendolyn, realizing the gravity of the journey ahead, and bolstered both by Della's encouragement and her reclaimed scarf, just kept taking one step after another.

The sun gifted her with invigorating energy. She came upon the long-awaited Granite Path as its darkened exterior became highlighted by white crystals. As Anna Gwendolyn looked down the path, she saw that she was travelling over dark and white stones that resembled something she recognized.

She stepped on one white, long-shaped crystal—then another and another, then another, and then she heard a sound. *Is that music? Where is that coming from? These darkened and white crystal stones . . . they . . . Oh! They're piano keys!* Music began to play. But not just any music! *Could it really be? The guild audition . . . Norwegian Concerto . . . ?*

Oh! Yes, it is! "This Granite Path is playing my eighth-grade piano recital piece, as I step on it!" she announced as if there was an audience. Taking a chance, she tested the keys. So what if it was an arrangement!!! "World! Now hear this! Now hear me!" she shouted. The pianist in her, and the dancer, were re-awakened, as her steps turned from "chancing" into prancing which became dancing, and down the "keyboard"

Anna Gwendolyn flew! Swirling pirouettes propelled her along the now glorious Granite Path!

As Anna reached a fork in the Path, she sat down on the giant C-sharp key, making one last climactic sound. "Oh, this is so much fun!" A feeling of victory overcame her. "I can dance! Look at me! I can leap! And . . . I can play the piano and it really sounds good! And I'm finding my voice! Bullies, beware!"

Then a calm feeling settled over her. Anna Gwendolyn understood that everything Della had told her was probably true. Bullies did steal dreams.

"Now that's victory!" Anna shouted, smiling from ear to ear. With the concerto still playing in her head, Anna heard a voice whisper: "Just dance." She was learning to trust the whispering voices; they no longer frightened her. She stood up very carefully, tucked in her behind, lifted her chest, extended her arms in graceful ballet fashion . . . and then stood on her toes . . . for the first time in many years! She was surprised at the pleasure it gave her. She became acutely aware of the joy she had deprived herself of for so many years.

Anna Gwendolyn turned right at the fork in the Granite Path. From within a whirl of turns, a magical Red Carpet unfolded; Anna Gwendolyn stepped onto it and froze. Then, a "voice" began directing her to sway, move, dance, to perform. As she did, an airy lightness took over. Anna Gwendolyn leaped into the air, executing tours jetés with the grace of a Giselle. The joy she felt was inexplicable. *Wow! A real Red Carpet! Just like in Hollywood!* "I'm ready for anything this Rhibbonosphere has to offer!" she shouted.

The Red Carpet led her onto the spectacular stage of an outdoor theater. Before she knew it, she was performing, improvising and dancing, while taking breaks to play the gorgeous grand piano! "If only they could see me now!" she laughed.

No sooner had the words rolled off her lips than an audience appeared: the teenagers from that pajama party that had gone so very, very wrong, where the girls threatened Anna and bullied her into lying. Now those same girls sat in admiration, watching Anna Gwendolyn perform flawlessly. Scanning the audience, she saw them cheering for her. When their eyes met, the haunting scowls and bullying voices that she had remembered for years melted into smiles. As they handed her a spray of coral roses, she said, "I forgive you. I've held you against my heart all these years, and it dragged me down. I truly forgive you all. Thank you for coming tonight!"

Anna Gwendolyn gathered the many flowers tossed to her, ran backstage, and completed another step to finding her dreams.

But her adventure was about to take a radical turn.

Ever Lost A Dream?

Chapter Twenty-Five

Nevah-Tu-Latte—Coffee and More

Stepping through the theater stage exit, Anna Gwendolyn found herself right back on the Granite Path. Somehow, she expected to be further down the road, but she was learning that traditional expectations were rarely realized in the Rhibbonosphere.

"Are there any coffee shops around here, I wonder? A latte would be nice, really nice for my walk." (Her preference for coffee was instigated by her coffee-crazed friend, Nevah, back in Parkersville.) Seeing a "Dream-Chasers Overlook" notice ahead, she walked to the side of the road. The view before her was spectacular. "Yep, a cup of coffee sure would be nice right now," she lamented. Seeing there was a little gift store next to the Overlook, she stopped.

"Is there a coffeeshop around here? I'm really tired, and my mouth is watering for a caramel latte, with whipping cream, chocolate and cinnamon sprinkles—the kind I can get in Parkersville."

The storekeeper responded, "Where did you get the idea that there is such a thing? In the Rhibbonosphere, we have a few places you can get coffee. But if you insist, and as it must be a habit of yours, you can try the Hatte-Latte Coffee Fountain run by a Miss Nevah-Tu-Latte. Well, it's not really a coffee shop, but it pretends to be. You can get coffee; I don't know if they have that caramel, cream, and cinnamon one you're salivating for, but you can get coffee. I must warn you, though, Nevah-Tu-Latte always has something more than coffee in mind for her customers."

Totally confused but still wanting a cup of coffee, Anna thought little about the storekeeper's strange answer. "Really? What's that name again? I think I remember seeing that name on a sign somewhere . . . ah, let me think . . . now I know. I saw it on that sign up in the sky. It was something about how it's never too late. How weird." Then Anna Gwendolyn asked, "Okay, well now, would you please tell me where this coffee fountain is?"

"First things first. I know you'll need to write this down. Do you have a pen and paper? Are you ready? Okay," the strange woman said.

"How do you know I'll need to write this down?"

"Because I've known you all of your life," the woman responded. She began the directions, ". . . walk three blocks down Smile-A-Mile Road and turn left on Wake-Up-Call. Then travel past Creamery and Sugar Mountain and make a right on Arome-ah Street. You will find the shop right on the west corner of Snooze-Ya Loose Lane. You can't miss the sign— Hatte-Latte's Coffee Fountain. There you always get more than a cup of coffee." The woman continued, "Go in and introduce yourself to Miss Nevah-Tu-Latte. It is not exactly what you are wanting, but trust me, in the end, you'll thank me."

"If you say so. As long as I can get an extra-large latte, with a mountainous mound of whipped cream, I'm game," Anna Gwendolyn said.

"Yes . . . yes, little one. I hope you find what you're looking for."

She followed the woman's directions, sure that she would get confused. Relaxing with relief, she saw the shop, as she finally made a left on Snooze-ya Loose Lane. But Anna Gwendolyn was disappointed by what she saw in front of her. The storekeeper was right. The place looked nothing like a coffee shop. But the aroma of brewing coffee spoke its name. She dug into her jean pocket for a comb, half-heartedly approved a mirror reflection but was frustrated with her hair. She wished that she could do something with her frizzing braids, however, the humid air had another plan. "Oh, well," she sighed, accepting that she'd done the best she could. Maybe her beautiful scarf would be enough to make her presentable.

Anticipating the rich beverage, she quickened her pace. Anna Gwendolyn found a big, red door framed in the center of a huge, front porch. Out walked a tall, thin figure, but one with great posture.

"Welcome to the Hatte-Latte Coffee Fountain, I'm Nevah-Tu-Latte" she said. Nevah-Tu-Latte was a bright-eyed woman, her shoulders back and her head held high, with a bizarre, red hat that had the distinct appearance of a pillow.

"I just need a large latte to go," Anna Gwendolyn replied, as she tried to take in this odd-looking person. *Was anything or anyone in this place normal?*

"Not so fast, speedy! Don't be in such a hurry. I know I might look strange, but I am really very nice. The pillow-top? Is that what you're wondering about?"

"Where I come from people don't wear pillows on their heads."

"Oh, that's just in case I get tired. It's for convenience only. Here," Nevah-Tu-Latte said, handing her a menu. "At least, take a minute and examine the menu. You just might find something that you need, not just want." Nevah-Tu-Latte met Anna Gwendolyn's stare head on.

"No thanks, I'm kind of in a hurry," Anna Gwendolyn said.

"Hold on. Just sit down here for a moment and listen. Give me a chance. You're here for a reason and you might as well take advantage of it," Nevah-Tu-Latte blurted out.

"But I'm on my way and in a hurry," Anna Gwendolyn said, beginning to fidget. This "person" was making her feel uneasy.

"Why? Are you trying to find a dream?" Nevah-Tu-Latte asked.

"Yes, I'm . . ." Anna Gwendolyn responded suspiciously. Everyone in this place seemed to know her and her business. She knew she should be getting used to it, but it was still unnerving. "Don't really know what my dream is, precisely, but yes, I'm trying to find a dream, even though I'm sure it's probably too late for me. How did you know?"

"Too late! That's what everybody says," Nevah-Tu-Latte replied. "Do they also say, 'That's not for you, honey'? Have you also come to the conclusion that you are not bright enough or pretty enough or sharp enough? People will say that, too! Well, I'm here to tell you, it is never too late to embark on your dreams!" Pausing for a deep breath, she continued, "However,

there's another thing besides one's negative Defining Moments that stops a dream in its tracks."

"What's that?" Anna Gwendolyn asked, genuinely interested. She still wasn't quite sure about all of this, but was starting to see how each character she met seemed to have some new insight regarding her, as well as their own ideas on how she could reach her goals.

"Lost dreamers sometimes miss the importance of serving their fellow man. Giving back to your community is one of the single most important acts you can do to help your dream become reality. Do more than one, too," explained Nevah-Tu-Latte, "because it's contagious! You can use your gifts or you can use your grit."

"What do I have to do? Where do I start?" Maybe this was the "next step" in her search for her dreams. *Might as well not fight it and just jump in.*

"Now you're talking! We can discuss the possibilities over a latte."

"How's that? So, you're really going to make me a latte?"

"Come with me," Nevah-Tu-Latte said. She guided Anna Gwendolyn through the eclectically decorated first floor, then up a rainbow-colored, spiral staircase to what seemed like the seventh story of the shop. Once in the room, Anna Gwendolyn was astonished to see what appeared to be a gigantic screen and rows and rows of desks with computers and high-backed chairs.

"Wow! This is like Mission Control I saw in the history books about the moon landing!" The twenty-five-foot screen was covered with what appeared to be stock market readings, letters, numbers, minuses and pluses.

In actuality, the listings were compiling the worldwide availability of volunteer opportunities. Information lines, by way of the internet, brought daily information from around the globe.

Nevah-Tu-Latte asked, "Are you ready to order? Our menu has changed. So, take a good look and you're sure to find something to suit you."

"Please take a seat," a waitress said from behind a '50s soda fountain bar, at the far corner of the room. Seven vinyl-covered, red and chrome swivel stools sat in front of the bar. The waitress was right out of the '50s too, complete with an updo, ruffled apron and a chrysanthemum made out of coffee filters, an artful accessory.

"Ah, eh . . . yes, I'll have the Raz-ma-taz-Chock-o-late Frappé-Latte, with a Snow Mountain," Anna Gwendolyn requested (without looking at the menu).

"What! Never heard of that one. But I can give it a try. One Raz-ma-taz-Chock-o-late Frappe-Latte Snow Mountain coming up," said the waitress, with a big smile. *This lady loves her job*, Anna thought as she watched the waitress enthusiastically prepare the experiment.

Guiding her by hand, Nevah-Tu-Latte said, "Now, Anna Gwendolyn, come and I'll explain the reason for your visit to the World-Wide Web of Altruistic and Charitable Opportunities—WWWACO for short. Please sit down here and study all the world has to offer in volunteer opportunities; your coffee will be brought to you when it's ready.

"President Kennedy began with the Peace Corps; this is just my way to continue his work. To be successful, every Dream Searcher must contribute generously to a community in some way. They need to give back." *(Where have I heard this before?)* "There is surely something on this screen that suits your talents."

"Do I have to pick something from this long list? I'm going to need more caffeine than a single *frappé* for this!" she said, resigning herself to this journey of self-discovery.

"I need to get back to the shop," Nevah said, as Anna's *frappé* arrived. "I'll leave you to study your options. Just remember, as Nevah-Tu-Latte says . . ."

"I know, I know," . . . Anna responded.

"It is Never Too Late!" Nevah-Tu-Latte piped up with a broad, toothy smile.

Chapter Twenty-Six

Pillars of Inspiration and Persevering Percy

Clutching her frappé, Anna Gwendolyn examined the massive screen, and became totally overwhelmed. "So many people need help!"

Studying the list, she selected an opportunity she knew would make her grandfather proud—making life better for the residents of Dreams Preserved Nursing Home Village. There were several opportunities:

1. Someone to begin a gardening program. There were many residents with green thumbs and the energy to use them, but no tools or resources for a program.
2. A sun-filled room full of painting easels and artist supplies.
3. Comfortable and fashionable exercise attire to inspire movement. It could be one size fits all.

Anna Gwendolyn had no idea how she could do this. But she had figured out, dream or no dream, that she had to find her way out of this place, wherever she was. And if volunteering at this nursing home was part of the requirement, she was all in. She went downstairs and told Nevah-Tu-Latte that she'd made a decision.

Nevah-Tu-Latte congratulated Anna Gwendolyn. "Your Pappy would be proud," she commented, once again shocking Anna Gwendolyn with the reference to Pappy.

When will I get used to these characters knowing everything about my life? Anna Gwendolyn remembered how Pappy would feel after visiting his friends in their nursing homes. He felt he could never do enough for them. Anna thought probably no single person could accomplish everything that needed to be done. But if responding to even one request, she could give back to this community and help her dreams come true, she would give it a try.

"OK, Anna Gwendolyn, here are the directions to Dreams Preserved Nursing Home Village. Leave the Coffee Fountain and turn left on Smile-a-Mile highway; walk one mile and turn right. Then walk straight down a short, wooded lane and you will see the Dreams Preserved sign. Did you get all that?"

"Oh, yes. I have it," she replied, secretly wishing she had written directions to refer back to. Anna Gwendolyn said good-by, actually remembering to thank Nevah-Tu-Latte.

Successfully finding her way to the Village with very few U-turns, Anna walked up to the front door. Dreams Preserved Nursing Home Village looked like it needed some care. Built fifty-four years ago, it had plenty of charm but was short on amenities, an all too frequent situation in retirement and nursing homes.

As she entered, "May I speak to the manager, or director? Oh, my name is Anna Gwendolyn Shaw," she quickly added. So far, everyone seemed to already know her.

"And I am Ms. Jones, the administrator of Dreams Preserved. Welcome! What can I do for you?"

"Ah . . . I don't have a complaint or anything like that. I just want to volunteer. Do you have any volunteer positions available? Nevah-Tu-Latte and WWWACO have directed me here. Do you need a volunteer?"

"Yes, yes, we have so many needs. You really could change some lives with some gardening tools, workout clothing and art supplies! Budget cuts and hurricanes have stolen a great deal from our community."

"Ah . . . oh yes . . . well, first of all . . . my Mama and Pappy taught me how to dig and how to plant and, most importantly, how we always felt better after a day of gardening. Secondly, I'm known as the town *Fashionista*; I know how to put an outfit together, even if it's just 'stitched' with a glue gun. I know I could help dream up some cute and sassy workout wear! And . . . of course, very sharp and stylish outfits for the men.

"And with some art supplies, there will have to be some easels! Ya know, I'll bet there are some residents who would love to do some woodworking." Anna rambled on enthusiastically, pretending to know what she was talking about, her mind buzzing like a hornet's nest.

"You might not know this yet," Anna pointed out, "but I'm sure you'll find out soon that everyone knows everything about everyone's business around here. I single-handedly created my own parachute! And it really worked! Well, almost! It's just that my train got caught in the . . . well, that's another story.

Ms. Jones, I can do this. Please give me a chance, I'm ready and willing to commit."

Touched by her sincerity and enthusiasm, Ms. Jones agreed to let Anna try, steering her to get assistance from the County. Mr. Green, of the County Extension Office, was thrilled to be asked to help. He listened intently to Anna's ideas. He had long wanted a way to provide a service to the senior community, and he loved inspiring gardening. This was perfect. *What an amazing, young girl she must be to come up with this solution,* he thought.

"I assure you that soon the residents will be eating their own freshly grown vegetables and beautifying the grounds and their personal living spaces with colorful flowers," Mr. Green told Anna Gwendolyn.

"That's wonderful, Mr. Green. Thank you so much for your support. Goodbye," Anna said sincerely.

Wow, one down and two to go! Anna was feeling better about her project. *Now all I have to do is locate art supplies and workout clothes,* she thought, hoping she would find similar success with these challenges. She headed back to Dreams Preserved to brainstorm with management.

"Wait a minute," Anna Gwendolyn said aloud in the meeting, suddenly hit with an idea. "Ms. Jones, do you have any residents, men or women, who can sew?"

"Why yes, yes, I'm sure we do. We have several. In fact, they call themselves the Stubborn Stitchers," she said, grinning.

"I have an idea. May I have permission to talk with them?" Anna Gwendolyn knew from her Pappy's visits to nursing homes that you could not just walk in. She assumed it would be the same, even in this strange world.

"Why certainly," the administrator answered. "In fact, you know, I believe they're meeting now; I'll take you there."

Anna Gwendolyn was welcomed by the group of Stitchers, and explained her idea. All were well known for their sewing expertise. As one might have guessed, the women and two veterans, men, were delighted to take on the task of making stylish, comfortable, workout wear for their fellow residents. They were excited by the challenge. How wonderful it would be to do something so important for their friends at Dreams Preserved. This definitely was going to be a change of pace.

Anna Gwendolyn could feel the energy expand in the room as they chatted among themselves, figuring out the logistics and allocating different duties to each other.

Fueled by their enthusiasm, Anna Gwendolyn went a step further. Putting the word out, residents' families donated fabrics, notions, and so many sewing machines, Dreams Pre-served didn't have room for all of them. Sharing the wealth of excess machines and materials, sewing projects were added to surrounding retirement homes' programs. Over time, The Stubborn Stitchers grew into an energetic, non-profit program that answered the needs of many senior communities.

Anna Gwendolyn had one more task to carry out. The last two had really worked. She had performed real volunteer work, giving back to the community. She was getting the hang of this and was kind of enjoying it. Now, she just had to find some art supplies; and maybe some easels. *I've been lucky so far,* she thought. *But good art supplies can be expensive and where am I going to find teachers?* Dreams Preserved didn't have a budget for these things.

There had to be a way.

"Ms. Jones, I think I can get art supplies through donations but not easels. I was wondering, do you think there are residents right here at Dreams Preserved who would love to do some productive work involving wood projects? It would be a project they could feel really good about. If I can find some donated wood, could they build some easels? What do you think?"

Ms. Jones nodded yes. And when a local arts college found out about the Dreams Preserved program for constructing easels, art students needing internships signed up to teach painting to the residents of Dreams Preserved.

And so, it was . . .

Dreams Preserved, always charming on the outside, now housed happier, more productive residents on the inside—beautiful flowers, fresh vegetables, healthier, stronger, active residents and lovely artwork gracing the walls were the fringe benefits. Anna Gwendolyn knew, from the confidence she gained with her own creativity, that dignity was the best gift to give the residents. These programs had enriched their lives, and their smiles were proof.

Anna Gwendolyn was not exactly sure how long she had been at Dreams Preserved. Time seemed to have a mind of its own in this place. But satisfied she had met the challenge required on this stop, she was ready to move on. *But to where?* she asked herself, as she waved goodbye to Dreams Preserved and headed down the path.

Just as most of the surroundings in this strange place were eclectic, the next landscape didn't disappoint. She passed skylines of skyscrapers, with views of rippling corn and wheat fields. There were mirrored lakes, streams and rivers flowing wildly, swans gliding on the water tops. Nothing was typical, no matter where she looked.

Walking further down the road, she saw in the distance, what looked to be three lone columns; the kind that held up buildings. They looked rather detached, or unattached might be a better description. Getting closer, she saw they were a bit worse for wear and were just a short distance from a pile of rubble and ruins.

"Hum, I wonder what stood there before?" Anna Gwendolyn asked the air. As she turned around to examine the site more closely, black clouds above signaled the close presence of a thunderstorm.

She needed to find shelter quickly. Flashes of lighting followed by booms of thunder threatened approaching rain. What quickly turned from a threat into a torrential rainfall frightened Anna Gwendolyn. Sheets of rain blocked her visibility. Drenched, she was desperate to find some sort of cover. "What on earth will happen next?" she cried. She was soaked to the bone.

Looking around, there seemed to be no form of shelter. *What other choice do I have*, she thought, *but to continue on this path and hope I find something? Maybe the rain will blow the other way.* She wished she had a car or at least a bicycle, but then knew the rain was so thick, they would have been useless. She was left no option but to trudge along the barely visible Granite Path. She thought with nostalgia of her snuggly bed at home and became even more determined to complete these steps that would get her out of here and home where she belonged. Pappy must be sick with worry.

The Granite Path narrowed and became increasingly bumpy and rocky. Anna Gwendolyn was certain she was going to be struck by lightning, but at least the rain was slowing somewhat. She could see the road now, but "How is that going to help?" she questioned, since she still had no idea of her next stop. Reaching the top of a small hill, she saw a billboard appear through the haze:

THE OBSTACLE-MULTIPLIER
1/2 Mile Ahead

Then she saw it in the distance—a huge boulder that must be the side of a mountain. And miraculously—at least it felt like a miracle to her—with all the lightning bolts still electrifying the sky, there appeared a small cave where she could find shelter. She stopped, and studied the details on her map. Where was her destination?

Anna Gwendolyn saw that if she was reading the map right, she had traveled over fifty miles. *How can that be*? Anna thought. This place seemed to have no patterns, no regard of time, days of the week or even distance. She had only been walking half a day . . . or had she? This place was truly a mystery and followed no rules.

Her journey continued on the Granite Path. She had faith in its direction. She couldn't see much in front of her though. Her black mascara, running down her face and into her eyes from rain and tears, hindered her vision and made her look pretty scary. When she glanced up from the map, she saw the road had come to an end. That "end" was that enormous boulder she'd previewed, now completely blocking the Path. But where was the cave she had seen? And those columns? Had her vision been that blurry or like everything else she encountered, had it just appeared out of nowhere?

"Well, I have no choice. I guess I better find some kind of opening. I wonder . . . could this be where my dreams are? They could be waiting for me on the other side." She tried to analyze the situation and be calm, but so overwhelmed, she screamed out into the air as if in agony, close to a breaking point. She was alone, in the middle of nowhere, drenched through to her skin, with no clear idea of where she was going or how she was going to get there. Plus, she worried she was hallucinating.

She reached out and felt the boulder in front of her. At least it was real. How would she ever get over this huge rock? Anna Gwendolyn needlessly shoved her shoulder against the boulder. *I can't move it; I can't go around it—there is no around; and I certainly can't jump over it. This is useless,* she said to herself. *Where is all that creativity that everyone said I have? It certainly isn't helping me now!*

Suddenly, she heard something.

A voice called, "Hello-o-o-o-o-o-o-o down there. You, looking for your dreams, could you use a hand? No, we don't think you can jump over that boulder either, but how *could* you get over it? You seem like the resourceful type." A large hand touched her shoulder. She looked up. Just above stood those three columns—the ones she'd seen in the ruins. Yes, they were a little worn, but still standing ever so proudly. They were alive! Speaking!

The tallest spoke first, "We'd love to give you a hand. We've supported dreams for centuries. That's our purpose. We've held up buildings that were supposed to hold up the dreams of the people. Well, sometimes the buildings succeeded, but often they failed."

"Like during times when integrity and responsibility to the people were lost in deceit," said another of the Column-Men.

"Well, I'm on my way to find my lost dreams." She was no longer startled by strange events or unlikely characters taking on human qualities. Besides, just maybe these very tall, strong creatures could help find a way around this boulder. *These guys seem like they want to help me. I bet this is where I'll find my lost dreams.*

"We see you've completed a most important step. You just made every day 'Christmas' at Dreams Preserved. So we're here to help. You need to get to the other side of that giant boulder, right?" one Column-Man asked.

"Yes, I do. It is so slimy and slippery because of the rain," Anna Gwendolyn lamented. "I do know how to climb but . . ."

"But what? You haven't done it in the rain? It's too big? Your hair will get tussled or you might tear your designer jeans? We're sorry if we sound sarcastic, but a little disarray is necessary for dream searching and retrieval."

They don't mean to be sarcastic. Then why are they? (She had a sudden flashback to Luv-Ern using that same exact tone!)

"You are very resourceful, Anna. Just think about it for a minute. You'll come up with a way," encouraged a Column-Man.

"That long, turquoise scarf you are wearing?" questioned the tallest Column-Man.

"Oh, this is my train," Anna Gwendolyn replied.

"Ah, what is a train, may I ask? Is it useful?" another Column-Man asked.

"Oh well, some day it will act as a train for my wedding dress when I marry," Anna Gwendolyn replied flippantly. She still hadn't abandoned the Cinderella-like thoughts that had been her safety net these past few years, and easily fell back into her flighty demeanor.

"When you marry a prince?" the same Column-Man asked.

"Well, I joke about it, at least."

"Oh, let's just say that's a pretty popular dream around here!" the Column-Man commented.

"Have any of those wedding dreams ever come true?" Anna Gwendolyn asked, feeling slightly wounded by the condescending tone of the Column-Man. "Surely, some came true," she continued, hopefully.

"That's a hard question to answer. May we suggest trying something with your train?" another Column-Man asked.

"Well, can't you use something else? This train . . . it's my prized possession, and I can't let anything happen to it."

"But Anna Gwendolyn, it might get you to your dreams."

"OK, but please be careful. It's very special."

"See that jutting rock, way up there at the top? Toss your train up there to catch on that rock and then you can shimmy up to the top," said a Column-Man.

"Can't you just lift me up there?" Anna Gwendolyn asked. *It's such an obvious, simple solution to my problem. Why can't they see it?*

"We are pillars of inspiration. We do not do the work. Only you can. In the Rhibbonosphere, there are rules. If you are of a certain age, thirteen in this case, and of certain health and mentality, one of the rules is that you must do things for yourself. You'll learn that you can figure everything out yourself," said a Column-Man.

Anna Gwendolyn was disappointed. "Why do I have to do everything myself?" she pouted.

"We're here to help you. Support and inspiration are our jobs and we have a long heritage of doing just that. Our relatives in Greece hold up incredibly beautiful and honorable structures, the source of inspiration for thousands of years," said the shortest Column-Man. "In order for you to be successful, you must learn to believe in yourself. You've been good at figuring things out in the past. You will do it now. These are steps toward your dreams and intended destiny."

Anna Gwendolyn sighed. She could see she was not going to win this one. A ray of sunshine broke through the clouds and illuminated the rocky ledge, as if giving her a "Go" signal. She took a deep breath and almost angrily threw her train into the air. It floated skyward like a hot air balloon and then draped itself over the jagged rock. Anna Gwendolyn crawled up onto a five-foot mini-boulder to make herself taller, and then reached up high over her head. Her fingertips brushed the bottom hem of the train—just beyond her reach.

"Jump, jump, jump," the Column-Men called out in unison.

Anna Gwendolyn jumped up as high as she could and grabbed the train in each fist. Like an expert rock climber, she pulled herself up the side of the boulder, slowly inching and fearfully slipping with each pull towards her ascent to the top. "I'm not even halfway up!" she shouted, but with the help of her "climbing rope" scarf, she persevered.

At last, at the top, she stood breathless, now looking at the Column-Men face to face. She did not want to admit it, but her heart was pounding with pride at her victorious ascent.

"Would you like a refill for the road?" Nevah-Tu-Latte asked, suddenly appearing next to Anna Gwendolyn, with an ear-to-ear grin and her coffee fountain in hand.

"What . . . Nevah-Tu-Latte? How did you get . . . ?" asked Anna Gwendolyn, looking around for some sort of explanation.

"You'd really better get on the road because there's a lot waiting for you. Don't forget your train."

Flabbergasted by Nevah-Tu-Latte's appearance, Anna Gwendolyn pulled up her train and wrapped it around her waist. "Now wait just a minute! I successfully made it through a roaring thunderstorm, climbed to the top of a gigantic boulder and all you can say is 'You better get on the road?'"

Nevah-Tu-Latte explained, "Anna Gwendolyn, have you not yet learned completely how important it is to do things for yourself? You had a few obstacles. So what? Well, you have definitely arrived in the best place to learn about obstacles and their effect on your ability to make dreams come true. Percy Press-on Verance will meet you at your next stop, the Obstacle-Multiplier."

She continued, "In short, it's a place where living, breathing Obstacles can rob you of your will to dream. The Obstacles can depress you, deter you, anger you, frustrate you, and extinguish even blazing fires of passion. It's at the Obstacle-Multiplier that you will learn about the dangers of falling over the side, into its pit . . ."

Nevah-Tu-Latte warned, "You don't want to end up in that Multiplier; it can rob you of your confidence, self-esteem, and dignity. It can literally 'steal' your treasured dreams. Besides, as the name implies, its expertise lies in the ability to multiply obstacles you already have! That's why you'll need Percy Press-on Verance. He's our Rhibbonosphere expert in the art of persevering against any and all dangerous obstacles. Everything about him exudes his 'press-on at all odds' mentality."

"Has anyone seen Percy?" asked one of the Column-Men. They were so very tall that their faces could actually see over the pit of the Obstacle-Multiplier.

"Anna Gwendolyn, while we are waiting for him, I want you to jot down, on this tablet, those things you see as obstacles to your dreams," said Nevah-Tu-Latte.

"This place is the obstacle to my dreams!!!" said Anna Gwendolyn emphatically, still stinging from not getting accolades or at least a little credit for all the things she had accomplished so far. She felt forced to begin thinking about obstacles—hers in particular.

"How will I know this Percy, what does he look like?" Anna Gwendolyn questioned, trying again to get the attention she felt entitled to.

"His hair is pressed. His shirts are starched and the pleats in his trousers are legendary," Nevah answered. "He has pleats in his trousers that could slice a Thanksgiving turkey! It's been whispered throughout the community that he was the

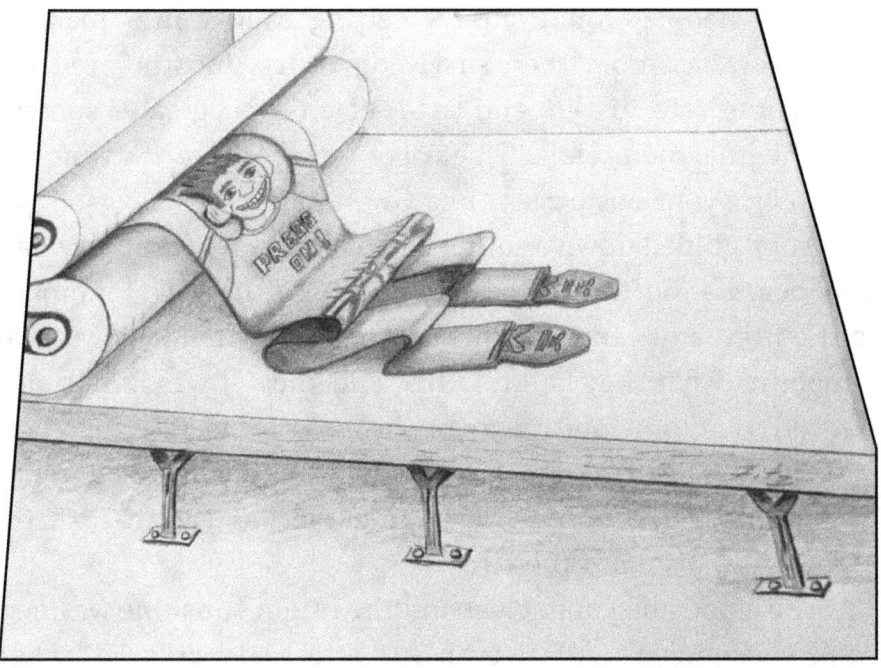

unfortunate victim of an ironing mangle. He got caught in its steam rollers.

"Percy's interesting trait is his unique commitment to recycling. He has created a triangular vehicle he christened the Roll-On! (with an exclamation point at the end because he said, 'as a reminder that, no matter what obstacle, we have to keep rolling on!'). It is truly a sight to behold. It's made from the very 1950s ironing mangle that almost took his life. The mangle's ironing roller is the front wheel of the Roll-On!. That man can zip around faster than the speed of light. His mission is to help dreamers recognize obstacles before it is too late, and teach them to 'press on' against all odds. Percy Press-on Verance can single-handedly take on any dream that has lost its way or been destroyed, by teaching the dreamer to persevere and face obstacles head on.

"Few people would survive getting caught in a mangle. But Percy has more than survived; he has incorporated his misfortune into his life and made it an even greater success than he imagined. He will be eager to meet you. It's time for you to face your obstacles, Anna Gwendolyn."

Anna gulped down another cup of coffee. She probably had only heard a fourth of what had been said, her ADD jumping to the front and center of this conversation. She was trying to remember what they had told her; she knew it was important, but she could only put fragments of the conversation together.

Then Nevah-Tu-Latte gave her a hug, and whispered in her ear as she said goodbye, "Just remember, as Nevah-Tu-Latte always says, it's never too late!"

The clouds began to clear and the bright sunshine warmed Anna Gwendolyn's skin. Nevah-Tu-Latte's words played in her head, "It's never too late. It's never too late. It's never . . ." Anna Gwendolyn was humming, lost in thought as she traversed the rim of the boulder.

"What do we have here—another lost soul?" a male voice said. Anna Gwendolyn jumped with fright.

"Who are you? I thought I was going to fall into that . . . pit," Anna Gwendolyn said, startled and looking around.

"You say you are going to fall into the Multiplier?" the male voice asked.

Anna Gwendolyn couldn't see where the voice was coming from. "Who's there? Show yourself." *Oh no, I've got myself into another mess*, she thought.

The voice said, "At least you're showing some spunk. You've made it this far without falling into the Obstacle-

Multiplier. Almost nobody, and I mean nobody, does that on the first try."

Shocked as the creature became visible, Anna Gwendolyn stumbled back and fell over the side of the boulder, right into the pit of the Obstacle-Multiplier!

"I see you're still in the business of creating obstacles for yourself. You really should start listening and refrain from those trips you take in your mind." The voice was Percy Press-on Verance.

It was too late. Anna Gwendolyn was now the potential prey of the greedy hands of ever-multiplying Obstacles. Worry, Self-doubt, Low Self-esteem—all the Obstacles were quickly multiplying around her. A Grandfather Clock—like Father Time—held out its hands grasping at her hungrily and marking her arms. He would not let go. "Young lady . . . you think you have all the time in the world! Times up!"

Anna Gwendolyn cried, "What's going on?? Oh my, my train! What's happening? My train is becoming a tapestry of negative messages." All along her beloved scarf, neon signs reiterated what she had been told all her life:

YOU DO NOT HAVE ENOUGH MONEY! YOU ARE NOT SMART ENOUGH! YOU ARE TOO FAT! YOU ARE TOO SKINNY! YOU DON'T LISTEN! YOUR HEAD IS IN THE CLOUDS!

"Hello, young lady, down there. Yes, you have fallen into the dreaded Obstacle-Multiplier! I'm Percy Press-on Verance. And I'm sorry you've now met the Obstacle-Multiplier where, if you don't watch out, the Obstacles will tear your dreams apart at the seams," Percy warned.

"Percy, is that really you?" For a moment, she thought that she, indeed, knew this Percy Press-on Verance, or at least she thought she did.

"You always helped me when I was little in Parkersville, especially when I was in trouble, and gave me a huge bag of tiny, colorful building blocks. And you could fabricate anything out of recycled material," Anna Gwendolyn remarked, remembering the happy hours she'd spent watching her neighborhood friend, Percy. "You could fix, rebuild, recreate, well, almost anything."

Percy Press-on Verance said, "I still can. The Roll-On! I drive helps me do what I do best—mainly, begin the repair process on salvageable dreams by diagnosing their early demise."

"Do you know Luv-Ern?" Anna Gwendolyn asked. *Sure sounds like her.*

Percy answered, "Of course, how else would I have arrived here—the place where my wildest dreams would come true! You know, she also had to earn her dreams. They're not handed out freely."

"What should I do then? Could I please just go home?" Anna Gwendolyn begged—but only half-heartedly—hating to admit the Rhibbonosphere and all its characters were growing on her.

"First you have to quiet the Obstacles, which will continue to multiply before your very eyes. They have one mission—to eradicate your dreams. You must pretend that obstacles have no effect on you."

"But, how do I get out of here?"

"Learn to defend yourself against the ever-multiplying forces that are getting in your way and holding you back."

"Can you help me?"

"My work here, with the help of others, is to teach you how to conquer any obstacle." Percy replied, rather proudly. "Hard as it is to believe, sometimes an obstacle can actually help a dream." Percy extended his hand down to Anna Gwendolyn, but told her the rest is up to her. "You climbed the boulder; you should be able to climb out of the pit."

Anna Gwendolyn painstakingly squirmed herself through the Obstacles, trying to escape, searching for a wall she could climb. She was a sight to behold, covered from head to toe with soul-crushing criticism, insults, indignities, and other obstacles meant to thwart a dream. There was the giant Clock again with its outstretched hands still greedily grabbing at her arms. Her treasured train was laughed at.

Finally, with great relief, she emerged, bedraggled and exhausted from the pit.

She had experienced the full weight of the Obstacle-Multiplier, and although out of the pit, felt unable to free herself from their grip. Unknown to her, if she could manage to stay outside the pit for just five minutes, the Obstacles would disintegrate and vaporize before her very eyes. But even with their absence, they could return again. This was another lesson she would learn along the way.

Anna Gwendolyn screamed, "Forget my dream; please forget my dream. I just want to get away from these awful Obstacles." Her thunderous statement brought back the rain, which poured over her. She already felt drowned in fear.

"Are you going to allow a few silly, nagging obstacles to get in your way?" Percy asked.

"What do you mean a *few* silly obstacles? I'm inundated with them. There are literally hundreds," shouted Anna Gwendolyn.

"They've always been there. You just couldn't see them. You could only feel them."

Percy stood looking at his watch, waiting for the five-minute period to be over, at which time he knew the Obstacles would disintegrate.

Anna Gwendolyn pleaded, "Could you please get me away from here? It's raining harder and harder."

"It's not too late to realize your dreams. I've known you most of your life and I know how creative and resourceful you are."

Anna Gwendolyn was surprised at the sudden turn of his words. The critiquing had changed to caring. "So, you believe in me?" she asked.

"Of course, and I'm not the only one. The world is waiting for you to find your dreams."

Anna Gwendolyn persisted, still unsure. *The "world" may think I'm capable, but they don't really know me,* she thought. "Then why do I feel so weighted down?" And just as she said that, the five minutes passed. The weight on her shoulders shifted and her posture straightened, which lifted her head.

Percy remarked, "The only way to get rid of any obstacle is to learn how to handle it, and to persevere. You need support. I'm here to support you. Obstacles do not go away; they just fuel up and return for another onslaught."

"So how do I overcome them?"

"Keep your guard up. And decide to outlast them. Sometimes, simply pretending, with a giant smile, can scare away even the toughest ones. Are you ready to face the obstacles in your path?"

"Yes, I'm ready to take them on," Anna Gwendolyn answered. She was comfortable with this Press-on character and felt a growing confidence inside. She realized she truly meant "yes" when she agreed to take on the next challenge. Her fears were becoming smaller as her eagerness and self-esteem grew.

On hearing her affirmative answer, one Column-Man responded, "First you will need to recognize your own magic." It would have been a simple task to lift her from the pit, but they had stood by, patiently waiting for her to save herself; how else would she gain confidence?

"Magic?" Anna Gwendolyn asked in a puzzled way. Now they are asking for magic; what else would they demand? She knew she was growing stronger, but she wasn't sure about magic. *Was this the magic that Pappy was talking about?*

The same Column-Man said, "Yes, magic. It's in you, and when you find its voice, you'll be in awe of your newfound strength and empowerment, as you single-handedly take on your obstacles. But you're about to learn a delicate, complicated process. Now, you'd better get started, because the longer you wait, the more obstacles you'll confront."

With Percy at her side, Anna Gwendolyn was ready, with or without this so-called magic.

Ever Lost A Dream?

Chapter Twenty-Seven

Detective Bun-Cover & the Tell-Tale Apron

Percy Press-on Verance and Anna Gwendolyn piled into the Roll-On! and rode down the long and meandering side of the boulder, with Percy at the wheel. A paved road stretched before them as they traveled through a shiny city with gleaming, towering skyscrapers and large, picture windows of inviting storefronts. Finally, they reached a long, outdoor, walking mall, with a glass, atrium-like roof. Exiting the Roll-On!, Percy and Anna Gwendolyn walked down the mall as Percy described the sights in each window. Each store window displayed acts of perseverance.

"What do you mean by 'acts of perseverance?'" Anna Gwendolyn asked.

"Before long, you will instinctively know," Percy said. "The people in those windows were protecting their last ounces of dignity. They stayed committed to their goals, no matter how many assaults or obstacles came their way. That's perseverance. You learned from your accidental dive into the Obstacle Pit that if you persevere, obstacles just fall away. You passed that test with class and stamina, Anna Gwendolyn.

"After too many hits to a person's dignity, their dreams disappear. The group, Whistle Blowers Anonymous, prides itself in rehabilitating people who unknowingly have sold their souls, at the cost of their self-respect, character and dignity. You'll learn about that on the next leg of our trip.

"Now, on a less serious note, it's time for you to have an appropriate memento of your accomplishment," he continued. "Come on. I want to take you to 'Wear It & Blare It,' my T-shirt & Blouse-A-Blaze boutique."

Anna saw an increased perkiness in his step. *He must be really proud of this T-Shirt shop*, she thought. "You have a T-shirt shop along with all your recycling business? What do you do? Recycle old T-shirts?"

"Actually, I do recycle old T-shirts, and even silk and satin blouses, too. Once refurbished, they're individually hand painted by artists in the colors of the . . ."

"I know, I know," interrupted Anna, "in the colors of the Rhibbonosphere, just like everything else around here."

"Well, yes." Percy said. "But more than that, each blouse and T-shirt is designed for a 'personal declaration' to be printed on the front by the wearer. There's a steady line of Dream Searchers, like you, who make pit stops here to create one-of-a-kind motivators to inspire them. Come on, Anna Gwendolyn, you're going to love this."

She followed him up the street. A large, multi-colored sign read

Wear It & Blare It

Percy went behind the counter, "What's your favorite color, Anna Gwendolyn?"

"Teal—or any shade of purple, even lavender."

"Let's see. Think I can find some purple shirts over here, under this chest. There! I have a couple.

"Sleeveless, short or long?"

"Oh, sleeveless. It will look better with my Renaissance skirt," Anna Gwendolyn answered. Magically, her skinny jeans suddenly transformed into her billowing skirt! (Anna was so used to these bizarre happenings she didn't even flinch.) The T-shirt matched the skirt perfectly!

"Good. Take this purple shirt and think about what you want to say to the universe. You have often stopped yourself from doing something because of obstacles—the doubters, those people who have faith in nothing. What would you like to tell them? Now that you know you're on the road to perseverance, you can shout your message to the world.

"Slide this cardboard inside the shirt to secure the surface. Use these paint markers to write on the front. Remember your frustrations when people doubted you or made fun of your hopes and dreams? Think back when you wanted to accomplish what others said was impossible. Something like 'I am reaching for the Stars!' or 'Going for the Gold!'"

Oh, that's really original, she thought, attempting to keep her eyes from rolling.

Anna thought for a while. She laid down the shirt, inserted the cardboard Percy had given her, and in big, block letters wrote:

WATCH ME!!!

Then she slipped it over her head, straightened it over her chest and displayed a mile-wide smile.

"Perfect," Percy said, pleased that Anna seemed to be reclaiming some of her spunk. *Yes, she is moving along this journey quite nicely.* "Let's get a quick bite," he urged, hopping into the Roll-On!. "I'll have to be getting back to the Obstacle-Multiplier soon. Lost dreamers will be lining up. But before we eat, I want you to meet a friend of mine."

Anna Gwendolyn was escorted to a sort of unusual storefront. *OK, is this a burger place?* she asked herself. There were lots of buns, but no burgers. She wondered where the burgers were. It was not a burger place, but a bun shop. *Why would someone sell only burger buns?* she wondered. She exited the Roll-On! and got closer to the sign that read:

Sal's Selective Bun-Covers
Satisfy your Cravings. Select a Bun-Cover Today!

"Here we are," Percy said.

"What in the world . . . ?" she asked, as she approached the counter. Her stomach was beginning to growl with hunger. Above the counter:

Welcome to Sal's Selective Bun-Covers!

"Can I get a sandwich here?" Anna Gwendolyn asked.

"Of course—our specialty is the Bodacious Bun-Witch," said Sal, the owner.

"What's that?" Anna Gwendolyn asked.

"Here, take a look at our menu. Take your time. You've probably never had anything quite like our Bun-Covers. You have your choice of fresh and delectable ingredients—greens, dairy, poultry, fish, and meat to name a few. They are baked to perfection inside our trademarked, patent-pending Bodacious Bun Baker. They are deee-licious! I make them myself. What fillings would you like?"

Her mouth was watering. Anna Gwendolyn delighted in the surprise food offerings. She didn't want to embarrass herself by taking her usual fifteen minutes to order. "I'll have the mini roasted shrimp and rémoulade sauce, with sprinkles of endive, zucchini fries and a Pomegranate Fizz."

Many piping hot Bun-Covers, on special plates, were strutted out of that kitchen like a marching band, with every individual plate displaying the artistry of a Picasso painting. Anna chose hers and savored every bite. "Please, I will have one mega Marshmallow-Mountain Milk-Dud Marvel."

"What flavor bun?" the waiter asked.

"Ah Oh, that Chocko-Mocha one looks yummy! Please."

She finished off her outrageous meal with a Loco-Latte.

"Now you'll have to meet the proprietor formally." Percy went over and whispered something to the man behind the counter. The man took off his apron of multi-colored bars and walked to where Ann Gwendolyn sat.

He was an interesting looking man, kind of short and stout, with a lock of red hair on one side of his face, wearing a rather disheveled looking outfit.

"Hello, I am Sal, owner of Sal's Selective Bun-Covers. Good menu choice, by the way. Percy tells me you are pursuing your dreams. I know exactly what you are going through. I've done that journey; it is not for the weak of heart."

"What do you mean?"

"Well, I used to work at a big corporation. I was there during the takeover and subsequent downfall . . . you might even say that I was part of the downfall. Actually . . . I was the reason for the downfall."

"Were you a . . . uh . . . ?" Anna Gwendolyn's voice trailed off in confusion.

"Was I a crook?" Sal asked, with a grin. "No. But I guess I might as well have been; I lost everything. You see I was a whistle blower. I just couldn't stand by and watch intelligent men do what only crooks do, and think it was O.K. I blew the whistle on them, uncovered their lies, and, in doing so, I lost my job. I lost my insurance, retirement, and a fortune in stocks. But, most of all, I lost my peace of mind. I could no longer provide for my family."

"They took everything from you," Anna Gwendolyn asked, "because you exposed them?"

"That's right, everything physical. But I guarded my self-respect and my dignity. Keeping those intact is how I was able to rebuild my life. That's why I had to blow the whistle. I could not stand by and see my co-workers be cheated. You might think everything has been taken from you, but if you don't let them steal your dignity and your soul, you have still won the battle. You can survive and thrive. That's why I have this business."

"You were willing to risk everything?" Anna Gwendolyn asked.

"I saw what was happening and knew it wasn't right. I tried to tell my manager what was going on, but I was ignored. No one wanted to make 'waves.' The top bosses found out what I was doing and wanted me to be quiet, follow the rules. Managers wanted me to cover their buns and do what I was told," Sal said.

"Sounds like school," Anna Gwendolyn interrupted. She was very familiar with being cut off when she had something to say. People just didn't understand how things flew out of her head, if she didn't say them immediately.

"In a way, it was, but I was not learning anything. I became very nervous because I had to make a choice. Was I going to listen to them and do what they said or stand up to them and expose bad things that were happening?" Sal responded. "Was I going to let them cover their buns with lies?"

"Were you afraid?" she asked.

"Sure, I had this horrible feeling in my gut. I was shaken and depressed. Conforming meant I might have to sell my soul. In my wildest dreams, I never thought I would become a whistle blower. I was never that assertive. Wimp was my middle name."

"What made you change?" Anna asked.

"I saw what was happening to my co-workers, and I couldn't stand it any longer. It wasn't just about me. It was about other people's well-being. That gave me the strength I needed to blow the whistle—loud! I may have saved my soul, but my family, income, and financial security took major hits. I hit rock bottom." explained Sal.

"How did you get back on your feet?"

"Well, founding Whistle Blowers Anonymous helped a lot; I decided to take what was hurting me and turn it into something that would help me. I thought surely there are others like me; people who are not willing to sacrifice their souls and principles just because others say they should, just to feel 'safe' no matter the cost. All of us here at Sal's Selective Bun-Covers have gone through an experience that taught us we could have more—be more. All of my employees have traversed the Rhibbonosphere, learned its valuable lessons, and have taken back their lives. They are now in school, training to open their own businesses and continue the survival of their dreams."

Before Anna Gwendolyn could ask Sal another question, he went to the counter to take another customer's order.

"Please excuse me for a moment," Anna Gwendolyn said to Percy. "Could you please direct me to the restroom?"

After fluffing her hair, primping her lips, Anna headed back to the table. She felt so much better after taking a few minutes to attend to her appearance—the rain had taken a real toll. Exiting the restroom, she caught a glimpse of Sal rushing out a rear door, rather sneakily glancing back and forth, as if watching for something. *Now, just what's he up to?* she thought. *One minute he's serving buns, all full of wisdom and positive words, and the next, sneaking about doing something he wants to keep secret. Why did he rip off that apron so quickly and head out the back door?*

She slipped out the back door and watched Sal weave through the mall's parking lot. Curiosity got the better of Anna Gwendolyn and she decided to follow this so-called, fancy, sandwich chef. *I've got to hurry, or Percy will wonder what happened to me,* she said to herself.

Crossing the street, Sal went into a tall, silver and brass office building. She followed discreetly behind him, until he disappeared into an elevator. As the elevator doors closed behind Sal, Anna Gwendolyn found the huge, glass-covered directory and looked for a clue that would explain Mr. Sal's behavior. A listing caught her eye: Detective B. Un-Cover, Defender of Justice. "B. Un-Cover . . . Bun-Cover . . . humm."

Anna Gwendolyn pushed the button for the elevator. She got in and selected "12" on the glowing panel. Stepping off the elevator, she looked to the left and right and saw a plain wooden door at the end of the hallway. The plaque on the door read

Detective B. Un-Cover & Associates

She walked up to the door and tried the knob. It turned in her palm. Sitting behind a plain, oak desk was a woman in a puffy blue chiffon dress and bright pink hair. She was chewing gum and blowing fantastic bubbles that turned from blue, to green, to lavender, to pink. Anna Gwendolyn thought, *Well, would you look at her. It must be close to Halloween.*

"May I help you," she said through the bubble gum, when Anna Gwendolyn walked into the office.

"I'm looking for Sal, the sandwich chef," said Anna Gwendolyn.

The woman answered, "Oh, you mean Detective Bun-Cover."

"Yes, I think so. What does he do? The name on the plaque is spelled B. Un-Cover. Is that the same person?"

"Of course, he's one in the same. Why Detective Bun-Cover is a defender of the people. He will find anyone who is in the business of covering their buns to hide their crimes."

"He fights buns?" Anna Gwendolyn asked, not exactly fully listening.

"Well, sort of. Yes. He investigates and eradicates anyone who is covering their buns!" she said, pointing to the wall. "Those who lie to exploit and demean others soon learn it is no longer fun or profitable to cover their buns."

Anna Gwendolyn read the plaque, framed in gold, on the wall . . .

> Detective Bun-Cover here.
> You cover 'um, we discover 'um.
> Think you can hide,
> The fact that you lied . . .
> No longer such fun,
> You covering your bun.
> Those dreams all undone.
>
> From Bun-Cover you'd better run . . . .
> Before your plot's undone!

"How does he do it?" Anna Gwendolyn asked.

"Simple. Microwaves," she replied, looking at Anna Gwendolyn in amazement. *Didn't this girl know anything?*

"Microwaves? Really? How would a microwave help?" That made no sense. Microwaves were for cooking, not detective work.

"Not the cooking kind," the woman answered, seeing that, as usual, this lost dreamer was thinking in black and white. "You surely noticed those colorful bars on his high-tech apron. The bars are special sensors Sal wears. Any time it senses that bun-covering is imminent, they send out a condiment-color coded signal: red, yellow, green, and white for ketchup, mustard, relish, and mayonnaise. If someone sees these colors light up, they just assume he's spilled something or simply advertising his condiments. But it's an alert to Sal that someone is covering their buns and hurting someone else."

"Isn't he covering his own buns?" Anna Gwendolyn asked. "After all, he's not really a sandwich chef; he's covering up his true identity."

"It is not that unusual to have many talents and do more than one job." The receptionist accented her statement with a huge multi-colored bubble, that popped loudly.

"Well, he does make really good Bun-Witches!" Anna Gwendolyn admitted. She was playing with the funny sandwich name, "Bun-Witches."

Realizing she wasn't going to get any further with this protective secretary, Anna Gwendolyn left the office with a quick "thanks and goodbye." Besides, Percy surely must be wondering what had happened to her.

Percy was still sitting at the food court. "Where've you been?"

"Oh, I'm sorry, Percy, I just got a little carried away exploring the mall. Nothing is ever as it seems."

"No, it isn't," he laughed, realizing Anna Gwendolyn must have discovered the not so-carefully hidden secret of the Bun Shop. "Keep that in mind as you continue your adventure," he cautioned. Then he generously added, "Anna, you've made most of your journey by foot; that's great for mind, body and soul. However, I would love to loan you one of my Roll-On!s for the remainder of your trip."

"What? Thank you, Percy. Does that mean I can have a few driving lessons?" Anna asked, thrilled at the chance to drive the vehicle, not to mention how much easier her travels would be. This would be first time she had driven anything, but she wasn't frightened. Maybe there was something to this fantasy journey; normally she would have wondered if he had lost his mind by loaning a custom vehicle to a thirteen-year-old, but this seemed perfectly normal.

Out in the parking lot, nervous but determined, Anna Gwendolyn aced the lesson and couldn't help but give Percy a big hug. *What an experience,* she thought. *No getting mixed up, no forgetting what he said; I just followed the directions as they were given and, now, I can drive. What a relief!*

"Good job, Anna Gwendolyn, but it's time to go," Percy told her. "Jump into the driver's seat. Off with you!"

"To where?" she asked.

"You'll figure it out." Percy answered as he waved good-bye and disappeared over a hill.

Chapter Twenty-Eight

Viewing with Visuella

Anna Gwendolyn searched her map. The Picture Palace was next. She'd been so distracted by Percy Press-on Verance and Detective Bun-Cover she hadn't thought about this next step. She pulled onto the road in her newly borrowed Roll-On! and headed toward Picture Palace. *I wonder what lesson I'm supposed to learn there,* she thought, *I like photography but why would a Picture Palace be on the list? It'll probably be like all the other crazy stops in this place,* she thought, remembering Luv-Ern's words—"*Nothing is ever as it seems.*"

After twenty-three miles, she pulled the Roll-On! into a roadside rest stop that overlooked a green valley. Shafts of sunlight illuminated a dome-like structure at the center of the valley. Vibrant purple and yellow flowers bordered the winding path leading to what must be the Picture Palace. Anna Gwendolyn took in the view before her; the flowers reminded her of her mother's garden. She was on her mind a lot lately. That had been her favorite flower combination. *I should be arriving soon at the Picture Palace. Looks like thirty minutes by Roll-On!*

She had barely pulled back onto the road when she saw a trailing message written with clouds, apparently from Percy:

Press on.
Depend on yourself.
Take risks.
Take the road less traveled.
Find other modes of transportation.

Anna Gwendolyn smiled, feeling more encouraged about the challenges ahead. "Thank you, Percy," she called out to the clouds. But she wondered about "other modes . . ."

Finally, Anna Gwendolyn arrived at the farthest end of the valley, where she found herself staring straight into a ravine that bordered a what looked like a mile-high retaining wall. "Now what am I going to do?" she questioned. These obstacles had not been visible from the overlook. It was clear that if she wanted to get to Picture Palace, she had to find a way over or around the ravine and wall. Struggling to find an answer, it appeared on the dashboard of the Roll-On!:

Alternative Transportation Modalities
Press button 1, 2 or 3.
Transport options in manual.
Fear and anxiety solutions included.

Anna worried out loud, "OK . . . Gosh, there's an awful lot of stuff in here. Let's see . . . Registration . . . Service Reports . . . Operating Instructions. Oh, there it is: *Alternative Forms of Transportation*. OK, looks like I just have to press this combination of buttons and I'll be able to get to the Picture Palace. As she pressed the three buttons, she heard a slight commotion. Looking up, she saw her new mode of transportation: a seat similar to a ski lift attached to a cable, which meant she would be hoisted into the air. Oh no! Would this contraption be safe? Was this going to be yet another test? But the Picture Palace was standing in all its glory, waiting for her. She had to get there . . . it was the next stop on this outlandish odyssey.

"The ravine is almost the size of the Grand Canyon," she aired to no one, having no idea how really big the Grand Canyon was. "I don't know how, but I have to cross it. I have to face this fear."

Anna Gwendolyn was starting to see that challenges in the Rhibbonosphere had exposed her to the crazy idea that she could do anything. She wasn't a full believer yet, but, still, she seemed to find her way out of whatever was put in front of her. *Maybe I can do this, too*, she thought.

Anna Gwendolyn grabbed onto a cable and carefully got herself into the seat. She held her breath and pulled the cord. In 12.5 minutes, she made it victoriously to the other side of the ravine.

Safely standing on the ground once again, she was still faced with a giant challenge. The wall.

It looked like a huge billboard, but on closer examination, she saw it was pictures from her scrapbook and clippings from various magazine covers and movie posters she'd saved, plastered all over this wall. (She had always dreamed of looking like the models in those magazines, but now the pictures depressed her. *Compared to the magazine versions, no one in real life looks like that,* she reminded herself.)

Directing her attention away from the pictures, she focused on some way to get over the wall. Maybe she could use the tools the Column-men had taught her.

Without even thinking about it, Anna Gwendolyn threw her train over the top of the wall, grabbed the end, and scaled the wall. *There! I did it. That was much easier this time,* Anna thought to herself. At this moment, she was very proud of herself and wished Pappy had been there to see what she'd accomplished.

As Anna was rearranging her skirt and train, a woman who looked like the identical twin of Detective Bun-Cover's secretary, stepped through a *marquee-like door.* Looking up at the blazing marquee, Anna read:

Welcome to the Picture Palace
Your Visualization Station

It was the same woman, complete with pink hair and rainbow bubbles, and she appeared to be manning the ticket booth. Except today, she had fairy wings. *Not at all a surprise.* Anna Gwendolyn approached her.

The woman greeted her as if it were their first meeting, "Welcome to the Picture Palace where, if you can 'visualize' your dreams in your mind, your destiny will be much easier to find!"

Clearly, she didn't remember Anna Gwendolyn. Maybe that was a good thing.

"Wow! Now, I've really heard everything." Catching herself, she stopped just in time to block the sarcastic words that immediately came to mind. *Each thing I've had to do so for, as odd as it has been, has helped me,* she thought. *Seeing my Defining Moments up there on a movie screen certainly helped. So, I'd just better be patient and see what this lady has to offer. You never know around here . . .*

Swishing around in her blue chiffon dress, this woman reminded Anna Gwendolyn of the fairy godmothers she'd seen in picture books when she was a little girl. "I am Visuella, your Visualization Station Specialist. People need to learn how to visualize their dreams. You have come to the right place for just that. Are you ready to view the show?"

"I think so," Anna Gwendolyn responded nervously.

"Good, because you're the star of the show!"

Visuella's excited demeanor invited Anna Gwendolyn to take another chance on her dream quest. She had no idea what was next, but she decided to go for it. *I have to keep my mind, and my eyes, wide open.*

Visuella continued her presentation. "I'm going to teach you the benefits of visualizing your dreams in your own mind. If the mind can visualize it, then the soul can achieve it."

Anna Gwendolyn was the only person in the theatre. She climbed up the aisle and picked a choice, middle seat, just as waitresses on roller skates brought her a sparkling water and popcorn. Then all went dark.

What was wrong? *What's the malfunction? Did Percy know this could happen?* Then, just before Anna Gwendolyn called out, the Picture Palace screen illuminated, but remained blank.

"Would someone please tell me what is going on? Visuella, are we experiencing technical difficulty?" Anna Gwendolyn asked, trying to be polite.

"You might say that there is indeed a technical difficulty, but it's within your brain, not our Picture Palace's equipment. You see, Anna Gwendolyn, you and you alone are the creator of the movie," Visuella said. "The only way this works is for you to project the images. Picture what you want to be, where you want to be and how you can arrive there. Picture your goals and how you're going to achieve them."

"How am I going to know how to achieve my goals?"

"It's not magic; you must be diligent in your efforts. Humans are constantly bombarded with images on billboards, in magazines, over the internet. All kinds of images . . . positive and negative, good and bad . . . it can get confusing. Too many negative images can cause the 'Movie in your Mind,' to short circuit. People have every right to impose those images on you; but you have every right not to let them affect you, too."

Anna Gwendolyn actually was understanding what Visuella was saying.

"That huge wall outside is plastered with magazine pictures that often make you feel bad." Visuella said. "When someone feels they are not good enough to begin with . . . magazine models and social media stars taunt that they're probably right!

"Time for you to try to find your movie again . . . Just follow my cues."

Anna Gwendolyn closed her eyes very fast, a needed retreat from rolling them, and listened to Visuella's instructions. She was learning how to meditate and visualize. She breathed deeply. Minutes passed. More minutes passed. *OK. My mind's eye . . . uh . . . I am supposed to picture my dreams, with my mind's eye. OK. Here goes. OK. I can do this.* She opened her eyes. *I'll start off easy, just visualizing myself dancing on that stage or playing the piano like I did back there, on the Granite Path when I left Delphinium. Then I'll get to the big stuff.* Anna Gwendolyn continued creating pictures of everything she'd always wanted to do. And they were all appearing in living color in Visuella's Picture Palace. She saw herself on her own "big screen" as a famous architect, world class climber and world explorer.

"Wow, I sure do want to do a lot of stuff! Do I have to make a choice, Visuella?"

"You can make a choice, or you can try all of them and see which ones spark a passion," Visuella answered through the speaker. "And more importantly, remember that you've a right to dream whatever and how many dreams you want!"

Anna Gwendolyn hit re-play and watched the cinematic show of her dreams, over and over. As the star of her own movie, she saw herself as an architect, building creative waterfalls in suburban castles; as an adventurer, fording rivers, climbing mountains; and as a performer, she saw herself dancing at Kennedy Center. The visions were breathtaking, but she still was skeptical about them becoming reality. For one thing, there was probably a lot of work involved.

As if reading her mind, she heard Visuella's voice through the speaker, "Huge dreams are often, if not always, accompanied by doubt."

"What did you say the cost of all this dreaming is?" Anna Gwendolyn asked.

Visuella replied, "Oh, just a lot of energy and sacrifice of blood, sweat, and tears and sometimes plain old commitment. You've already proven yourself, since you were catapulted out of the Peacock Plane. I know you'll continue to do well. Now, it's time for your next stop." Visuella continued, "Study the map. It is only about seventeen more miles. You should take the Zavanuu Zip Line. The roads are quite rough. I'll get the Roll-On! there."

Feeling an unexpected sense of confidence, rather than the fear she usually felt when she heard the words zip line, "That would be great. I feel very in control. How long will it take?" she asked confidently. "Oh, by the way . . . I forgot to ask, where is 'there'?"

"You're going to love it. It's the Coliseum of Commitment. By zip line, you'll arrive in twenty-three minutes. The Roll-On! will be waiting." Visuella responded.

"The Coliseum of what? Sounds scary."

"Oh, it can be pretty scary if you're are not prepared, or if you haven't learned the lessons of the Rhibbonosphere! Many a person have run away from commitment, and they can't get their dreams without it. But don't worry though, Anna Gwendolyn, you are skillfully and completely prepared.

"I believe you're ready for anything! Goodbye, dear Anna Gwendolyn. You're on your way!"

Anna Gwendolyn approached the Zavanuu Zip Line and strapped herself in. With a push of her feet and a giant leap of faith, she was suddenly flying back over the strange terrain, forgetting her fear of heights. She was reminded why they were called zip lines, hearing the whirring of the wire zipping above her head.

After landing smoothly and an uneventful short walk, Anna reached her next destination—sure enough, the Coliseum of Commitment. She walked around looking for the proprietor of the place. There were no voice directions from a loudspeaker, there was simply no one around. As soon as she decided it might be closed, she saw the sign written in big, bold letters:

COME IN
Hours: 24/7

24/7, Anna Gwendolyn thought, *Then where are the people?* Looking closer, she saw instructions written in much smaller letters:

Push the bright green button on the huge boulder at the front entrance.

Anna Gwendolyn spotted the boulder and dutifully pushed the bright green button.

"Hello, Anna Gwendolyn, master trailblazer of the Rhibbonosphere!" a voice said, coming out of the boulder. *A boulder is talking to me! Can this place get any weirder?*

"I see you're ready for your final venue," said the boulder. "The other stops were lessons. This is a venue you have earned. There's nothing to learn here. Actually, what you are going to do here is use what you've learned to get on with your dreams."

Oh great, Anna Gwendolyn thought. *I'm going to have to do all that stuff again! And directed by a boulder this time!!!!*

The Boulder continued, "You've arrived at the Coliseum of Commitment. Will you or will you not commit to the dreams that have been dormant in your psyche for a very long time? Here you must commit to your dreams by inscribing them on the hieroglyphics wall."

Concluding this bizarre presentation, "Your willingness to put your dreams in writing is evidence of your intention to follow through on what you started. I speak from experience!"

"What was your dream? Anna Gwendolyn asked.

"If you look to the left of my nose," said the Boulder, "about in the middle of my cheek, you'll see my dream written in stone. It was simple and uncomplicated: to help lost dreamers do the same, 'write their goals and dreams in stone.'

"Now, my dear lost dreamer, it's time for you to commit . . . Just press the green button at the side of the stone door."

Anna Gwendolyn accepted the absurdity of a talking boulder; there was no longer anything in the Rhibbonosphere that could surprise her. She placed her hand on a massive, cold, stone door and pressed the green button. The heavy doors swung away from her, revealing the entrance to the Coliseum. She headed down a long, dark corridor that appeared to lighten with each step she took. As her corridor became brighter, she could see what looked like ancient hieroglyphics on the surrounding stone walls. Looking closer at the writings, she saw it was not hieroglyphics, just roughly cut sentences in stone. She read them, one by one:

I will be what I want to be.
I will be a teacher.
I will be a mother.
I will be a master scuba diver.
I will be Counsel Executive of Boy Scouts of America.
I will change the world.
I will be a ceramic engineer.
I will be president.
I will be an occupational therapist.
I will have a career with Make-A-Wish.
I will build cities.

I will find a cure for cancer.
I will help people dream.
I will, I will, I will . . .

The declarations of dreams went on and on. There were so many. Too many to count or even to read. But what she did figure out, from those she read, was that they were dream declarations chiseled in stone, lasting to the end of time. She continued her walk down the corridor, realizing the significance of these walls. This was the point where dreams had been ignited by countless lost dreamers visiting there before her. The thought that others had traveled this same path gave her chills.

Anna was surrounded by interesting mementos left behind by previous Dream Searchers. Lying near was a fully loaded carpenter's tool belt, bursting at its seams with hammers and chisels—everything a sculptor would need. She wondered why it was there, but not for long.

Anna Gwendolyn gazed at the amazing selection and, driven by her instincts, carefully selected the large, well-worn, teal, blue, silver and gold chisels. She could create wonderful art with these. She had never seen gold and silver chisels but this was the Rhibbonosphere where anything was possible. Time to honor Pappy by leaving his spirit in this place; he was always talking about writing things in stone. Choosing a suitable place on the wall, she began to chisel out his picture. Each chisel left its color in the stone as chips of rock fell to the ground. The result was a kaleidoscope portrait different from anything there. Pleased with the result, she next chiseled a bouquet of over-sized peacock feathers. On each, she chiseled one of her dreams. Using a tool named "Magic Flame Stick," she signed her name to the sculpture, officially committing her dreams to stone. Immediately, a giant, gated, boulder-like door rumbled opened.

"Oh! Look! Flowers! Like Pappy's flowers . . . Oh!"

A walkway, bordered on either side by magnificent hanging gardens of sun-kissed sunflowers, roses, peonies, tulips, iris and daffodils entwined throughout traveling bougainvillea vines lead her to a walkway.

A crimson carpet lay out before her, emblazoned with the message:

VICTORY PATH!!
CONGRATULATIONS!!!!!

Wow! The next step is here and appropriately called The Victory Path, she thought in awe. "I must be close to my destination, wherever that is," wondering out loud where in the world that might be.

Anna Gwendolyn stepped out of the Coliseum onto the Victory Path. She had done it. She had been victorious one more time. A gentle breeze and rays of sunlight soothed her skin. The wind grew stronger and out of nowhere came a tornado-like wind-spurt spinning wildly in front of her. *Oh c'mon. Where is this coming from?* She had gone through enough. *What next?* She was almost ready to crumble when she noticed it was simply reflective scraps of paper from the Delphinium's Collide-A-Scope—her Defining Moments—but only the positive notes, swirling all around her. The twister spun out another long message in the sky:

This way to the Roll-On!

Anna Gwendolyn thought back on her journey, and of all that had tried to block her progress. *I've learned that we all have obstacles that try to keep us from doing what we dream of doing. But I can prevail, if I focus on my dreams instead of on the obstacles. I used to complain people didn't believe in me; now I think the problem was that I didn't believe in myself!*

The Rhibbonosphere had provided Anna Gwendolyn with many mentors who taught her that everyone is born with special talents and skills. It is their job to use them! She was pleased with all that she had accomplished!

- She learned to take risks and leaps of faith.

- She learned that to receive you have to be willing to give.

- She learned the importance of visualizing and committing herself to her dreams.

- She learned that challenges can be overcome and there are more people willing to help you, if allowed, than to deter you.

- Most of all, she learned about the power of believing in yourself.

She said aloud "I'm not as afraid as I once was. I feel different . . . I feel like . . . like I could move mountains and ford streams . . . and build buildings. I'm beginning to believe in myself. Believing in myself is what enabled me to get through all this!"

Anna Gwendolyn now knew she could go anywhere, but despite her amazing experiences in the Rhibbonosphere, the one place she still wanted to go was home.

Chapter Twenty-Nine

A Taste of My Power

Anna Gwendolyn had received the best preparation that the Rhibbonosphere could offer. She felt ready to chart a course for her life . . . and she had the knowledge and tools to do so. Now, she needed to figure out how she was going to make it through the final phase of the Rhibbonosphere to, hopefully, retrieve her lost dreams and find home again.

Continuing to roll on (like Percy had preached), she found the Roll-On! and stepped on the gas. "I've learned what I have to do to re-claim my lost dreams. So, I might as well give it a try."

As she drove, the roller-coaster roadways magically succumbed to the steadfast Granite Path that would ever so faithfully re-appear.

Oh, I wish I wasn't such a bad listener. Mother was right. I miss half of what people say to me. I'll bet I've been told countless times by different Rhibbonosphere characters . . . how to get home. But I wasn't listening. I wonder how much I've missed. I just remember hearing that if I passed all of these "tests" and did all these crazy things . . . that I'd discover the way to my dreams and my home.

She turned a sharp right at Celebration Way. "What in the world? Never seen anything like that!" Out in the distance, a group of men and women, especially older men and women, appeared to be exercising energetically. *They are too old to move like that! Who in the world are they? Where did they come from? Somebody's gonna get hurt. Are those workout clothes?* The group was dressed in multi-colored leggings and tops. As Anna drove closer, she saw that their tops were painted with words. The group was singing energetically and triumphantly waving their fists through the crisp air. *Who in the world are these people? I wonder what they're celebrating—old people don't have anything to celebrate.* A fiery, red-headed woman, on the third row, caught Anna Gwendolyn's eye and waved to her. She walked forward, reached down, plucked a handful of Indian Paintbrush and approached the Roll-On!.

"Hello! My name is Marvelous Marie. Where, may I ask, are you going, my dear? Can we help you with anything?"

With no other options and a bit startled, Anna Gwendolyn answered, "I'm on my way . . . ah . . . I'm on my way home to find my lost dreams." Afraid she might miss something, she then turned off the engine and stepped out of the Roll-On!.

"Home is where we found our lost dreams, right at home at Dreams Preserved Nursing Home Village."

Yes. This confirms I'm right about going home and finding my dreams! Anna Gwendolyn thought. *Looks like that's what they did.* Not fully listening, she missed the reference to the nursing home.

"Ah . . . ah . . . I really have never seen such an energetic . . . oh, I mean . . . ah, I have never . . . ," Anna Gwendolyn stammered.

"Yes, dear. We understand. You have never seen a group of old people, dressed to the Nines, exercising, and having the time of their life! Right?"

"Well, yes, I guess that's what I mean," she said, turning red with embarrassment.

Marvelous Marie prattled on . . . "Our exploration through the Rhibbonosphere, to re-claim our lost dreams, directed us to Dreams Preserved Nursing Home Village. Of course, first we had to prove ourselves, with all those often silly but treacherous feats! And yes, dear, we too made our own parachutes! Just like you! Some of us jumped tandem, others solo. Luv-Ern is something else, isn't she??

"These joyfully colored, spandex exercise tops and leggings are painted with our personal empowerment statement. These statements acted as our voices, while we were practicing to use our own. Watching re-runs of Erin Brockovich did the rest!" she added, with a wink.

"And the songs that you hear empower and motivate us to be active and move . . .

"Oh, wait a minute!!!" she interrupted herself. "Oh, my goodness! Wait until I tell everyone! I knew you looked familiar! You're the one! You're Anna Gwendolyn, volunteer extraordinaire! As Marvelous Marie, I know I speak for all of my friends. We are so honored and thrilled to officially meet you! You're the reason we have these beautiful workout cloths."

Another character who knows my name, Anna Gwendolyn thought. *So weird. They think they know me.*

"We thank you, Miss; your volunteer work at Dreams Preserved changed our lives forever! Don't you remember? Don't we look great? Because of you, we can work out at any gym in the Rhibbonosphere, looking fashionable and sharp! Athletic spandex! Not just for young people!

"And . . . our Master Gardening classes are awesome! We share our abundant garden's harvest with anyone in need. It makes us so proud to actively participate in our community."

Anna Gwendolyn listened carefully. She had no idea her little projects had made such an impact. Her chest expanded with pride.

"Ms. Anna Gwendolyn, you have given our resident seamstresses purpose—a feeling of productivity. As I mentioned earlier, everyone feels so sassy in their new work-out apparel. Makes you want to move! Our personal mantras on the shirts tell our story. Our self-confidence and self-esteem rocket to heights unknown in the Rhibbonosphere!

"And our carpenters love making the painting easels! It's so much more fun, to paint on a real easel. Everyone is motivated to pick up a brush! And no one can resist the official painting smocks the Stubborn Stitchers made for us. Plus, you have never witnessed a bigger smile then when a proud grandpa gives a newly hand-carved race car to a grandchild. It's magic!

"Your gift of time, energy and perseverance continues beyond the walls of the Dreams Preserved. The Crystal Ballroom studio instructors caught the excitement and teach bi-weekly lessons at Dreams Preserved! The county's mobile dentist now makes regular visits. See my teeth? And thanks to Hats Off/Nails On Mani-Pedi, our Mondays are in full swing! Their cosmetology internships come to Dreams Preserved every Monday to practice on us." She held up her manicured hands. "Ready for the red carpet!"

Marvelous Marie just couldn't stop raving, "Being proud of ourselves is unbelievably motivating to quality of life. We have a sparkle in our step, a feeling of usefulness and productivity, and our minds are buzzing with activity.

"So, Anna Gwendolyn, we have placed a bronzed newspaper article in our entry way describing the vast improvements at Dreams Preserved with our attractive exercise cloths, art supplies, and gardening program. The improvements help residents engage, socialize and enjoy their lives more than ever. The article ends with a personal thank you to you, Anna Gwendolyn Shaw.

"Now, here is a little token of our gratitude." One by one, the men and women stepped forward and handed her a spray of Indian Paintbrush.

"Oh, thank you. I really don't know what to say." (But her eyes said it all.) Anna Gwendolyn cradled the growing bouquet of wildflowers and was overwhelmed with emotion, witnessing how her volunteering efforts had given so much happiness to so many.

"We will never forget the generosity in your gift of time and energy. Your selfless acts of kindness have changed our lives forever," Marvelous Marie said.

Nervous and fumbling as to how to say good-bye, Anna began, "So glad to meet all of you. Thank you! I think . . . I think that you all have taught me and given me more than I have given you." Waving goodbye to the group, Anna Gwendolyn, tearful and overwhelmed, began to realize the good that she had done.

I really did this . . . me!!! Wait until Pappy hears about this. Hey . . .seniors enjoying life, just like Pappy and his Alligator Bayou fishing excursions . . . I gave a group of seniors—in fact an entire community apparently—a chance for much of the very same thing. A second chance to experience joy, to feel important, to be productive and to re-claim, along with their dreams, their self-worth, their dignity and maybe even their destinies. Did I do all that? Yes, little old Anna Gwendolyn did all that!

As she thought back on her odyssey, there had been an entertaining parade of other-worldly characters, with unbelievable demands and requests. "I'm certain I haven't met all the Rhibbonosphere characters yet," she said aloud. Flowers clutched, she headed back to the Roll-On!. With a sigh, she hopped in and started to turn the key, but stopped suddenly. Without warning, a wave of fatigue swept over her. The realization of the good she had done had exhausted her.

"A nap would be perfect about now . . ."

Chapter Thirty

Rhibbonites Show Their Stuff

A voice boomed in her dream through the Roll-On's speakers, blaring "FAME, FORTUNE, POWER, BEYOND YOUR WILDEST DREAMS. CHANGE YOUR LIFE; DISCOVER YOUR DESTINY, IN THREE EASY STEPS."

Still asleep, a strange sensation enveloped Anna Gwendolyn. Dreaming, she felt the Roll-On! being pulled off course. The voice beckoned her—"POWER, FAME, FORTUNE, PERFECT LOOKS AND ANYTHING YOUR HEART DESIRES. THESE CAN ALL BE YOURS. JUST CALL WITH YOUR CREDIT CARD NUMBER." But this time, the temptation of this Dream-O-Tron didn't interest her. It's as if she'd forgotten about it. The lessons of the Rhibbonosphere were taking hold. She pulled herself back on course. Pappy had been right all along.

Anna, still slumped and dreaming in the Roll-On!, victoriously changed the station. The Top 100 extravaganza was interrupted by a special news bulletin: "This just in. A whistle blower has just accused the Dream-O-Tron company of making false promises. According to Detective Bun-Cover, the company has been selling false dreams and has been willing to take in a sucker at every opportunity. The company has been taking advantage of people's self-doubts and despair for decades. Detective Bun-Cover has proven that all the promises of fame, fortune, and power came at a heavy cost—not just money but a person's self-worth."

"How stupid do those Dream-O-Tron people think I am?" Anna Gwendolyn said to the radio. But she hadn't always been so self-confident. Right when her dreams and self-confidence were at stake, she was dropped into the Rhibbonosphere. The people she met there, including Detective Bun-Cover, had helped her save herself. Anna Gwendolyn changed the station again. The music was interrupted by another special news bulletin: "This just in. A whistle blower has just accused the Dream-O-Tron company of a home theft. According to Detective B. Un-Cover, the manufacturers of the Dream-O-Tron dream machine weren't even waiting for people to call in their credit cards; they were hacking into personal computers and stealing people's livelihoods."

Snoozing away and dreaming she was still driving, Anna Gwendolyn pulled to the side of the road, put the car in park and answered a call.

"Anna Gwendolyn, this is Sal."

"Detective Bun-Cover?"

"Yes," he answered, sounding urgent.

"They're talking about you on the radio."

"I know. Listen, Anna Gwendolyn, you need to get to your grandfather as quickly as possible. The Dream-O-Tron Corporation has stolen all of his private information. They are no longer just selling dreams; they are stealing them. You have to save him."

Anna Gwendolyn knew that all the progress she had made in the Rhibbonosphere could be derailed, with the stealing of Pappy's dreams.

"You get home to your Pappy and I'll call the others from the Rhibbonosphere to come help."

"If I drive too fast, I'll get pulled over for speeding. Besides, I don't know where I'm going or how to get home."

"Leave your car and take your 'train'—your scarf!" he instructed her. "You can fly on your own fuel now. You've worked so hard for it. Just use the power you've gained on your journey. It will take you to Pappy. Go now. Luv-Ern, Visuella and the others will be on their way aboard Peacock Airways."

Anna Gwendolyn jumped out of the Roll-On! and shook out her train. It had transported her before in the Rhibbonosphere. Why not now? Using the same commands that Luv-Ern had used, Anna Gwendolyn was airborne. Soon, she was hovering above her home, witnessing the spectacle of her friends, the Rhibbonites, parachuting out of Luv-Urn's plane.

As they pulled their ripcords, Anna Gwendolyn saw that each parachute was an exact replica of the Dream-Chute she had created for her own descent.

With Detective Bun-Cover, Anna Gwendolyn ran into the house. Pappy was asleep on the sofa; faithful Briggs slept at his feet. A rhythmic pulse coming from the television seemed to have hypnotized both of them. They heard a strange sound coming from her bedroom. Pressing his finger to his lip, he tip-toed up the stairs. Anna Gwendolyn followed. The man from the info-mercial was sitting in front of her computer!

"Hey!" Anna Gwendolyn shouted loudly (almost waking herself from her dream!). Detective Bun-Cover blew his whistle.

The others from the Rhibbonosphere hurried up the stairs, surrounding the dream thief. There was a suitcase laying on the floor, wide open and filled to the brim with Pappy's memories. The getaway car at the curb was already full of Pappy's stolen money, personal information, and retirement account numbers. All his vital information was there; enough to destroy Pappy and his dreams for the future.

The Rhibbonites bombarded the car and retrieved all Pappy's goods. Bun-Cover caught the thief red-handed and refused to let him cover his buns. But, before Anna could stop him, the thief grabbed a mattress and jumped out a window. He landed in an early blooming holly bush. "OUCH!" Off he ran!

Anna Gwendolyn looked around. *Oh, my goodness! Everything, every single thing these characters, these Rhibbonites, have told me is true! They really do rescue dreams! All of this time I've been running around in this place thinking I'm all alone and wondering why everything is so hard, and they've really been working to save my dreams.*

Deep in her dream she spoke out loud again, "Okay, gang, it's time to celebrate. Come on with me. I want you all to see our backyard—Bling Swing and Pappy's hammock. They were both little dreams of Pappy's and mine once upon a time."

"Anna Gwendolyn! . . . Anna Gwendolyn!! . . . wake up, time to wake up!" It was Percy, not knowing he was shaking her out of a horrible nightmare. "We heard the news! You made it to the Victory Path! We're all going with you to the Island of Lost Dreams. It's finally here—your trip to Dream Garden Beach, your ultimate destination! Sit here on these pallets and wait for

Luv-Ern and the Peacock Plane. That will give us time to tell you our stories and about the magic of your next journey," Percy said.

"What stories?" she questioned, still a little groggy.

"It's time to tell you how we ended up in the Rhibbono-sphere. We were all just like you. We were ordinary people with sometimes extraordinary dreams," Percy said. "We were focused on our dreams of helping people rediscover their dignity, self-esteem and self-confidence. It was harder to do then we thought. People made fun of our goals and dreams and rolled their eyes at us. No one believed in us. Obstacles surrounded us. Before we knew it, we'd given up on our dreams."

Detective Bun-Cover agreed. "Oh, just like me, Percy . . . just like me."

Anna Gwendolyn could almost feel the serious demeanor of the group. She knew they'd all experienced something phenomenal, life-changing; something most people would have trouble even believing.

"Somehow, probably with the help of some Rhibbono-sphere-type nudging and our belief in ourselves, a little bit of magic happened," Nevah-Tu-Latte said quietly. "All of us you see here . . . somehow magically crossed paths with each other and formed our group.

"Just like you, Anna Gwendolyn, all of our unrealized dreams—dreams of Luv-Ern, Della, myself, Percy, Bun-Cover, Visuella, and even the Column-Men—had flowed into the vast ocean. Our dreams dashed against boulders and rocks until they washed far out to sea, thought to be never heard of or seen again," Nevah-Tu-Latte related.

"After years of painstaking research, we found they'd been washing ashore on the Island of Lost Dreams at an alarming pace," Percy noted. "We learned what happened there."

"As the dreams arrived, Dream Combers (the workforce for the entire Island of Lost Dreams, by the way), collected our dreams, cleaned and catalogued them, placed them in giant conch shells and then crated them until they could be transported by Seaphairies and Clipper Ships to Dream Garden Beach." Nevah-Tu-Latte loved telling this story.

"What are Seaphairies?" Anna Gwendolyn asked with skepticism. She was committed to the story, but she had never heard of such a creature. *Are they teasing me?* she wondered.

"They are winged creatures that carry the crated lost dreams to and from the safety of the ships," explained Nevah-Tu-Latte.

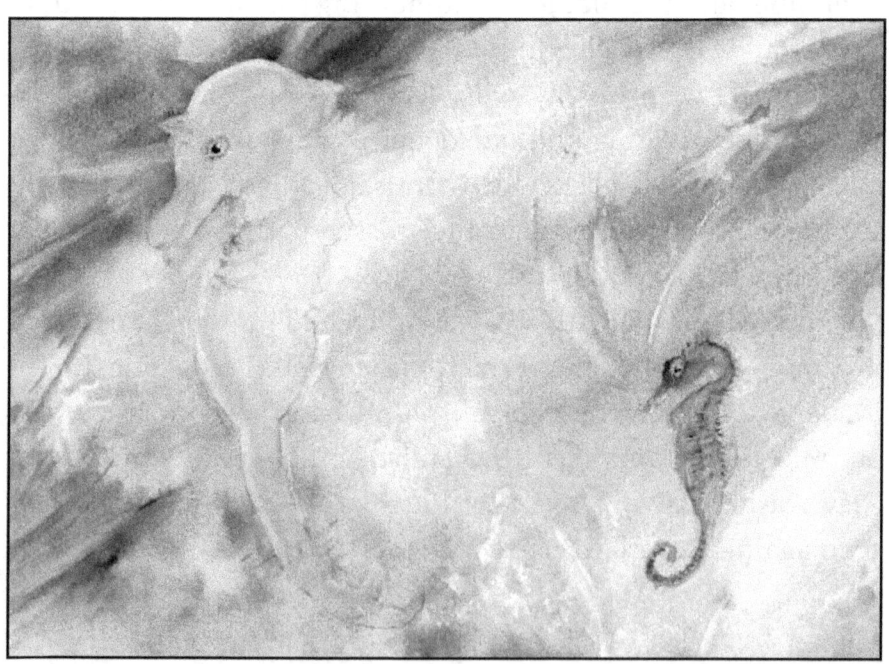

"But where do they come from?" Anna Gwendolyn asked.

"They were formerly seahorses. One day, many years ago, a lone seahorse named Sam dreamed of being a fairy. She thought, 'Well, I have these wings, but all I do is swim . . . I want to fly.' And the rest is history. Of course, Sam is now the founder of the Seaphairies Brigade, who live solely for the purpose of helping rescue lost dreams around The Island of Lost Dreams and delivering them to Dream Garden Beach," Nevah-Tu-Latte continued.

"Anyway, back to my story, at Dream Garden Beach our dreams were uncrated and nourished in giant, tree trunks in Tree Trunk Trove, until we finally earned our right to reclaim them."

"The security there is better than that at airports," asserted Percy.

"So much potential would be lost forever without this place. When a dream arrives at Dream Garden Beach it has traveled thousands of miles—just like your own dreams. When Dream Searchers, like you, conquer the Rhibbonosphere and find their lost dreams, the Garden comes alive with a huge celebration much like the Fourth of July!" said Percy, eyes reflecting his excitement.

"Whose lost dreams end up there?" Anna Gwendolyn asked.

"The rich, the poor, the healthy, the unhealthy, the very young and the very old. Everyone has dreams, often threatened by doubt, indecision, bullying and a host of other obstacles," Nevah-Tu-Latte answered.

"Unbelievable, but this is all beginning to make sense! It's what Pappy was always talking about. And I've learned probably everything I need to find my lost dreams, right? It seems frightening, but exciting at the same time. Are my dreams in this place called Dream Garden Beach? Do I really get to go there???" Anna could barely breath.

"Anna Gwendolyn, you've met the challenges of the Rhibbonosphere," Percy confirmed. "You've learned to give of yourself, to persevere, to visualize, and to trust that, no matter what, it's never too late. You've learned to teach those lessons to others. You've succeeded in a major part of your journey to find your dreams."

As Anna Gwendolyn took in his words, applause broke out. No, it was more like a standing ovation. Anna Gwendolyn was receiving accolades from her friends for her efforts and accomplishments. It took her by surprise.

"There is just one catch," said Luv-Ern, having joined the group. "You have to take a couple more short jaunts, on your way to Dream Garden Beach."

"Oh, no. Please, how many more 'jaunts' are there? And where will I be going? Maybe I wasn't listening?" Anna Gwendolyn asked, a little frustration oozing into her voice.

"To the Island of Lost Dreams," said Visuella.

"But this time you don't have to go alone," comforted Nevah-Tu-Latte. "We're all going with you," she added. " Luv-Ern will fly us."

Chapter Thirty-One

Touch Down: The Island of Lost Dreams

All aboard!

Captain Luv-Ern flew the plane expertly to the Island of Lost Dreams. The sky blended into the water, then into land.

"Look, everybody! There it is! There's the sign!" broadcasted Luv-Ern happily.

Island of Lost Dreams

A security detail was ahead, waving and welcoming the group. Another sign out the aircraft window said:

Welcome to the Island of Lost Dreams
Where lost dreamers ready themselves for rediscovery

Anna Gwendolyn and the Rhibbonites descended the steps of the Peacock Plane full of anticipation.

"Take a look at the waves marching into the beach," Luv-Ern pointed out. "Think of it . . . They're full of lost dreams."

After a brisk exploration at the ocean's edge, the Rhibbonites and Anna Gwendolyn situated themselves on blankets in the sand. Promised to everyone was a seashore dinner, sprinkled with music by the Crashing Waverly Brothers. The Dream Combers, taking a break from rescuing dreams and doubling as waiters, chefs, and cooks, made up the entire service staff. They treated the weary group to a beach-side feast of Stopped in Their Tracks Crabs, Ogling Oysters, Swashbuckler Sword Fish, and Succulent Seaweed Salad.

The stories of dream rescues peppered the conversation. The spectacle of waves crashing on the shore provided a mesmerizing backdrop.

While everyone was finishing a desert of Sea Sprayed Sherbet and Conch-Shell Coffee, a ritual going on a few yards down the beach caught Anna Gwendolyn's attention. She felt drawn by something appearing on the tops of sparkling sand dunes. Surveying her friends, confident that they were all busy talking and wouldn't miss her, she hurried over to get a closer look.

She could see giant boulders strewn with huge, tree-size branches of driftwood along the way. Something was out there.

Then, she saw it . . . a glassy, mesmerizing garden, mere feet before the shore line. Little flowers, purple and yellow thistle, though short in stature, stood proudly in sand, just far enough from the edge of the rolling tide to be safe. *This is just like my Pappy's backyard garden. Mama taught me how to grow thistles in the sand. And there, in front of me, is that garden. Are my Pappy or Mama around somewhere? Are they listening in on my strange adventure? After all, it's looking like Pappy's dream doctor lessons might be right on target.* Anna Gwendolyn's intuition was dependable, and it was talking to her. She sat down on a flat-topped boulder to think about what she was seeing.

Three pastel and shocking pink butterflies, as if called to attention, landed on Anna Gwendolyn's arm, coming very close to her face. Then, as if on cue, they resumed their flight. She followed their flittering wings with her eyes as they disappeared into the blue skies. "Butterflies?" she questioned aloud. "My mama's favorite? That's strange. Why not a seagull? What's going on here?"

Now something was on the boulder tabletop that had not been there before.

It was a petite bouquet of purple and yellow thistle flowers, tied with a long, green palm stem.

"Where did that come from?" Anna Gwendolyn asked the sea breeze suspiciously, with a quiet gasp. And in that moment, she banished any doubts she might have had about the purpose of the Island of Lost Dreams.

Ever Lost A Dream?

Chapter Thirty-Two

Top Secret Spectacle

Anna Gwendolyn knew she'd better get back to the group before she was missed. She would keep this special place to herself.

The evening entertainment, The Crashing Waverly Brothers, had started performing. As she saw the group dancing around in the sand, she thought, *I can just dance myself back into the fun without anyone noticing*—a typical Anna Gwendolyn antic. The music, dancing and laughter acted as the perfect camouflage. Anna Gwendolyn took a dancer's leap, hoping to land gracefully within the merrymakers. She had performed that leap many times, but not within the atmosphere of the Rhibbonosphere. Her efforts for a "graceful" leap landed her spread eagled, in the middle of the dance floor. But as luck would have it, the partiers were impressed as they saw Anna Gwendolyn shoot back up from the ground without missing a beat; *Not a graceful landing, but a very graceful recovery*, she thought, laughing at herself. (Any other time, she would have been mortified. Her new-found confidence was paying off.)

It was dusk. Some were still dancing, others finished up their dinner and were watching the waves running from the lavender sunset. The Crashing Waverlys played their guitars, singing a song that seemed very familiar . . .

> *Dream tonight, by starlight,*
> *Or while the sun is shining bright,*
> *Catch a ride upon Dream Spinner,*
> *Time to catch your dream in flight.*
>
> *One hundred years of witness,*
> *The life-long legend can't be wrong.*
> *Listen, you'll hear the melody*
> *Of the lost dreamers' anthem song.*
>
> *Fall asleep upon the Spinner,*
> *Your dream, the grandest show!*
> *That dream your heart's been guarding?*
> *The Dream Spinner might just know!*
>
> *The Spinner's on a mission,*
> *Slumber's magic, dreams come true.*
> *Pick a swing to take you dreaming,*
> *Swirling light whispering a clue.*
>
> *The legend's age-old question—*
> *Ever lost a dream or two?*
> *Where did they disappear to?*
> *Would you like to take a view?*
>
> *A brave view of possibility,*
> *Visions glowing 'til they gleam,*

Whirling winds of passions calling,
Your dream now waiting to redeem.

Find your dreams! Find your dreams! Find your dreams!

That's the song the Dream Spinner plays! How, how in the world did this happen? Anna didn't have time to ponder the question.

She was looking forward to whatever this great adventure had to offer, but the thought of the special garden she had discovered was still top of mind. "Nevah, can we talk for a minute?" she said, singling her out of the group.

"Why, sure, Anna Gwendolyn."

"I was reminded of my Mama earlier this evening. I saw purple and yellow flowers growing out of the sand. It reminded me of how, as little girl, I planted seeds in the sand at her urging. Everyone told me nothing would come from our attempts; but to everyone's amazement, an enchanting garden thrived on our shore. Mama and I had such fun with our garden that year. Do you think anyone would mind if I plant a garden in the sand here? It would be just for Mama," she whispered.

"Of course not. You can call it your very own Dream Garden," Nevah said, smiling sweetly at Anna. *This thirteen-year-old girl has a lot of heart,* she thought. *I hope she grows to see that in herself.*

"But let's go now, Anna Gwendolyn. It's time to line up for a tour of Lost Dreams Observation Bunker."

"Good evening, everyone," the Dream Comber bellowed as Nevah and Anna joined the others. "We'll be leaving for the Lost Dreams Observation Bunker in ten minutes." The Dream

Comber motioned for Anna to move to the head of the line, as she was the honored guest.

"Miss Anna Gwendolyn, your success in the Rhibbonosphere has earned you the right to tour the Lost Dreams Observation Bunker before your trek to Dream Garden Beach. It will give you incredible knowledge that, until now, you couldn't have comprehended.

"Everyone ready?" he continued. The group replied in unison, "YES!" Anna Gwendolyn felt a little half-hearted about her answer, concerned a little about going underground, below sea level, to a bunker. She hoped this was not going to present her with another challenging learning experience. She'd had enough for a lifetime!

Led by the Dream Combers, the group walked a little over a mile before coming to a densely wooded area on the side of a hill. The Dream Combers used their golden rakes to clear an area marked *KEEP OUT*. Swish, swish went the rakes, until a rusty, dented, steel door was exposed, almost laying on the side of the hill; the slanted door reminded Anna of the entrance to an old, tornado cellar.

The three Column-Men, as if on cue, crouched down and pulled open the massive door, illuminating a narrow, crystalline tunnel. The Column-Men, twisting and folding into ribbon-candy bends so the tunnel would accommodate their stature, entered the tunnel and held the door open. With Anna Gwendolyn in the lead, the Rhibbonites followed down the darkened shaft. The group traveled what seemed like several hundred yards to a green door that read OBSERVATION BUNKER. It was flanked by two security guards.

The head Dream Comber began, "We are now in the Observatory, the top-secret viewing room where the arrival, retrieval and protection of the world's lost dreams can be witnessed.

"It is your privilege to be privy to the nighttime procession of the Clipper Ships spectacle, which only happens every full moon. It's one of our favorite parts of dream rescuing," beamed the Dream Comber.

The awe-struck Anna was speechless. What in the world was she about to see?

"Captain Luv-Ern, please pull the Golden Cords and open the curtain to the Observation Windows," suggested the leader.

"With pleasure, sir." Luv-Ern pulled the very long, velvet cords and the massive viewing windows were exposed. A brilliant, state-of-the art flat screen periscope allowed the observers to see anything and everything happening above sea level. Their eyes adjusted, and they saw the full moon had kept its promise: One by one, by the light of the moon, they could make out the three Clipper Ships anchored in the harbor, awaiting their cargo, the lost dreams.

"What are those Dream Combers all over the beach doing with those rakes?" Anna Gwendolyn couldn't contain her curiosity.

"They're gathering lost dreams, and freeing the ones that get stuck in the reefs. As bullying and negativity increase on earth, the number of lost and broken dreams increases, too, all making landfall right here."

The Dream Combers were tall, lean people with very muscly legs and arms, and feet like swim fins. They practically lived in the ocean coaxing lost dreams ashore. To exercise, and develop team-building, too, the Dream Combers played underwater hockey in their off time. Holding their breath for long periods, two teams, the Wonder Waves and the Dream Divers, steered glowing, heavy lead pucks stamped "Island of Lost Dreams" along the ocean floor. Using fourteen-inch, white or black "hockey" sticks, they wrestled with each other over control of the puck as they scraped and steered it toward their perspective goals. The game kept them in shape for capturing lost dreams and raking them ashore.

"You're watching my fellow Dream Combers gather lost dreams, a job we have day in and day out. Look to the left: We're cleaning and sorting the dreams over there. Look to the right: At that station we place each retrieved, tattered and torn dream in a beautiful conch shell. Look down by the beach now . . . See? There we're crating the conch shells, not only to protect the fragile dreams but to ease shipment. (Understand, they have to get to all the way to Dream Garden Beach on the other side of the island on those Clipper Ships, and the sea can be rough.) We store those precious crates—holding thousands of lost dreams—and wait.

"On every full moon, like the one tonight you're lucky enough to witness, official dream transporters called Seaphairies carry each and every crate, stored since the last full moon, onto the waiting ships. That spectacle is what you're about to witness."

On his cue, the Seaphairies started their parade, passing the heavy crates hand over hand, all the way out to the ships. Some Seaphairies were on land, some in the water, and certain very strong ones were the designated flyers who flew the crates up to the ship's deck.

Because the Seaphairies only work at night, they glow with the colors of the ocean. The effect created what seemed like a tidal wave of shimmering, liquid color swells rolling back and forth between the ships and shore.

"Once the cargo has been loaded, the majestic Clipper Ships weigh anchor and sail off to Dream Garden Beach. Those ships can have a rough ride, too, because of the currents and the tides. That's why we crate the dreams so carefully. Luckily for us and every Dream Searcher out there, the ships always make it to Dream Garden Beach, because forces of good will always win over the forces of evil."

"Truly amazing," Anna Gwendolyn said, now fully engaged. "I never knew anything about these things happening to a dream. I guess my lost dreams traveled here and got all this special treatment. I wonder if they've travelled to Dream Garden Beach yet or if they're tucked into one of these crates right now!" she pointed.

"Well now, Miss Rhibbonosphere traveler, speaking of traveling, it's time to go again," Percy interrupted the faraway look he saw in Anna Gwendolyn's eyes.

"On the Peacock Plane?" Anna Gwendolyn asked, enthusiastically.

"No dear, we will be walking," Percy said.

Ever Lost A Dream?

Chapter Thirty-Three

A Very Fake Smile

"Walking? That means hiking! You are kidding me, right? And why don't those Clipper Ships have dinner cruises?" Anna challenged Percy.

Then, with a change of heart, "OK, OK. Where do I go? When do we start?"

"It's a rather short hike that ends at a train station, Destiny Depot."

"Train station . . ." Things were looking up in Anna's Gwendolyn eyes. "You said 'train station'? That makes me think of my Pappy."

"Oh, one thing," Nevah-Tu-Latte added. "You must take the lead in the group. There is a security reason. The Obstacles may be targeting your presence. They'll expect you'll be in the middle of the group, and certainly not be the leader. You'll have the element of surprise if you're in the lead."

Anna looked at each face staring at her. *Can I really do this?* She knew everyone was waiting on her to make the first move. *Well, I sure hope they're right; everyone seems to think*

I have what it takes, so I guess I better start believing it, too. And I certainly don't want to be a target of the Obstacles. I had enough of them at the Obstacle Pit. She didn't really know what was ahead, but *I'll just have to figure it out*, she thought.

"OK," she addressed the group, "there are a few things we need to consider first: Does everyone have proper traveling attire? Comfortable, strong shoes? Drinking water? Potty break now or forever hold it!" She took a head count: "Percy Press-on Verance, Nevah-Tu-Latte, Detective Bun-Cover, Captain Luv-Ern, Della from Delphinium, Visuella and all three Column-Men! OK. That's nine. Housekeeping complete."

Anna Gwendolyn was officially exasperated by now, though she tried not to show it. This legendary Dream Garden Beach, the place she had worked so hard and sacrificed so much to get to, was still miles away. She wasn't crazy about the idea of leading the group, but she was ready to do just about anything to get there.

"Is everyone ready? We should make Destiny Depot in a little more than an hour." She took a big breath and stepped out onto the trail as everyone filed in behind her. They were on their way.

Here the Granite Path, mostly uphill, was winding and littered with tree branches and slippery, moss-covered rocks. No one had told her it would be so rugged. She questioned just how much real hiking her companions had done. Oh, yeah, they could dart about here and there and show up at the most convenient and inconvenient times, but this was steady trudging and she wasn't sure it was in their skillset. Taking her leadership role to heart, she decided to check on them. Stopping, she faced her charges. "Ok, how is everybody doing?

Let's take another head count . . ."OK, we're good." But to herself: *But I'm scared out of my mind . . . I've been intimidated by those Obstacles . . . how am I ever going to do this?*

The group began trudging up and over the wooded trail, following Anna's lead. She was busy trying to figure out how to lead with confidence, Anna Gwendolyn style. She reviewed in her mind the many lessons she'd learned to get her this close, evidently, to her lost dreams. Someone had told her that when it came to confidence, she could fake it with a smile 'til she made it'—until she truly felt confident.

So, flashing her biggest and very fake smile, she led the group forward.

Ever Lost A Dream?

Chapter Thirty-Four

It's Up To Me

As the group moved cautiously along the wooded path, the brush became thicker. The travelers kept quiet, but they knew exactly what to watch for. They knew that each bush or piece of brush along the way could be laden with Obstacles. It had been only days since that last infiltration. They needed to stay keenly aware of their surroundings to avoid even a hint of any negative forces.

They were there to guide and support her, but Anna needed to mobilize her new-found courage and deal with the Obstacles by herself. The Obstacles could be very sneaky; they had an ability to surprise their prey, giving absolutely no warning.

Anna decided to concentrate on the view. "It's so peaceful out here! You can hear the birds singing. This is paradise. I know I'm supposed to be cautious and careful . . . but I think everything is going to be all right! I don't think anything could interfere with this atmosphere. It's absolutely hypnotic!"

"Well, yes, Anna Gwendolyn, that is true, but please . . . please beware of what you can't see," warned Percy. "Remember your time in the Obstacle Pit and how you thought you would never get out? Be careful not to slip back into that Pit; it's an easy slide."

"And remember, bravery, and even pretend confidence, have the power to chase away negative forces. They can save not only your dreams, they can save you," added Detective Bun-Cover. "Don't forget to keep them in your head and heart."

"Hello, Anna Gwendolyn! Hello there! Anna . . . Gwen-do-Lynn!!!"

"Is that you, Percy? Nevah? Which one of you is calling out to me? Bun-Cover?"

"No, I'm not calling you, Anna, and I don't think Nevah is either . . . wait . . . wait . . . Listen . . . There . . . Listen . . . is anyone calling out?"

Suddenly, Obstacles surrounded their targets. Even the unshakable Column-Men were surprised to see them. There wasn't an inch of the road ahead free of these menaces. What was happening? At their slightest movement, the travelers were bombarded by booming insults and blaming chants aimed directly at Anna Gwendolyn.

It was now time to use all she had learned on her journey through the Rhibbonosphere. Anna Gwendolyn bolstered herself and forged her way forward. Detective Bun-Cover had warned her; she would have to fend off these assaults alone or face the certainty of capture by the Obstacles.

Just as she thought she might escape, a loud commotion in the bushes and a familiar giant Grandfather Clock jumped out. Glaring down at Anna Gwendolyn, he shouted, "It's TIME for you to ditch that confidence! TIME to CLOCK OUT! You are out of TIME!!! No more silly dreams for you . . . they have all expired!" Greedy outstretched hour and minute hands waved high into the air and searched for Anna Gwendolyn to destroy her dreams.

The Clock looked exactly like the one from the Obstacle Pit, except with a much angrier face. Barely recovering from the first attack, Anna Gwendolyn was bombarded again. "You are too fat!" she heard. From another bush, out popped a twenty-foot hurricane of insults. "You are too skinny! Your nose is too big! You are too poor! You will never be smart enough! Dummy, dummy, dummy!" the insults continued. The hurricane's whirlwinds expelled a barrage of insults, criticisms, and bullying. An air of negativity spread from all directions—its target, Anna Gwendolyn. She felt powerless to escape its grasp.

All of the Rhibbonites were at risk of capture, too; these negative forces would do anything in their power to succeed. Anna Gwendolyn had to do something quick, or all progress could be lost.

"Oh! Oh! What am I going to do? How will I . . . ? I have to get out of here. Help! Help me, please!" Anna Gwendolyn began panicking. "I don't know what . . . !"

Percy asked calmly, "You don't know? Don't know what you're going to do?? Think! Remember the lesson you learned from all of us. You must be strong; don't give up. Stand up to these forces! Make them more afraid of you than you are of them. If you don't feel it, fake it!" Percy continued his efforts to get Anna Gwendolyn to reach inside herself for the resources he'd seen in her. "Don't let yourself be defeated before you give yourself a fighting chance!"

"I've worked so long and so hard; I've faced dangerous and crazy challenges to reach my dreams; and now . . . now I have to fend off all this negativity and I don't really know how to do it," her whining voice back in full force.

"Yes . . . yes, you . . ."

Suddenly, cut off by ear piercing, screaming insults, Percy jumped ahead of the others to advise Anna Gwendolyn. Looking her straight in her eyes, "Think, Anna Gwendolyn. Think! You do know how to save yourself! Think of your fall into the Obstacle Pit. What did you do? You saved yourself with just the power of your mind!"

Anna Gwendolyn tried to concentrate and remember what to do. The negative forces loomed closer and closer—surrounding her.

ANNANNNNNNAAA. GGGWENNNN-DOLYNNNNNN.

A A A A A A A A N N A N N N A N N A N N A . GWENNNNNNNDOOLYNNNNNNNNNNN.

The sinister sounds could be heard above the melee. Soon, those Obstacles would leave her unable to move; they would bury her! Smother her voice!! Steal her passions!!! Kill any hope of finding her dreams.

I'd better do something! I can't lose everything I've worked for! Anna Gwendolyn thought—Percy's words finally sinking in. *I guess it's totally up to me.*

"Stare that bully in the face! Show strength! Fake courage! Wipe away your tears. Stand on your own two feet," she repeated loudly, over and over.

Pulling herself up to her full height, Anna Gwendolyn summoned the courage to stand up to the Obstacles. Rejecting their words, laughing at their outrageous accusations and dismissing their lame excuses, she felt her strength and resilience grow. She felt empowered as she spoke her own mind, displaying her real voice.

"I have walked the empowering miles through the Rhibbonosphere. I've been lifted up and cared for by strangers. I've learned the lessons required to successfully dream . . . and in doing so, I gained the strength within me to stare my Obstacles in the face, and deny their power over me! I am doing that, as I speak.

"I wish for all of you the peace and happiness that I have been blessed to receive. So long, I am on my way to retrieve my lost dreams!" *Now that's a way to handle a bully!*

Then something akin to magic started to happen. The hurricane's whirlwinds reversed, sucking back the bullying, the insults, the degrading and domineering negative aura, until only Anna's friends, her positive forces, remained. The waving hands of the menacing Clock retreated; the place was no longer an obstacle to her future.

It's just like Pappy said. Negativity cannot survive in a positive environment.

The chaos cleared and heads were counted: "Anna? Anna?" No one answered. Anna Gwendolyn appeared to be missing. "Where is she?" Nevah-Tu-Latte asked. The Rhibbonites began to call her name when victoriously she emerged from behind the trees, beaming her megawatt smile from ear to ear. "Just always wanted to 'make an entrance!'" she laughed, so proud of herself and standing on a pile of glistening, white coolers filled with ice cold water, which she passed out to all.

Anna Gwendolyn was successful, her rescued dignity, self-esteem and self-confidence intact. She had rescued herself and her friends! She had applied the lessons of the Rhibbonosphere and they had worked!

The group felt a celebration was in order, to honor Anna Gwendolyn's conquest. Cheers by all, as they laughed, danced and applauded her victory. Anna had warded off negativity and embraced perseverance. They were very proud of her and she was proud of herself.

A newly empowered Anna Gwendolyn led the party down the re-emerging Granite Path. The group could not help but see the growing confidence in her walk and stature. Her smile, now the toothpaste-commercial kind, displayed Anna's message of victory and enduring gratitude.

The group continued on, laughing and reminiscing about what they had witnessed. Accolades and high fives for Anna Gwendolyn were so predominant, the travelers were unaware of the miles they had travelled.

Running ahead, Anna Gwendolyn saw something in the distance that resembled a . . . no, it couldn't be . . .the train station? "Are we supposed to? Is there supposed to be a building up ahead? Can someone check the map?" Anna Gwendolyn asked.

The Dream Garden quest had led Anna Gwendolyn and her faithful followers to Destiny Depot Train Station. "For real!! Wow!" a jubilant Anna Gwendolyn exclaimed. "Finally, a little bit of luxury . . . and a reminder of Pappy and home." Approaching the station, she thought her eyes were fooling her. The conductor looked just like Pappy. And there, in front

of Anna Gwendolyn, was an engine, just like Pappy's prized, 100-year-old steam engine, proudly leading its train cars behind it. "Wow!"

The conductor blew his whistle and hollered, "All aboard!" The huge engine filled the air with musty steam and sounded its call to action!

The Rhibbonites, a bit disheveled from celebrating, followed Anna Gwendolyn, as she crossed the wooden platform. She stopped to read the only sign she noticed.

DESTINY DEPOT
77 Minutes to Dream Garden Beach
Enjoy a Complimentary Ride
Bon Voyage!

With the return of her junior high school giddiness—and her terrifying run-in with the Obstacles almost forgotten—Anna Gwendolyn led the group aboard. The train, proudly built in another time, displayed an interior matching the colors and feel of 1950s Parkersville. There was even a bar with red vinyl barstools and booths taken straight from an old diner.

The conductor, taking a giant leap up the metal steps, grabbed the train microphone. Again, he called "All Aboard! All Aboard."

Anna Gwendolyn was ecstatic, scarcely able to control herself; they were on their way again, far away from rough terrain, and she had led them! Everyone settled into seats, the aroma of dinner talking to their tummies.

Waiters in tuxedos graced the train aisles as if they were serving a state dinner for the president. Oversized, silver trays displayed hors d'oeuvres to desserts: Steam Engine Train Truffles, Conductor Corn a la Cob, Whistle Blowing Prime Rib, Chug Chug Chocolate Chewies and Locomotive Lattes.

Everyone finally situated, Percy asked for their attention. "Here, here, let's raise a glass to honor our Lost Dreamer, Anna Gwendolyn. She proved herself in the face of adversity today.

To our Lost Dreamer; may her journey to the Dream Garden be successful."

"To Anna!" the group cheered.

The Rhibbonites enjoyed a relaxing evening sharing a wonderful dinner and stimulating conversation well into the night. With happy spirits, stuffed to the brim, one by one, the revelers retired to the sleeping cars. But not Anna Gwendolyn. Tired and exhausted as she was from her incredible day, she chose to stay awake for a while, to savor the day's events. She had much to digest. The gentle sway of the train was soothing; it reminded her of her days as a child, riding Pappy's train.

"Excuse me, excuse me, ma'am, may I have a pillow and blanket?" Anna Gwendolyn asked.

"Oh, at your service, ma'am. One fluffy pillow and peacock blanket coming right up," the stewardess said.

"Thank you so very much." *Of course it would be made of peacock feathers . . . what else would I expect?*

As the train roared over the tracks, memories skipped through the passageways of Anna Gwendolyn's mind. She was overcome with her love for Pappy.

How many times did Pappy try to tell me about Dream Prints or dreaming and I refused to listen? Mama always tried to help me listen better, she thought, trying to somewhat rationalize her behavior.

Banishing these discouraging thoughts, Anna Gwendolyn wrapped herself in the blanket. Caught in a twilight state, her head pressed firmly against the window, her mind struggled to ward off sleep. She wanted this day to last.

The big, black, steam engine chugged forward, lulling Anna Gwendolyn into a deep sleep. She succumbed to the tiredness of the day, the sound of the rhythmic wheels the last enticement. As her head fell gently against the train car's picture window, she felt as if she were being lifted up into the air. She felt velvety but powerful gusts of air pushing her up from her seat. Suspended in air, above the train, she could see for miles. She waved her hands in glee and celebration, feeling the wind on her face. Luv-Ern's training and teachings left her unafraid.

A blinding beam of light woke her. The morning sunrise. Looking around, Anna Gwendolyn realized she had slept all night in her seat. The conductors walked up and down the aisles alerting passengers of their momentary arrival at the Security Checkpoint for Dream Garden visitors.

Finally, have I arrived at the Dream Garden? What's going to happen now?

Chapter Thirty-Five

Vision of Love

The Rhibbonites were stirring in their sleeping cars. Anna Gwendolyn laughed to herself, *Am I ever going to get there?* The roar of a passing train broke the silence, awakening any still sleeping passengers.

Was this really the end of this ridiculously, long journey and the beginning of her trek to Dream Garden Beach? Experience had taught her that it probably was not. So far, with each journey's end, another challenging trek had begun. Nothing had been easy. And yet, she was proud she'd made it this far, with the end almost in sight.

As the group exited the train, "Security Clearance will be ready for you in about thirty minutes," the Station Master announced. "Please be prompt."

"What? Clearance! What do you mean clearance? Like security at the airport? This is supposed to be a train station," Anna Gwendolyn challenged no one in particular. "I have traversed the treacherous paths through the Rhibbonosphere and I'm required to have clearance?"

"Relax, Miss Anna Gwendolyn. No, it's not like the airport. The job of the Dream Garden Beach Security Detail is to ensure that negative forces, such as the Obstacles and any other dream stealers, don't infiltrate the gates of Dream Garden Beach," Percy explained.

Soon the Station Master drew back the heavy, velvet drapes and declared Security Clearance officially open.

"I guess it's time!" Anna Gwendolyn was shaking with excitement, as she was escorted by the Rhibbonites to the Clearance Station.

"Step right up, ma'am. And where may I ask are you going?" the officer asked.

"Oh, well, of course, I'm going to Dream Garden Beach. Isn't that where everyone's going?" Anna Gwendolyn asked.

"Ah, it is where everyone thinks they are going," said the officer.

Anna Gwendolyn was stunned, "Uh, you mean they don't all get the clearance they need to go through?"

"That's right. You see, Miss Anna Gwendolyn, if a person has not passed the challenges of the Rhibbonosphere, it will show up during the security check. One must be able to show their worthiness to enter DGB. Are you ready to see if you passed?" asked the officer.

"Well, yes, I'm ready," said Anna Gwendolyn.

"Please lay anything that you will be taking into the Garden on this red conveyer belt. You'll receive the green light to enter, once you have cleared security," said the officer.

"All I have in this world is my train; someday, it will be my wedding train," she told him with a wink and a giggle, momentarily shifting back to her pre-Luv-Ern persona, "and what's left of a wreath that I made. The rest of it turned into Luv-Ern's plane."

Anticipating the worst, Anna Gwendolyn hesitatingly walked through Security. She was terrified she'd be thrown out at any moment. *Ohhhh, Pappy, I wish you were here . . . and the girls and Jake . . . But look what I've done! Yes, alone! I'm going to find my dreams—if only I pass.*

And then, to Anna Gwendolyn's astonishment, a huge neon sign blared a shining, blinding

Congratulations!

Anna Gwendolyn had passed! She almost floated through the security gates. She was now worthy of rescuing her dreams. Tears cascaded down her face.

Pulling her shoulders back, Anna Gwendolyn held her head up high and repeated the words of the Rhibbonosphere: "Be generous! Believe! Commit! Persevere! I did it! It worked! I passed!

"Does everyone succeed in rescuing their dreams?" Anna Gwendolyn asked again.

"Ah well, we so wish that was the case. Sadly, there are always a few lost dreamers who took too many short cuts, passed over some of the requirements and arrived unworthy of dream retrieval and attainment," said the officer.

"What have they missed doing? What's missing?"

"That's simple: Lack of self-belief and the inability to persevere, to go the extra mile. But you've trained with the best. Now that you're hear, just concentrate on all the lost dreamers that made it through security! Look at this fingerprint board.

Those fingerprints with names beside them represent lost dreamers who earned the right to Dream Garden Beach.

"And now it's your turn, Miss Anna Gwendolyn. Put your fingerprints on the board," he invited. "Go ahead!"

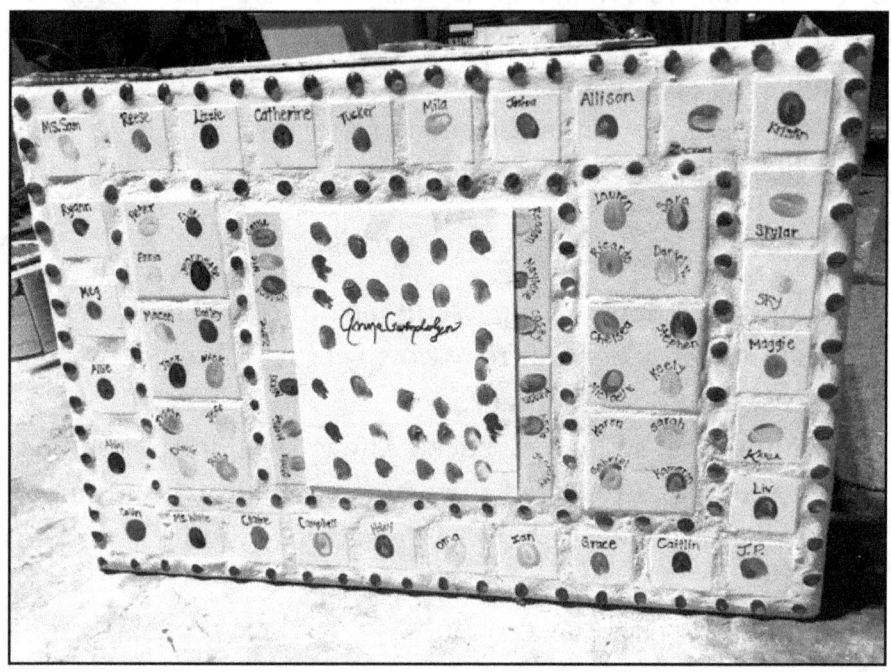

Anna was so thrilled to have made it this far that, in her enthusiasm, she couldn't *stop* fingerprinting the board! She wanted to make sure she left an indelible mark, attesting to her perseverance and renewed passion. In fact, she left many!

"OK, now, Anna, ready for the Dream Garden?" asked the officer with a grin.

"Yes, Yes, I am," Anna Gwendolyn answered confidently. *I don't think this guy has any idea of what I've done to get here,* she said silently to herself.

Witnessing their protégé's excitement, the Rhibbonites almost skipped to the Beach to keep up with her running.

All of a sudden, Anna started yelling, "There's the beach!! There's the beach!! Oh, it's beautiful; coral, pink, and white sand that sparkles. I can't believe I'm here. I'm really and finally at Dream Garden Beach. Oh . . . it's true! I know I'll find my lost dreams here!"

The huge sign up ahead read:

DREAM GARDEN BEACH
Welcome Dreamers!!!

That mystical, meandering Granite Path bordered by sunflowers appeared out of nowhere, rolling out in front of Anna. Looking ahead, she saw that the Path headed directly to an ornate golden gate—the entrance to Dream Garden Beach.

Anna Gwendolyn stepped onto the path that had led her from Delphinium all the way to the front gates of the Garden. She said quietly to herself, "Well, from taking a chance on a flimsy dream ladder, look where I am now! One step at a time. I will take one step at a time. I will get there. This is really it! I can't believe I'm finally here!"

But she was.

Her lost dreams were now within reach.

Then, a change of pace . . .

"Anna, Anna Gwendolyn," Percy nudged, kindly interrupting her state of awe. "The Dream Garden Beach staff has been expecting you. They will appear any minute at the Garden Gate."

"What is that? What do I hear? Music?" Anna Gwendolyn asked.

A voice uttered, "Ladies and Gentlemen, Rhibbonites and Dream Seeker . . . May I introduce you to Geraldine, the Guardian of the Garden and Hostess for your visit here." As the music played and the heavy gate opened, an ethereal creature appeared.

The Rhibbonites stood grinning as their newly introduced hostess welcomed them with a sweet serenade.

Come to my special garden
Growing far beyond the Earth
A place where dreams once broken
Can celebrate rebirth.

A place where dreams once frozen
By the predator of fear
Escape from their captivity
And find safe harbor here.

Dreams upon the threshold
The fog they must break through
To christen their beginning
Celebrate their coming true.

Nestled safely in your Dream Trunk
Your lost dreams are now quite near
Your heart will lead the way, dear,
As it has through any a fear.

You've proved to be unstoppable
Casting foes at dreamland's door
You've freed yourself of Obstacles
Your dreams, as eagles will soar!

"Thank you, Thank you," Geraldine bowed as the Rhibbonites applauded her performance.

"Welcome to you, Miss Anna Gwendolyn, our honored guest, and to all the Rhibbonites. We know you've worked diligently to complete your challenges and learn the lessons of the Rhibbonosphere. We're here to help and support you on your final endeavor—retrieving your lost dreams."

She then told a story. "Ever think it's too late to go after your dream? I know one seventy-four-year old dreamer who thought so. She'd always wanted to study painting and be an artist, but non-believers and horrible Obstacles bullied her into believing she could never be good enough, certainly never make a living at it. She'd lost her dream long ago. But then she fought her way through the Rhibbonosphere, and today, she has a lucrative painting career—at the age of ninety-six! Her work graces the walls of museums, hospitals, homes and a book, always reminding the viewer it's never too late."

Ah, yes, Anna Gwendolyn thought with a smile, *perseverance really does pay off!*

"Now, are you ready for the tour of a lifetime? You, my dear Anna Gwendolyn, are in for the surprise of your life. Everyone ready? I will direct you, pointing out special sights and describing various parts of the Garden. Just raise your hand if you have a question or don't understand something. Follow me, please."

Stopping just a few feet from where they had been, Geraldine said, "I'm sure this is the best starting point. Scoop up a handful of our sparkling sand. The mystery behind the power of the waves, to guide dream-filled ships to the safety of our Bay, can only be explained by Mother Nature. Just for

review: On the other side of the island, Dream Combers rake the waters for lost dreams, clean and sort them, place them in conch shells and pack the shells into crates. Seaphairies assure that, when the moon is full, each crate gets stowed safely onto one of three Clipper Ships. When the ships arrive in our Bay, the Seaphairies unload them here. Once safely ashore, the dreams are bathed in Garden Waterfalls to extricate any lingering negative forces."

Geraldine had their attention.

"Our Dream Garden Beach staff makes special arrangements for lost dreams. A metropolis of tree trunks speckled our hillside, and, well, there was an army of senior woodpeckers out of work. We requested they hollow out the tree trunks for us. Why? So, the rescued dreams would have a safe and protective refuge to wait for their owners to find them.

"Look as far as you can up and down the rolling path until you see a menagerie of dots in the landscape. That, Anna

Gwendolyn, is where your dreams are," Geraldine explained. "The dots? Those are the tree trunks where the lost dreams of the world are secured. We call it Tree Trunk Trove. Watch for the "Nathan's Way" sign and you'll know you're close."

The touring group followed directions, watching for the special sign.

"There it is," Anna Gwendolyn yelled, pointing ahead. "We must be close!!"

A sign, amidst fields of sunflowers, hinted the way to Tree Trunk Trove.

NATHAN'S WAY
Ahead

The breathtaking, mystical menagerie of tree trunks seemed to rise within the camouflage of sunflowers.

"And there you have it, Miss Anna Gwendolyn!" stated Geraldine. "Your victory awaits you! Yes, within one of those dream-filled tree trunks are your lost dreams."

I've arrived at the Dream Garden . . . and somewhere out there in that field, my lost dreams are waiting.

"So, ladies and gentlemen, that concludes our tour of Dream Garden Beach," Geraldine said, breaking the spell. "Miss Anna Gwendolyn, is it everything that you dreamed about?"

"Well, I haven't exactly dreamed about it because I didn't know it existed. What I do know is my Pappy's teachings have come to life throughout the Rhibbonosphere and here at Dream Garden Beach. And soon, I will bring my dreams back to life!"

"Yes," Geraldine agreed, "but first, some food—Dream Garden Beach style."

Anna was about to experience another style of fine, beachfront dining with music provided by The Crashing Waverly Brothers.

Anna Gwendolyn was escorted to her place—an azure, high backed, cushioned beach chair, in the sand.

The feast included Slam-Dunk Salmon, Dancing Octopus Legs, Sun Bathing Shrimp, and Seaweed & Serpentine Salad. The sweet tooth pleasing Crab Cake Romanoff and Coral Reef Pie followed, as they all watched the sun set. With a closing toast of Sunset Sea Splash, the group relaxed, relishing their desserts.

"We have a little extra time here, Anna Gwendolyn," offered Geraldine with eyes twinkling. "Go explore the beach or take a run through the warm water. Check out this place!"

"So, it's alright? I can go explore the shoreline?"

"Sure, it's tradition!"

Her Rhibbonite friends were busy celebrating her success. This group of mentors had achieved its goal. These zany characters taught Anna Gwendolyn to become a leader, not a follower. They reminded her how to be resourceful, to look for answers within herself rather than wait to be saved. They helped her learn to face her fears, no matter the outcome. And now, soon, they would witness Anna retrieving her long-lost dreams.

Anna Gwendolyn meandered away from the group, trading the sounds of laughter for the more serene sounds of the sea. *Look at the shoreline . . . the waves lap against the sand, teasing me to catch them.*

That's why I like waterfalls so much! The sound of flowing water is so healing. My waterfalls could put the sound of healing water into every home I build. I could actually help people feel better, she thought to herself. *Waterfalls could be my trademark!*

Looking up from the sand, Anna Gwendolyn saw that she had traveled farther than she'd planned. She could no longer see the beachfront activities.

Anna straightened her back, as Captain Luv-Ern had taught her. The Column-Men had taught her to figure things out for herself. Percy had taught her to persevere. Visuella had taught her to visualize her wants and that weird talking Boulder had taught her to inscribe her desires in stone!

"Ok . . . Here goes. I trust myself," she said aloud, hoping to reaffirm her thoughts. Step by step, she followed her instincts. Further and further she traveled. "Just one step at a time will take me back," she reassured herself. She knew her friends would be worried if she didn't show up soon, assuming that by now they knew she was missing. Then, up ahead, she thought she saw something. *Is that a mirage?* The sand appeared to be covered by a layer of color—yellow, bright yellow. *Is something else there?* Intrigued, Anna Gwendolyn headed toward the yellow sand. *Sunflowers?*

Then a sudden movement caught her eye. *Is that a shadow?* she asked herself silently, not sure if her curiosity or fear was winning. *Oh, no! Is one of those crazy Obstacles following me? What am I going to do? I'm moving as fast as I can and I have no idea where the Rhibbonites are.*

The thing came closer and closer; it looked more like a shape now than a shadow. *Am I seeing a vision; is that a person?* "Who's there?" she asked timidly. "Are you an Obstacle? Who are you?"

The sparkly, shadowy figure came into clearer view.

Anna Gwendolyn watched as the figure began to slowly transform itself . . . She said aloud to no one, "It's a person; she has pink flowers on her dress! Is it a woman? Who could it be? Nevah wouldn't want pink flowers and Della, the robot with all her gadgets, certainly wouldn't wear a dress."

Wait, I think . . . Ohhh!! I must be seeing things!! It looks like a figure . . . ah, it's a girl or . . . Oh my goodness! Is it . . . Anna's mind raced. *NO, what would SHE be doing here? But it is . . . It's my mother. It's my mother!!!*

How can that be? Am I seeing things? Did I make this happen? Boy, Visuella's lessons . . . I guess I really did listen to her! Anna had visualized being with her mother many times, but she never really believed it would happen.

The woman reached out to her . . ."Is this real, Mama?" Anna said, shaking with doubt and hope at the same time. In a haze of bright yellow turning turquoise, Anna Gwendolyn's mother was standing right in front of her. "OH Mama! OH Mama! Oh! Oh!! I've found you . . . at last!!! It's really you! I have so much to tell you!" Tears rolling down her cheeks, Anna Gwendolyn fell into the warm, inviting, outstretched arms of her beloved mother!

"I've been waiting my whole life to talk with you, Mama! I can't believe you found me here."

Mother and daughter sat together, clutching each other, doing the seemingly impossible—catching up on all the lost years. They couldn't stop crying, smiling, absorbing each other's love and inner beauty, and talking non-stop. Anna confided in her Mama all her secret fears and disappointments, as well as all the lessons she'd learned on her odyssey through the Rhibbonosphere. But of course, her mama already knew.

Then a soft grey cloud hovered ever so gently over Anna's face . . .

"You're wondering how long I'll be here . . . Just long enough to inspire you, Anna Gwendolyn, and your belief in your goals. I'm here to celebrate the re-discovery of your dreams!"

Sunflowers surrounded mother and daughter, creating a golden glow which encircled them and then illuminated the Granite Path, as it lay ahead of them. Mother and daughter, hand in hand, took the first steps onto the Path, now bordered with purple and yellow thistle.

"Yellow and purple," Anna Gwendolyn said, smiling and remembering the special garden she had discovered at the Island of Lost Dreams, and how she had wanted to plant one.

Ever Lost A Dream?

Chapter Thirty-Six

Sanctuary of My Lost Dreams

Anna Gwendolyn was thinking, *I can hardly believe I'm here, walking hand in hand with my mother, my mama! Could my heart be any fuller than it is right now?*

"Anna Gwendolyn, my little girl . . . You are all grown up! Those few and precious times we shared; the lessons I taught you. You have grown into an incredible and beautiful young lady! Oh Anna! I am so sorry that I had to leave. But just look at you! You are my amazingly confident and generous Anna Gwendolyn—such a far cry from the lost, sad, insecure young girl who had lost her way—and her dreams—because of bullying. I saw you at the Renaissance Festival, and now I see you've had a renaissance of your very own! I'm so proud to see you using your voice!"

"Mama! Hugging you feels like . . . like . . . magic! I can hear a voice in my head saying everything is going to be all right again.

"Pappy's taking such good care of me!" *That sneaky, conniving Pappy! I haven't even opened the dream trunk and the magic is already happening!*

Anna Gwendolyn hugged her mother again, and again, soaking up the love she'd craved and missed for so long. She hung onto her every word, not wanting this visualization to end.

"You know, Anna Gwendolyn, Pappy has been teaching you straight from my lesson book. So, I like to think we raised you together. Just look at you. Anna Gwendolyn, you listened. You are ready for anything!"

"Ready for anything, Mama?"

"Yes, dear Anna Gwendolyn, ready for anything!" Mama said with pride.

Anna Gwendolyn and her Mother strolled on the welcoming flower-lined Granite Path. Serious talk behind them, they joked and giggled and compared habits and laughed some more. "Mama, now I see how much I'm like you. You tilt your head like I do. You sound just like me. We even giggle the same!"

Then she interrupted herself, "Look Mama! Up there coming from behind that cloud. It's Luv-Ern! and her Peacock Plane!

"What's trailing behind her? I can't quite make it out.

"I can't see, Mama! When she comes a bit closer, maybe I can make it out. Oh, Mama, it's a banner!"

YOUR DREAM TRUNK AWAITS!!
We will meet you there.
Love, your friends, The Rhibbonites

"Oh, Mama, they're all coming to watch me open my trunk! You'll get to meet all of my new friends. We have to hurry, Mama."

"Sweetheart. Look . . ." Mama said. "We must be close."

Nathan's Way

"That's it, I think, up ahead. That must be it, way over there beyond those hills," Anna Gwendolyn pointed out the sign. "That will lead us to Tree Trunk Trove. Geraldine called it 'the sanctuary of the world's lost dreams.'"

A beautiful bench, tiled with images to honor and highlight the dreams of other lost dreamers, sat at the entrance to Nathan's Way. Many dreamers contributed to the tiles, some even creating them, and lost dreamers from around the world have rested and refueled their perseverance there.

"Wow, how beautiful!" said Mama. "And just think, all those lost dreamers were just like you, so eager to reclaim their dreams."

"Oh, look, see the sign, way in the distance . . .

TREE TRUNK TROVE

"Mama! That's why I've travelled all this way. The dotted landscape they told us about . . . it's up ahead. OH!!! Those dots are dream trunks full of lost dreams!

"Now, Mama. Let's go! Somewhere out there is a trunk filled with my dreams! Let's go!"

Together, they seemingly flew to Tree Trunk Trove. There were no words to express the wonder they were now experiencing.

"I lost my dreams, Mama. Now I'm going to get them back!"

What lay ahead was miles and miles of rolling green hills, dotted with the trunks that appeared as thousands of sparkling black diamonds, as far as the eye could see.

The path meandered gracefully up and down and all around the rolling hills of the Trove, providing convenient one-to-one access to each and every Dream Trunk.

The wide, walking paths allowed ample room for trunk-opening celebrations. Focusing on a couple of tree trunks, Anna and her mother noticed some trunks were identified by computer print outs and others—simple handwriting. Each tree trunk had digital date and time documentation and all had bronze plaques naming their lost dreamers.

"Mama!! Mama, I'm so happy you're here to share this with me." Anna Gwendolyn's determination to find her trunk only strengthened, as she began to realize the magnitude of the task ahead of her.

"Anna Gwendolyn, up ahead . . . there . . . you'll have your answer soon!" Mama encouraged.

"Tree trunk after tree trunk has a bronze plaque," said Anna, "with the name and birthdate of its owner. Watch carefully as the years and dates get closer to my birth year, 2009." She walked faster with anticipation, almost running.

"We ought to be close to my trunk now." 2007, 2008, 2009. They were now only steps from her Dream Trunk. "It must be up ahead!" *I think it's finally time for me to find this thing and find out what's in it! I can hardly breathe!!*

"There's the row of R's.. So, there's the row of S's and my trunk must be very close since my last name is Shaw. I wonder . . . Where is it?? Where is it?"

"Anna Gwendolyn, honey . . . Your trunk's over here. I'm sure of it."

"Will you help me open it? Geraldine said you have to pry it to open it completely."

"That's exactly why I'm here!!!" Mama blurted out, with a huge grin.

Looking over the hillside, "All these thousands of dreams found refuge from the taunts and bullying of the world. These dreams had been written off, lost, including mine.

"Oh . . . I think we are closer!

"And there it is! My incredible odyssey of 2,650 miles is truly over. I'm going to take back my dreams!"

5/11/2009 ANNA GWENDOLYN SHAW
#DNC04261127010900823

Ever Lost A Dream?

Chapter Thirty-Seven

Unleashing My Future

"Oh, Anna Gwendolyn, there it is! Your Trunk! Oh! It so beautiful!

"Oh! You found it, Anna! You found your dreams!" Mama shouted.

"I can't breathe, Mama!" I've traveled all these miles . . . and I don't even know what to do!"

"Well, it looks like there's some people coming to help you."

Just then, her friends rushed over.

"I . . . Oh, it's the Rhibbonites! Mama, you'll get to meet my friends!!"

"Hello, Miss Anna Gwendolyn! We've come to celebrate with you and your Mama!

"We wouldn't miss this for the world!"

Anna thought, *They sound as if they've always known my Mama was going to be here with me!*

Humbled by the gift of their sudden presence and that of her Mama, Anna Gwendolyn dropped to the ground, overwhelmed with emotion. Then she eyed her Dream

Trunk. She looked at it, stared at it, and tried to pry it open. "Will anyone help me? You guys over there—my traveling companions—how do I open this thing? I think it's locked. Is there a key? Does somebody have a key? Maybe if I stand up. Well . . . If no one's going to help me, I guess I'll just take matters into my own hands!"

And with her renewed sense of empowerment, Anna Gwendolyn pushed, pried and pulled up the protective covering of her Dream Trunk.

"Oh my gosh! Look what's happening!! Rainbows of light are shooting out from the insides—I see architectural papers, geography spreadsheets, weathered drafting paper, the tool set that Pappy gave me for my twelfth birthday, sheet music— even the Norwegian Concerto! Pretty pink toe shoes, waterfall stones and adornments . . . All of these precious things of mine have been nestled safe and sound, for years, in my own special Dream Trunk in the Tree Trunk Trove of the Dream Garden. Thank you, thank you, thank you, dear Dream Combers and Seaphairies!!" Anna said through cascades of tears.

"Piles of wallpaper samples and floor coverings, and waterfall pumps and solar lighting, and countertop samples and marble remnants and stone varieties all are tumbling out, maybe hinting what I'll be working on years from now! Tucked tightly into one corner is even some brand new rock climbing gear next to a now empty conch shell!"

Anna's childhood passions burst back into her life.

Anna Gwendolyn now had the confidence, self-esteem and fire-fueled passion to re-experience the passions of her youth. She'd found her lost dreams.

She pondered and she stared and she cried and she laughed and then she said, "Thank you." Just like that, out of the sky, Anna Gwendolyn had remembered to be grateful.

"Oh . . . it's the digital ruler and set of rules that Pappy gave me when I started to build that house in fifth grade! And there are my architectural drawings and charcoal pencils. Oh, look, the tool kit and matching belt that I got for my birthday! And my architectural books and my world geography atlases! It's all here! But wait! There's something else at the bottom of the trunk!

"Let me see if I can grab this. Don't know what it is but . . ." A thought struck her cold, and she dropped the item on the bottom of the trunk. She turned a little red. Her beloved Frank Lloyd Wright books had been returned to her. It was a startling reminder of her fifth-grade stone house she had never finished.

"Why Anna Gwendolyn . . . you're, why, you're turning red." She was embarrassed.

"You know, Mama, Pappy always wanted me to finish that thing.

"Oh Mama! I am sorry. I let him down. I tried to finish the house but . . ." Tears rolled down her cheeks, as she sobbed.

"It's all right, Anna Gwendolyn. It is all right. You have not lost your childhood dream of building that little house. I promise. You see, I've saved these long-lost river stone for you. They're little, but tough! Just like you! They are symbolic of the hard work that you did to rescue your lost dreams! Because of your new-found belief in yourself, you took back your dignity and along came your dreams! From now on, no one is going to mess with your dreams—or your dignity!

"So now, take these river stones and finish your club-house! Build your castles! And make sure, you build those waterfalls . . ."

"Yes, those waterfalls. Waterfalls are good for the soul," whispered Anna thoughtfully.

"You'll do it all by yourself," Mama said.

"And, with the kindness of strangers!" Anna Gwendolyn grinned, as she flourished her scarf.

Chapter Thirty-Eight

Watch Me!!!

With the wave of her scarf, Anna Gwendolyn was suddenly back in Parkersville, waking up still circling around on the Dream Spinner.

As she saw Pappy walking toward her, he asked, "Well, hello, sleepy head, did you get a good rest? I was just out walking with Briggs, and decided to look for my favorite dream-searching granddaughter, and I find you here snoozing on the Dream Spinner! How about that Dream-O-Tron! Buy any dreams lately?"

"Oh Pappy . . . That's you, Pappy? Where am I? Is Percy here? or Luv-Ern? or Nevah-Tu-Latte? And Mama? Am I at the Tree Trunk Trove? Pappy, where am I? Where's my Dream Trunk?" The thought of her Dream Trunk roused Anna Gwendolyn immediately.

"Sounds like you've been off dreaming, in a puffy white cloud maybe! Who's Nevah-Tu-Latte, anyway? And what's a Dream Trunk?"

"Oh, Pappy!! I found my lost dreams!! Everything you told me came true!!! I found my lost dreams!!!

"You know that legend about the Dream Spinner and about your dreams coming true? Well, it's true, Pappy, it's true!! Yesterday, you know, when you said it was never too late to dream? You said I had time. You said I shouldn't buy my dreams from that old Dream-O-Tron commercial thing. You were right!

"There was this thief from the Dream-O-Tron company who actually *stole* dreams—I even saved you from him!—and a place called Rhibbonosphere full of crazy characters who kept telling me to believe in myself and that I could do anything and to never give up. My peacock wreath turned into a Peacock Plane and I climbed a ladder up to the sky and had to make a parachute so I could get out of the plane! I parachuted out!!!!! Me!!! There was this guy Detective Bun-Cover and I fell into an Obstacle Multiplier full of bullies, Pappy, but I got out, I figured it out and I got out! And this woman, Nevah-Tu-Latte, with a red pillow hat, constantly saying 'It's never too late'— And, Oh Pappy, Oh! Oh!! I saw Mama in the Dream Garden and Mama and me found my Dream Trunk and all my lost dreams were in there!!! Waiting for me!!!! Not a Dream-O-Tron in sight!!!

"I learned it's up to me, Pappy, it's up to me, just like you said. There was a train like yours and a conductor who looked like you and a red robot and a giant jigsaw puzzle of all my Defining Moments. And the food, Pappy, the food!!! You've never heard of such wild concoctions! Plus seahorses with wings carrying lost dreams and a funny flat guy named Percy Press-on Verance who got ironed in a mangle and preached persevering . . . Boy, did I have to persevere! I had so many obstacles! But I learned how to handle them. There were

Clipper Ships with piles of lost dreams in crates and . . . and . . . an unending forest of tree trunks full of lost dreams. I chiseled my dreams in stone, Pappy, and I even started a sewing program at a nursing home and a painting program and I got old people exercising and loving it and they all applauded me and . . ."

Then, she finally took a breath . . .

A big, long, deep breath . . .

"Pappy," she said seriously, "I've changed a lot since I've seen you."

Anna Gwendolyn smiled sheepishly, with her chin down and her eyes looking up at him.

"I found my courage, Pappy, and my self-confidence and self-esteem and dignity. And no one, no one, is ever going to bully me or shame me ever again! I found my voice, and I know how to use it! Believe me, Pappy, with what I just went through, I can handle anything now! I can take care of myself and I can handle anything! I'm reclaiming my dreams.

"Just watch me!!"

She took another breath.

Then she gave her Pappy a long, warm hug.

"Let's go find those river stones, Pappy. Maybe that old stone clubhouse can be a castle . . . with a moat . . . and a waterfall . . . and maybe even some goldfish . . .

"I have this magic train . . .

The End

"Why is it so hard
to believe in the person
you've known since your birth?"

—Deborah Zvanut Drake

Ever Lost A Dream?

Ever Lost A Dream?

Characters in Parkersville

Anna Gwendolyn Shaw—A thirteen-year-old girl, living in Parkersville, Texas, with her grandfather, desperate to find her dreams again—and ready to buy them from an info-mercial

Briggs—The family dog

Gloria—Anna's childhood friend in Parkersville with a talent (or curse!) for organizing

Jake—Anna's teenage cousin in Parkersville whose family owns the Heal & Soul Shoe Company

Nevah—Anna's childhood friend in Parkersville, flighty but driven (usually by coffee!)

Pappy—Anna Gwendolyn's grandfather, who's been raising her since she was five years old

Veronica—Anna's childhood friend in Parkersville, the free spirit of the group

Characters in the Rhibbonosphere

Captain Luv-Ern—CEO and owner of Peacock Airways and pilot of the Peacock Plane

Column-Men—Wise talking columns who teach self-sufficiency

Della, The Docent of Delphinium—A shiny red robot who explains to Anna the impact of negative and positive Defining Moments

Detective B. Un-Cover—Alter ego of Sal, defender of justice and founding father of Whistle Blowers Anonymous, the organization that exposes those who lie to "cover their buns"

Dream Combers—The labor force who gathers, sorts, catalogues and protects dreams as they wash up on the Island of Lost Dreams

Nevah-Tu-Latte—Pillow-hatted coffee shop owner in the Rhibbonosphere who believes it's never too late to find your dreams—"but service to your community must be involved"

Obstacles—Conniving, insult-shouting "creatures" determined to destroy peoples' dreams by crushing their self-confidence, self-esteem and dignity

Penelope—Flight attendant on the Peacock Plane

Percy Press-on Verance—A flattened victim of an ironing mangle and the owner of Wear It and Blare It T-shirts, Percy's "press on at all odds" mentality makes him the Rhibbonosphere's expert in persevering

Rhibbonites—The collection of characters who inhabit the Rhibbonosphere and guide Anna Gwendolyn on her search for her dreams

Sal—The owner of Sal's Selective Bun-Covers, a unique specialty sandwich shop (Detective B. Un-Cover incognito)

Seaphairies (pronounced Sa-fair' ies)—Winged seahorses, crew of the Clipper Ships, who live solely for the honorable purpose of transporting lost dreams from the windy side of the Island of Lost Dreams to calm Dream Garden Beach

Visuella—A quirky operator at Visualization Station, who helps Anna Gwendolyn visualize the dreams in her head onto a life-size movie screen at the Picture Palace

Places in Parkersville

Parkersville, Texas—Initial setting, Anna Gwendolyn and Pappy's hometown

Memories Park—A community gathering place in Parkersville, home of the iconic amusement ride, The Dream Spinner

Steam Engine Park—Community gardens where Pappy's steam engine is displayed, and the scene of one of Anna Gwendolyn's worst memories

Heal & Soul Shoe Garden—A fundraising venue at the Renaissance Festival, with a whimsical high heel slide entrance, that provides free shoes (and a launch pad for dreams) for the community's children

Places in the Rhibbonosphere

Candlewood Castle—The place in Delphinium where Anna Gwendolyn explores her Defining Moments

Coliseum of Commitment—The destination where Anna Gwendolyn chisels her dreams in stone

Delphinium—The outer-most orbit of the Rhibbonosphere, the place where Anna Gwendolyn timidly explores her negative Defining Moments

Dream Garden Beach—The secret haven on the calm side of the Island of Lost Dreams where lost dreams—numbered, dated, and stored in tree trunks—await their rightful owners

Dreams Preserved Nursing Home Village—A senior facility in the Rhibbonosphere which attracts Anna's attention because its residents lost their dreams

Island of Lost Dreams—Home of the Dream Combers, Seaphairies, host Geraldine and the temporary refuge for lost dreams . . . Lost dreams wash up on the windy side of the island and are stored on the calm side of the island in the Tree Trunk Trove above Dream Garden Beach

Lost Dreams Observation Bunker—Top-secret underground place on the Island of Lost Dreams to observe Dream Combers retrieving and storing lost dreams, and Seaphairies loading them onto Clipper Ships bound for Dream Garden Beach

Obstacle-Multiplier—A massive pit that Anna Gwendolyn falls into, full of bullying, dream-robbing Obstacles

Picture Palace—The movie theater where Anna Gwendolyn, through her mind's eye, projects her dreams on the huge screen

Rhibbonosphere—A far-away galaxy where a community of characters caretake lost dreams and guide lost dreamers through challenges to reclaim them

Sal's Selective Bun-Covers—An outlandish specialty bun shop in the Rhibbonosphere, owned by Sal (Detective B. Un-Cover in disguise)

Tree Trunk Trove—On Dream Garden Beach, the forest of tree trunks housing the world's lost dreams, categorized and numbered and awaiting their owners

Wear It and Blare It—A T-shirts and blouse shop owned by Percy Press-on Verance where Dream Searchers add their own personal messages to recycled T-shirts

Objects Along the Way

Anna's Train—The fantasy name for the magical long scarf Anna buys at the Renaissance Festival

Clipper Ships—Vessels that pick up lost dreams for delivery to Dream Garden Beach

Collide-A-Scope—The steeple-like structure in Delphinium made up of reflective paper messages of Anna's memories and Defining Moments

Defining Moments—Positive and negative life-changing, life-rearranging moments in everyone's life

Destiny Depot—The depot on the Island of Lost Dreams where Anna Gwendolyn boards the train to Dream Garden Beach

Dream Direct-tionary—Pappy's book of directions about what it takes to attain one's dreams

Dream Print—A hint of one's talents, often evident early in young children by observing their obsessions

Dream Spinner—An iconic amusement ride with a century-old legend: Fall asleep on it and your dream will come true

Dream-Chute—Anna Gwendolyn's hand-made, sky-diving parachute that drops her off in Delphinium

Dream-O-Tron—Sold on info-mercials with a toll-free phone call, the blazing, new, technological device promises to make buyer's dreams come true, for only $49.99/month

Fingerprint Board—Security detail at the entrance to Dream Garden Beach where lost dreamers place their fingerprints and names

Granite Path—The road to finding lost dreams in the Rhibbonosphere

Memory Bench—The welcoming bench at the entry of Nathan's Way, a gift of gratitude from Dream Searchers, showcasing ceramic tiles with artistic, personalized memories of their trips through the Rhibbonosphere

Nathan's Way—Entrance to Tree Trunk Trove, the home of lost dreams

Peacock Plane—The whimsical vehicle that takes Anna Gwendolyn on her dream hunt

The Cheshire—Jake's customized vintage car in Parkersville

The Roll-On!—Percy Press-on Verance's vehicle, recycled from an old ironing mangle

Thinking Table—In Candlewood Castle, the desk that helps Anna sort her memories

Zavanuu Zip Line—Anna's transportation from the Picture Palace to the Coliseum of Commitment

Waves of Gratitude

Grandpa Ernie, **Darren & Sarah**, **Nathan**, **Catherine & Stephen**, **Baby Drake:** Like eagles, dancers and trailblazers soaring, because of your inspiration, love, patience, and tolerance, so soars Anna Gwendolyn; **Dennis:** You're always listening, always inspiring; **Carol:** Your support always felt, always helped. **My Nana:** This is for you, love; **Angels Jason, Paul, and Brian**: From Ocean Cove, to Lago Land, to the fifty-yard line of Jonesboro, our love and hearts are close by. I love and miss you to the galaxies! **My patients, clients & students, 3-101:** Your courage in sharing your most personal stories of challenge and victory cemented my resolve to tell Anna Gwendolyn's story. And, by no coincidence, many, many years ago, another empowered young girl named Anna directed me on a path to do just that. **My Sister Cynthia,** published author & phenom editor extraordinaire: this sea captain set out to steer my ship to Dream Garden Beach, saving Anna Gwendolyn from many a tsunami. My "all over the place" penning of plot, storyline, narration and dialogue was further camouflaged by abysmal punctuation and grammar. Your brilliant, laser-sharp editing fueled many chapter-chopping, clutter-clearing marathons. Emerging from the darkness, the dust would clear, but always left in its wake clarity, organization, inspired chapter titles, and a glossary. Your compass streamlined the once complicated Lost Dreams/Seaphairies/ Dream Comber "transport operation" and inspired the glowing Seaphairies and underwater hockey pucks, too! Cynthia, with me for this twenty-three-year odyssey, Anna would never have made it to the Dream Garden without you! And **Winston,** sea captain, engineer, published author: Your extreme patience, tolerance and dedication to assisting in the safe arrival of Anna to the Dream Garden is so appreciated. Your ability to live your life amidst our constant chaos trying to get her there is mind boggling! You are my hero! And Cynthia's too. **My friend Linda,** designer & creative, extraordinary editor and author of the Foreword in this book: Remember? "I've some time, Deb, need some decorating?" you had asked. "Oh, well ah, (shaking) "Ah Linda, what I want, what I really need is, well, could you, a, read something I've written?" Your words after reading 30 pages, "Deborah! I'd love to show this to my grandchildren." In spite of work and personal commitments, and living thousand miles away, you were not deterred. Mentoring by technology or during several week-long marathons, your extraordinary talent taught me with your heart. You believed in Bun-Cover, the dream-trunks, and Tu-Latte. Your quips, "You have a screenplay, yes, a novel, no. Where's the yearning? Why's Anna smiling? She's just been shoved out of a plane!!" Like Cynthia, you understood my soul's yearning and heart's purpose. Your 2009 challenge to me: Write poems about using your voice, Deb, your vision, belief, and bullying, and self-publish them. An all-nighter phone call at the expense of your last nerve . . . and my poetry book, *Dream Gardening,* was born. I did not know I had it in me. That night, your challenge, a game changer! Forever grateful; **Barringer Publishing, Jeff Schlesinger & Editors:** For your commitment to and pursuit of excellence in publishing. The strange case of Anna Gwendolyn presented a monumental task, requiring unfathomable patience, tolerance, understanding. I get it. My search for this dream became a nightmare. I am deeply grateful to Barringer for the victory of Anna's struggle and the freeing of her once silent voice; **Launch Pad Editors** who got me out the starting gate: **Dr. Betsey,** musician & published author, you dedicated your Saturday mornings to help me and encouraged me to give talks; **Lavergne**, creative with a wild & wonderous wit, you were the muse for my Peacock Plane pilot coined Luv- Ern; **Mindy,** owner of The Author's Assistant, you taught me the building blocks of writing and encouraged the writing of and implemented the self-publishing of my Dream Garden poems in *Dream Gardening*; **Paddy,** you cleared my mind and set Anna's path through the Rhibbonosphere. **Artists: Gail**, for your fairy tale Shoe-Slide that introduced the children's charity! An enchanted fantasy, making your sons so proud! **Janice**, your watercolors perfectly grace the cover and pages of *Ever Lost a Dream?* **Tom:** On my gosh! Your drawings, the Dream Spinner, Percy with the Mangle, and Tu-Latte's coffee cup and pillow captured the characters beyond perfection. To all you artists, your beautiful artwork gave life to my story! **Writer's League of Texas, Annual Agents & Editors Annual Conference:** Mentoring, inspiring, motivating from the heart. With you, any aspiring writer never feels alone, always has someone to show the way to get passion on to paper and into a book. WLT can become any writer's new best friend; **Texas Conference for Women**: Comradery, motivation, inspiration; a fueling station for boldness, risk taking, leadership; I took your dare, took the stage shaking, "How, a . . . do you, write a book?" Gretchen answered; **Genie Sayles**: Bestselling author & brilliant teacher, for your stories of vulnerability and personal, candid experiences, which granted me permission to believe, and never give up; **Mrs. Coker**, my high school teacher: "Good story, you should try writing!" "Oh, it's nothing, just from watching Twilight Zone." "That's ok! You used the inspiration!" Your encouragement was priceless; **Texas Woman's University & Professor Harriet Davidson**: Critiquing my final paper on occupational therapy, you called me to your office and encouraged my passions, "You will do this someday!" **Russel Music Studio, Don & Johanna:** You're still my inspiration, masterful musical training in a 1-mile radius; **Rachel:** In 2001 you told me "a fabulous story, a good piece that deserves mounting & workshopping. Call me," you offered generously; **Judith:** Brilliant writer, mentor and sifter of my thoughts. **Cynthia Hall:** Your natural, contagious and authentic humor commands attention. I know I "caught" some, and it sure helped me with these characters! **Cheryann:** Magic and motivation upon request, in 2000, sitting on your couch, your words, "Yes do it! I know you can do this!" **Kathy Evans Peters:** Unwavering support, you listened long ago and believed; **The Pucinni's**: watchers of the first video of the 2001 Dream Garden! **Tracy**: Your idea, a display for Anna's tools, helped so much! **Maryann H**, Poetry-partner inspiration and sustenance; **Jo-Ann F**, for renewed energy to chase this dream;

Bernadette, Carolyn, Christine, Christi, Cindy, Doris, Kyra, Martin, Natalie, Trina, Rosmin, Mona, Scott, Maryann, Sharon, Greg and Marilyn: Motivation stations, dedicated to my dream; **Dale & Stacy:** Bastrop support fueling station; **Patrick & Janet:** I learned from you. Love; **Keely & South Briar Swim Team**: Your forethought and generosity. Coach Nathan's swimmers created the Thumbprint Board, still keeping the Garden safe! **Wanda of wandicolor.com:** You inspired the memory benches now forever in Dream Garden to rest tired dream searchers, forever grateful; **Maryann Polhemus,** former principle of Ashford Elementary School: The Granite Path and Nathan's Way street sign that you encouraged on your campus now forever directs Anna to find her dreams. **Mary Jo and Caroline**: Your wisdom and heart inspires me daily; **Tamara:** You were a lightning rod for this story, so very grateful. And that beautiful cross; **The Lorfings:** Inspirers of love, patience, perseverance and all that is good in the world. **Diesa**, Director, 1999 & 2000 YMCA Home-School Arts Program: Your guidance and faith in me encouraged the child-written performances of "Garden *Party,*" "Fairytale *Reunion"* and "*Dream Garden,*" planting the seeds for Ever *Lost a Dream?* **Suzanne Semans Dance Studio**: I am forever grateful to you for the full-scale theater production of my 2001 Dream Garden, my little, bitty play. You gave us all the bells and whistles! **Erik Zvanut:** As musical director, you transposed Dream Garden poetry into whimsical songs, and a mini-musical was born! **Rudy:** You transferred my error-filled 2000 version of Dream Garden into a succinct, polished script for production; **Elaine:** You brought to life the characters of Dream Garden with your imaginative, enchanting hand-designed and creative costumes, all the while with littles ones climbing and husband Dirk calling . . . "Oh, Dirk, just 13 more fairy wings!" **Shout out to West Houston Medical Center 3rd Floor Geriatrics**—the amazing Dream Garden Lunch Bunch whose daily doses to me included belief, support, inspiration—you gave roots to my mission and always listened; **Heartland, ManorCare and Sharpview Nursing Homes**—Daily doses: Listening, supporting, and understanding; validation of my mission. Thanks for letting me rant and rave . . . and cheering me on for it. **Ashford Methodist and the West Houston and Ashford Hollow communities:** You've been blessed places to grow my Dream Garden obsession. No seeds, no garden tools, or idea of what I was doing, just the steely resolve that I had to do it. Year after year, loyal co-workers, teachers, students, friends and neighbors listened, with their hearts, to my concocted tale of outlandish places and bizarre characters. Yawns, eyerolls, or "ad nauseam moments" (yes, I get it), "Wows" and "Ah's" were plentiful. All, which bolstered my belief in answering the question, "Ever lost a dream?" And . . . if so, "Where did it go?" Your listening strengthened my resolve and armed me with the passion and purpose needed to go the distance.

A letter to family, friends, neighbors, co-workers and clients and everyone I missed: The ocean, immeasurable in size and splendor, glows at sunrise and sunset, requiring never-ending, passion commitment, dedication, loyalty and respect, as does writing a book. That's where you come in; my loyal friends who have wondered about or believed in my mission. I can describe the last twenty- two years of your faithful support in the same descriptive words: immeasurable, never ending, loyal, respectful. Those words symbolized your blessings, instrumental in keeping Dream Garden afloat, year after year, after year. Be it by osmosis, mental telepathy, or by some strange entity, your kind offerings made a bee-line to my heart, renewing my spirit and energy for the work ahead. To the untrained eye, anyone might have wondered, "What the heck is she doing?" I often wondered myself. Be it a chance meeting, or a 20-year celebration, your greeting was always the same, "How's Dream Garden?" or "What's Bun-Cover up to now?" and "What's a Defining Moment?" It has been the honor and delight of my life to have had your trust, loyalty and support on this journey. Thank you, and see you in the Dream Garden.

Freeing my voice I have found my place,
I now have a recognizable face.
My convictions the story of whom I've become,
In this crazy world; battle fought, battle won.

www.ingramcontent.com/pod-product-compliance
Lightning Source LLC
Chambersburg PA
CBHW051245260626
47162CB00002B/613